Praise for Br[illegible]
Previous Novel

Scandalous Virtue

"Hiatt handles the story beautifully . . . fast, witty, and fun."

—*Publishers Weekly*

"Witty and clever. . . . Brenda Hiatt beautifully captures the era."

—*Romantic Times*

"An exciting romp about two wonderful and interesting people. . . . Ms. Hiatt's tale keeps your interest throughout the whole book. I thoroughly enjoyed this tale and would like to read more by this wonderful and talented author."

—Robin Peek, *Under the Covers*

Also by Brenda Hiatt

Scandalous Virtue

SHIP OF DREAMS

Brenda Hiatt

HarperPaperbacks
A Division of HarperCollins*Publishers*

HarperPaperbacks
A Division of HarperCollins*Publishers*
10 East 53rd Street, New York, NY 10022-5299

For information address HarperCollins Publishers Inc., 10 East 53rd Street, New York, NY 10022-5299.

ISBN 0-06-101380-3

First HarperPaperbacks printing: April 2000

Printed in the United States of America

❖ 10 9 8 7 6 5 4 3 2 1

For Leroy Barber, without whom this book would never have been written.
Thanks, Dad!

ONE

The bride hath paced into the hall,
Red as a rose is she;
Nodding their heads before her goes
The merry minstrelsy.

—SAMUEL TAYLOR COLERIDGE,
The Rime of the Ancient Mariner

San Francisco—August 1857

"MURDER? IMPOSSIBLE!" DELLA STARED AT her landlady in disbelief, but the woman only nodded her neat gray head.

"Murder," she repeated. "That's what they're saying in the streets. Mr. Potts claims it was the Dr. Mirabula's Sovereign Remedy for Ague you sold him that carried off his wife last night. And that apothecary, Mr. Willis, is telling everyone who will listen that it must be true."

The bristle brush she'd been pulling through

her thick, carroty curls hung suspended as Della absorbed the words. "That's preposterous! I mixed that remedy myself. It contains nothing but vanilla, quinine, and a jigger of brandy. It may not cure the ague, but it's perfectly harmless. More likely it was one of Mr. Willis' own brews at fault."

Mrs. Lewis shrugged. "I wouldn't be surprised. But be that as it may, I've turned away four people already this morning wanting their money back for medicines you'd sold them, and I fear there'll be more. This could take an ugly turn, dearie."

"Yes. Yes, I suppose it could." Remembering the vigilante sweeps of the previous year, Della shuddered. More than a few accused "criminals" had been hanged without benefit of trial, and on evidence that was sketchy at best. Standing up from the dressing table, she crossed the tiny room in three steps and cautiously parted the yellow chintz curtains to peer out at the dusty street below.

A crowd had gathered two blocks away, in front of the *Euphemia*, once a landlocked ship and now converted to a hotel. Even from this distance she could hear the high, nasal voice of Mr. Willis as he shouted and gestured toward Mrs. Lewis' boardinghouse. The apothecary had been trying to put her out of business for months, seeing her as his greatest competitor. Now it looked as though he might succeed.

Selling patent medicines had been Della's most successful enterprise yet, first in the outlying mining towns, then in Sacramento, and now in San Francisco. A dash of this and a dash of that, and she could command far higher prices than her sewing or produce had ever brought in. Of course, most of her remedies were useless, which caused her the occasional twinge of conscience. But she'd always made absolutely certain they would cause no harm, in accordance with Hippocrates—and in contrast to others peddling medicines, to include Mr. Willis.

"They're getting louder. What will you do?" The landlady wrung her hands vigorously, as though to compensate for Della's immobility.

"Do?" She turned from the window and shrugged with resignation. "Why, leave, I suppose."

Mrs. Lewis stared. "Leave? Leave San Francisco, you mean? But if you're sure your tonic did no harm—"

At the moment, Della felt far older than her twenty years—far older than Mrs. Lewis, even. "Of course I'm sure. But that may not matter." Quickly she weighed her options.

She could face her accusers, attempt to prove her innocence and clear her name. But the coroner was a longtime friend of Mr. Willis, as was the chief of police. And even if she prevailed against all odds, most of her customers would likely desert her.

Two weeks ago she'd squandered most of her money on a new dress, in hopes it might elevate her social standing—a business investment of sorts—and she had yet to be paid for most of the past two weeks' sales. Now she likely wouldn't be, which meant she'd have nothing to pay *her* creditors when they came knocking. And they might come at any moment, as today happened to be steamer day, the twice-monthly date when all San Francisco businesses—and individuals—settled up accounts.

"At best, my business is ruined," she said to Mrs. Lewis at the end of her ruminations. "At worst, I'll be charged with murder. Leaving is the sensible thing to do."

She left unsaid what they both knew: Once a charge was brought, the verdict would depend as much on public sentiment as on the truth of the matter. Though the vigilantes had officially disbanded, justice was still frequently swift and careless in this exuberant young city—especially when a prominent man such as Mr. Willis had an incentive to affect the outcome.

"You're paid through the end of the month," Mrs. Lewis reminded her, pale blue eyes crinkled with worry.

Della smiled at the woman's kindness. "Consider next week's rent my gratitude for your help in this matter." She glanced out the window again at the milling crowd. "They'll be heading over here any time now. Hold them off as long as you can while I slip out through the kitchen. You've always been kind to me, Mrs. Lewis, and I thank you." She absently kissed the landlady on the cheek, already planning her escape.

As the woman bustled out of the room, clucking to herself, Della's mind worked rapidly. With a decisive nod, she pulled out her largest valise—the trunk would be too heavy—and began throwing necessities and her most valuable possessions into it. The brooch and rings that had been her mother's, her real silk scarf, the silver-handled hairbrush. No room for her bottles of Carter's Consumption Cure or Dr. Brown's Brain Tonic. Nor for her new hooped dress, the beautiful but expensive green dimity with the seed pearls that had taken her savings.

She'd wear that, she decided. Being dressed like the cream of society might give her more choices. Besides, she couldn't bear to leave it behind. She'd pack the old lilac one she had on. She slipped her mother's wedding ring onto her left hand, thinking she might pose as a married woman or a widow. That would give her more freedom.

Unable to afford a maid, Della owned only dresses with front closures, so she was able to change quickly and without help. Throwing an ivory shawl over her telltale red hair, she tucked her few remaining twenty-dollar gold pieces into her bodice and headed down the back stairs, suitcase in hand.

"She's not here, I tell you!" came Mrs. Lewis' shrill voice from the front of the house. "She went out just after breakfast to make some deliveries."

Dear Mrs. Lewis. Della would miss her—the nearest thing to a mother she'd had in years. Just now she had no time for sentiment, however. At any moment someone might think to check the back of the house.

Lifting her skirts out of the dirt with one hand, her valise clutched tightly in the other, she set out at a brisk walk up Front Street, toward the wharves, grateful that at least there was no mud. What a stroke of luck, after all, that this had happened on Thursday, the day the steamer sailed!

Lady Luck had always been Della's good friend, getting her out of more than one tight place in recent years. She trusted the good dame to come through for her again today. With a glance at her pocket watch, she quickened her pace. This was going to be close.

When she neared the crowded docks a few minutes later, passengers had already begun boarding the elegant Pacific Mail side-wheel steamship *Sonora*. Steerage passengers, from ragged to respectable, stood in lines to have their tickets and papers checked, while those sailing second and first class proceeded with more decorum. Della focused on the latter, thinking hard.

She'd be safest in first class, and she could just about afford a ticket, assuming any were still available, but it would take every bit of her money. Many of those aboard did not plan to sail, she knew, but were merely seeing friends off and would debark at the final boarding call. Perhaps she could pretend to be acquainted with a first-class passenger, then buy a steerage ticket once aboard? It would be risky. . . .

"Hoy there!" came a shout from behind her. "Has a Miss Gilliland boarded this ship?"

Her heart in her throat, she forced herself to keep walking along the wood-planked street, which at this point became a wharf, extending out into the bay. Out of the corner of her eye, she saw a uniformed policeman hurrying to question the crewman taking the steerage tickets. What a mercy she hadn't joined their line! Without slowing her stride, she veered toward the first-class section, keeping as many people as possible between herself and the police officer. Dressed in her finest, she easily blended in.

A loud cheer from behind her made Della glance back. A luxurious, decorated carriage had stopped, and as she watched, a couple, obviously just married, stepped out. Their wedding party and other well-wishers cheered again. Then they were being swept toward the steamer—toward Della.

Seizing her chance, she donned a bright smile and joined the throng. Carried along by the crowd, she hurried up the gangway and onto the elegant promenade deck—and away from the police search, which had now progressed to the second-class passengers.

Hordes of wealthy people jostled each other politely as they made way for the large wedding party. Even in her tight situation, Della couldn't help analyzing the faces and voices, trying to guess which ones had made a killing in the gold fields, which had made fortunes in business, and which had been born into money. Experience had made her an excellent judge of character.

Moving a little bit away from the wedding party before someone realized she didn't belong with them, she scanned those on deck for a likely face—someone who might be persuaded to help her. The nouveau riche tended to be less generous than those who'd had their wealth longer, she'd discovered. . . .

Ah! That tall, dark-haired man. He had the aristocratic bearing of one who'd grown up with a sense of his own importance. At the same time, something in his handsome, patrician features told her he just might listen to a hard-luck case. He appeared to be alone at the moment, too, which would make this easier.

A glance back at the dock showed that two other police officers had joined the first, one of them now questioning an important-looking man with a top hat and walking stick, probably a first-class passenger. She had no time to lose.

Pasting a winning smile onto her lips, she moved toward the man she hoped would save her.

Kenton Bradford, of the New York Bradfords, stood near the top of the gangway, irritation warring with impatience. Where the devil was Sharpe? They were supposed to have met an hour ago, before he boarded the *Sonora*. He had important business to discuss with the man, but now it looked as though they might miss each other altogether.

The riverboat bringing Bradford south from Sacramento yesterday had hit a snag in the river, necessitating repairs and delaying him by several hours. When he'd finally reached San Francisco late last night, he'd immediately sent a message to Mr. Sharpe explaining, and suggesting they meet at the *Sonora* before he sailed. But Sharpe had not yet appeared, and the ship was due to depart in a quarter of an hour.

Though he had done so only a minute or two earlier, Bradford pulled out his finely chased gold watch and consulted it yet again before thrusting it back into his pocket. Sharpe had been the one to convince him to attempt establishment of a California branch of Bradford Shipping and Mercantile, and had promised to become an important investor. Without his support and influence, its success would be far from assured.

He had run across more than a few slick-talking shysters since reaching California six months ago, men adept at parting the foolish from their money. Was Sharpe such a one? He'd had nothing beyond a few letters from the man since meeting him in New York last year, when he'd so enthusiastically expounded upon the opportunities for established businesses expanding to California. Those opportunities still abounded, no doubt about that. But to convince local businesses to patronize his company over others would take some doing. Competition was fierce.

Already Bradford Shipping had received pledges—and gold—from numerous merchants eager to take advantage of the lower shipping rates he offered. Not enough, however. If only Sharpe—

Ah! Was that him? Tilting back his silk top hat, Kenton scanned the shifting, richly dressed throng on the promenade deck and caught another glimpse of the man. Yes, it was definitely Sharpe. He'd seen Bradford now, and angled toward him, laboriously making his way through the press of bodies.

Kenton stepped forward, raising a hand in greeting. "Sharpe! I was afraid you wouldn't make it."

"Bradford! Kenton Bradford! It's good to see you again. I only received your note this morning, about having been delayed on the way from Sacramento," explained the shrewd-eyed, sandy-haired young man, raising his voice to be heard above the general clamor. "It's been all of a year, hasn't it? How have you been?"

"Fine, fine," Kenton said quickly, impatient with this small talk. "We have only a few minutes, I fear, and I have a lot to tell you."

"A lot to tell, indeed," came a feminine voice from behind him. A slender hand took his arm, and he turned in surprise to discover a flame-haired vision—a striking young woman he had never seen before in his life—extending her other hand to Mr. Sharpe.

"I'm so pleased to meet you at last, Mr. Sharpe," said the young lady. "I'm Della—Della Bradford. Kent's wife."

TWO

The ship was cheered, the harbour cleared,
Merrily did we drop
Below the kirk, below the hill,
Below the lighthouse top.

—SAMUEL TAYLOR COLERIDGE,
The Rime of the Ancient Mariner

FOR A MOMENT, KENTON WAS TOO ASTONished to speak—then the girl smiled up at him, holding his eyes with her remarkable gray-green ones. Even as he opened his mouth to deny her outrageous claim, he read the urgent plea in those eyes—and hesitated.

"Well, that's just splendid! Splendid!" Sharpe exclaimed. "I take it this is a recent event?"

"Very recent," said Kenton dryly, still staring at the woman. She looked to be no more than eighteen or nineteen, and was becomingly—and expensively—dressed in a green frock that made the most of her unusual coloring. Feminine and lovely, she was not at all his idea of a typical thief or swindler.

The moment Sharpe left the ship, Kenton decided, he'd find out what sort of trouble she was in that could possibly prompt her to make such a preposterous statement, trusting a total stranger to support it.

Now she shot him a grateful glance before nodding brightly. "Yes, this is to be our honeymoon trip."

"Excellent! Most excellent! And you won't be the only newlyweds aboard, you know. Kenton, Mrs. Bradford, I'd like you to meet my friend and onetime business partner, Ansel Easton, and his new bride, Addie Easton."

A handsome couple stepped forward, the petite Mrs. Easton still in her spreading white wedding gown. "Congratulations to you both," she exclaimed, taking the bogus Mrs. Bradford's hands in her own. "I'm sure you'll be as happy as we will. What fun that we can share our wedding trips!"

Della—if that was really her name—smiled back most convincingly. It occurred to Kenton that while she might not be an outlaw herself, she could quite possibly be a decoy for one.

"Easton here is one of the other investors I mentioned," Sharpe said then. "He has a lot of influence here in San Francisco, and can help you to establish your shipping business. I've told him a bit about it—and you. An excellent thing, isn't it, Easton, that Kenton is married now?"

Mr. Easton smiled and nodded, but Kenton chose his words carefully while at the same time straining to hear what was passing between the two women. "I very much look forward to making your acquaintance, sir. Before we sail, though, I must have a moment with Mr. Sharpe. Nelson, I'd hoped to have time to tell you what I was able to accomplish in Sacramento, but—"

"You'll have all the time in the world," Sharpe assured him. "Did I forget to mention that I'll be taking ship with you? I've business in New York, and this will give me an opportunity to discuss other investments, as well as take another look at Bradford Shipping."

Kenton abruptly exchanged one worry for another. Nelson Sharpe would be aboard for the entire voyage? Even after the introduction to the Eastons, he'd intended to explain this Della woman away as some kind of misunderstanding or joke. But Sharpe would know otherwise. Now his only course would be to expose the girl—something he felt oddly reluctant to do.

He glanced in her direction again and saw that she was now chatting amiably with two other women, as well as Mrs. Easton. Worse and worse! Clearly, the longer he waited, the harder this would be.

". . . in Sacramento," Sharpe was saying, "but I was thinking that a branch in San Francisco, either instead of or in addition to—"

"Yes, yes, but as you said, we'll have plenty of

time now to discuss business plans," Kenton interrupted him. "I fear I must tell you—"

A clanging bell cut across his words, signaling the final boarding of the *Sonora*. Near-pandemonium broke out as those not sailing scrambled for the gangway while those who had lingered ashore simultaneously tried to push their way aboard. Kenton was temporarily separated from Nelson Sharpe and the others, though he saw that the red-haired girl, Della, managed to remain with the small knot of women she'd just met.

Jostled and buffeted, he finally managed to work his way back toward Sharpe, but saw that he was deep in conversation with a man he had not yet met. This would be awkward enough without witnesses, he realized. He veered toward the group of women. Since he hadn't denied her claim at once, the least he could do was warn the girl that he planned to do so now. Perhaps she would be able to devise another way to get out of whatever trouble pursued her.

"Isn't it amazing that we could all have been married so recently and not known of each other before this?" Addie Easton was saying as he drew close. The crowd on the deck had thinned somewhat now that the majority of those staying behind had disembarked.

"Not so strange, in my case," said Della reasonably. "Kent and I were married in Sacramento two days ago, and were not engaged long. I'm not surprised it didn't make the San Francisco papers."

"Is your family in Sacramento, then?" asked another of the women, a pretty young blonde holding a caged canary, of all absurd things.

Kenton paused to hear Della's reply. "They were," she said. "Both of my parents are gone now, God rest them, and my sister was recently married herself. She sailed for the Carolinas last month."

For a moment, he felt a twinge of pity for the lovely young woman, so alone in the world. Then he shook himself. This story was as likely to be a fabrication as the one she'd told about their marriage. It was clear the girl was an accomplished liar. But sympathy was reflected on all of the faces surrounding her.

If he charged in now to deny their marriage and have her removed from the ship, he'd appear a complete villain. The women would tell their husbands, and he'd probably be ostracized for the remainder of the voyage. And many of those men might be in a position to help—or harm—his fledgling business interests in California. Kenton sighed.

Stepping forward, he greeted the women with as much geniality as he could manage. "Kenton Bradford, of the New York Bradfords," he said by way of introduction. "We'll be shoving off in just a couple of minutes," he added, with a significant look at Della. How long did she plan to maintain this charade?

She glanced over his shoulder to scan both the

deck and the wharf beyond. Though she schooled her expression remarkably well, he was able to recognize the sudden anxiety in her eyes as she apparently saw whatever it was she feared. Casually he glanced behind him, but saw nothing out of the ordinary.

"I can hardly wait!" she declared brightly. "This will be my very first sea voyage."

Two of the other women spoke up then, to assure her that she was in for quite a treat, unless they ran into a squall. Against that possibility, various remedies for seasickness were suggested.

Kenton frowned. This was becoming stickier and stickier. Della caught his eye then, and sent him a smile and the ghost of a wink, as if to reassure him. Though he still wanted to strangle the woman, he did feel reassured, oddly enough. She seemed in control of the situation. No doubt she'd already planned for a way to extricate herself from her lie once it had served her purpose.

"There you are, Bradford," exclaimed Nelson Sharpe, coming up behind him. "I have a few more people for you to meet. These voyages are excellent opportunities for making and maintaining business alliances, you know—one reason I decided to take this one. I daresay some of the most important deals I've transacted over the years have occurred aboard some ship or other."

He lowered his voice and leaned closer. "I couldn't say it in front of Easton, but it's the greatest good fortune that you managed to get yourself married just now. Stroke of genius, in fact! After some of the tricks your brother has pulled, this is just the thing to convince the investors that you're settled and stable, not the sort to go haring off before they've made their money back."

A knot formed in Kenton's stomach, but he lifted his chin haughtily. "I had no idea word of my brother's exploits had spread so far—not that they have anything to do with me. The family no longer recognizes him."

Sharpe shrugged. "Doubt it'll make a difference now, anyway. Respectable married man and all that. Come and tell me what you've accomplished in Sacramento while I find those gentlemen I mentioned."

Ruthlessly suppressing his growing unease, Kenton complied. It would be some time, it appeared, before he could speak with this Della alone. He might as well make the most of that time.

Della allowed herself a small sigh of relief when Mr. Bradford moved away to speak with his business crony. For a moment, she had been sure he meant to expose her, and at the worst possible time! That man with the walking stick, the one the police had been questioning earlier, had indeed boarded the ship. Until they were well away from San Francisco, she couldn't afford any kind of commotion that might draw his attention.

Letting the chatter of the other women flow over her, she followed Kenton Bradford with her eyes. He was even more handsome up close, with his thick, dark hair waving above compelling golden brown eyes. The firm planes of his face, clean-shaven in defiance of fashion, as well as his very stance, exuded authority. But had she misjudged his character? She knew that Lady Luck had intervened on her behalf again, when that quick series of introductions had prevented him from denouncing her at the very first. He gave the impression of a man with little tolerance for falsehood.

". . . all so very elegant!" the woman with the canary, who had introduced herself as Virginia Birch, was saying. "I confess I didn't expect such luxury."

Della tried to pick up the thread of the conversation, which had shifted to the ship and its amenities. One of the other ladies suggested a tour of the next deck, to escape the smoke now belching from the steamer's great stack. With a last glance at Mr. Bradford, then another to reassure herself that the man with the walking stick had not yet noticed her, she accompanied the ladies down the curving staircase at the rear of the deckhouse.

Emerging behind the others into the dining saloon, Della caught her breath. With its thick carpeting, graceful chandeliers, and richly carved woodwork, the room could hold its own against the highest-class hotel in San Francisco! Just as well she didn't intend to remain in first class, she thought. All of this luxury might easily go to her head.

As they paced along the rows of long tables and benches where the upper-class passengers would take their meals, Della's thoughts returned to her situation. Sooner or later she would have to explain herself to Mr. Bradford. Perhaps a heart-wrenching tale of woe . . . ?

Quickly she rejected that idea. She instinctively knew he would not be easy to deceive, and if he suspected for a moment that she was lying, he might well denounce her after all. No, her best course would be to tell him the truth, risky as that seemed.

She would simply trust to Mr. Bradford's sense of justice—and to luck. Again.

Though business was normally able to claim his complete attention, Kenton's curiosity about the mysterious Della kept interfering with his concentration. He was more than ready to speak with her alone and hear her explanations, but nearly three hours passed before they were finally shown to their—no, *his*—stateroom.

Opening onto the main dining saloon, it boasted three berths, one above the other, on the right, and a porthole across from the door that let in the noonday light. A padded locker under the porthole, a mirror, a washstand, and their luggage took up most of the remaining space in the minute but luxurious cabin. Della's hooped green skirts took up the rest.

If the steward was surprised at Mr. Bradford's mysterious acquisition of a wife, he was careful not to show it as he took his ticket. As Kenton had paid the extra three hundred dollars for a private room already, no ticket was demanded of Della. Whether he was relieved or irritated by this omission, he couldn't decide.

Closing the door behind the steward, Kenton finally turned to face this presumptuous woman who had distracted his thoughts all morning. But even before he could form the obvious question, she began to apologize and explain.

"Mr. Bradford, I can't begin to tell you how grateful I am that you've played along with my little charade, nor how sorry I am to have put you to such inconvenience." She smiled uncertainly.

He had noticed before how her smile lit up her face, and now strove to ignore that unsettling detail as she continued.

"You see, I had to leave San Francisco in a terrible hurry, and as the steamer was about to sail and I had no time to buy a ticket, this was all I could think of. I promise you that I'm no criminal," she added quickly, in response to his sudden frown.

"Oh?" He made no attempt to soften his expression.

"Not at all! A business competitor was

attempting to bring trumped-up charges against me, however, and law enforcement in San Francisco . . . well, I imagine you've heard of vigilantism. I considered it the better part of valor to leave, rather than wait to see which way the winds might blow justice's scales. But I assure you, I really am completely innocent!"

He raised a skeptical eyebrow. "Might I ask what you were about to be charged with, Miss . . . ?"

"Gill—Gilley. Della Gilley. I, ah, was accused of murder."

He rocked back on his heels. "Murder? Quite a serious charge, wouldn't you say, Miss Gilley?" What sort of trouble had he brought on himself by shielding this woman?

"Exactly!" she agreed eagerly, apparently unaware of his shock. "So you see, I didn't dare wait around. I could have been hanged if Mr. Willis had been able to convince the police chief of his story. As he's been a prominent San Francisco resident for some time and knows the chief well, I feared his chances were good."

"Even though you were innocent?" He couldn't quite believe that he, Kenton Bradford, of the New York Bradfords, was having this conversation. He'd made it through thirty years of life without the slightest breath of scandal ever touching his name. Now, suddenly, he was an accessory to murder!

"I told you, justice in California rarely follows

the civilized paths it does back East. Given the chance, I should have been able to prove my innocence, but I felt the risk was too great should public sentiment turn against me. In any case, my business would be ruined, so I had no real incentive to remain."

"I see," he said, though he didn't see at all. A thousand questions fought for supremacy, but before one could win, she was speaking again.

"Now that we're nearly three hours out from San Francisco, I should be safe enough. We can explain to everyone that it was all a hoax, and I can buy a steerage ticket for the remainder of the trip." She smiled brilliantly, clearly expecting everything to be forgiven.

He shook his head. "I'm afraid it's not that easy. For one thing, I overheard the steward say that the ship, including steerage, is full to capacity. I doubt they would be able to find you a berth. More importantly, recanting your story now will make me look a fool—or worse—to some very important business associates."

In fact, if he admitted to such a hoax, they would assume he was just like his feckless brother. His potential investors would dry up, and his new business venture would die before it began.

But Della waved his arguments aside. "Oh, don't worry about me. Steerage quarters can be cramped, I know, but I'll manage to squeeze in somewhere, I'm sure. As for your friends on board, surely you can tell them it was a joke. Put all the blame on me, if you like. I'll be careful to stay away from everyone I've met so far, so as not to risk contradicting whatever story you see fit to put about."

"I fear I'm not nearly so facile a liar as yourself, Miss Gilley." Kenton felt his jaw tighten at her effrontery. "Nor will these people appreciate having been tricked. I have no wish to alienate them." He literally could not afford to, in fact.

"But—" She fluttered her hands in confusion.

"No," he continued, ignoring her distress—and her loveliness. "We shall simply have to continue as we have begun. You will pose as my wife for the remainder of this voyage."

THREE

Till noon we quietly sailed on,
Yet never a breeze did breathe:
Slowly and smoothly went the ship,
Moved onward from beneath.

—SAMUEL TAYLOR COLERIDGE,
The Rime of the Ancient Mariner

DELLA STARED AT HIM, AGHAST. WAS THE man mad? "Surely you're not serious!" Despite her best efforts, her voice sounded shrill to her own ears. "I can't stay here with you. That wasn't what I'd planned at all!"

Mr. Bradford shrugged, broad shoulders moving powerfully under the fine black twill of his coat. "You should have thought of that before imposing yourself upon me in this manner. You've been so convincing, the others would think me the most heartless man alive if I were to banish you to steerage now. Either you'll play along for the balance of the trip, or I'll inform the captain that we have an accused murderess in our midst. I imagine your quarters then would be rather more unpleasant than those in steerage."

She sucked in her breath, then regarded him closely, ignoring as best she could his masculine presence, which seemed to fill the small room. No, she didn't think he was bluffing. Just as well she'd thought better of giving him her real name! Quite a few passengers must have been questioned about a Miss Gilliland, and there was no telling what story the police had given about her supposed "crimes."

She tried another tack. "Do you really want me sharing your stateroom for the next two weeks? It's fairly obvious that you don't even like me."

"No, I don't." She wondered whether he was referring to her question or her statement. "But I consider it the lesser of various evils, under the circumstances."

Della relaxed marginally. "Then I presume that our, ah, roles will be played out only in public, not in private?" She couldn't think of a more delicate way to ask the question that most preyed on her mind.

His mouth twisted in a mockery of a smile. "I don't intend to take advantage of the situation or of you, Miss Gilley. Your virtue—such as it is—is safe enough. Perhaps I should seek the same assurance from you."

"How insufferable!" she shot back, her temper flaring. "Handsome you may be, Mr. Bradford, but my opinion of you is clearly far lower than your opinion of yourself. I'll have you know that my virtue is quite intact, thank you very much . . . and I intend to keep it that way!"

His smile became more genuine. "It's a bit late for outraged modesty, Miss Gilley. Or should I say Mrs. Bradford? You can be as abusive to me as you wish in private, but in public you will play the doting new wife. I've already seen a sample of your acting ability, so I trust this particular role will not strain it unduly."

"And you'll play the doting new husband?" Acid skepticism dripped from her words.

"Of course." His slight bow mocked her.

She gave an unladylike snort. "Ha! That I'd like to see," she muttered under her breath.

He opened his trunk and began setting his toilet items on the washstand in regimented order. "I suggest you unpack, then, and join me in the dining room for luncheon. My acting experience may be more limited than your own, but I'll endeavor to give a creditable performance."

Ten minutes later, Kenton was wondering what had possessed him to promise such a thing. How on earth was he to convincingly play a devoted newlywed husband to a woman he'd met only that morning? A woman, furthermore, whom he didn't even particularly like, and certainly didn't trust.

He and Della shared their long oaken table with the Eastons, Nelson Sharpe, and the Pattersons, another honeymooning couple. Beyond the Pattersons sat Billy Birch, the famous San Francisco singer and actor, and his new bride, Virginia—the one who had earlier carried the canary. Sharpe made an unending stream of cheerful observations, while the various honeymooners exchanged secret smiles. Kenton felt distinctly ill at ease.

His unease increased sharply when Addie Easton turned to Della and said, "I've told you all about how Ansel and I came to be married, but I've not heard your story. Where and how did you and Mr. Bradford meet? Was it love at first sight?" Her eyes sparkled with her eagerness to hear the romantic tale.

Della hesitated only marginally before replying. "I suppose you could call it that, though we began our association with an argument. Kent nearly knocked me over in the street, you see, and I was most put out, for I dropped all of my weekly shopping."

Addie and the other women laughed, and Della went on to describe his supposed gallantry in retrieving her parcels. "I knew at once that he could be counted on to assist a damsel in distress." She glanced at him as she spoke, and he saw both gratitude and rebuke in her eyes before she turned back to continue her story.

Kenton mechanically ate the excellent food before him, mesmerized by the fiction Della wove so glibly. When asked about his background, she paused, and he stepped into the breach to add a welcome bit of truth to the story, mentioning the hoped-for business expansion that had brought him to California.

"Will not your family be surprised to have you return with a wife?" asked Mary Patterson with a giggle. "Or were you able to send a letter to precede your arrival?"

"Er, no. Things happened so quicky, there was no time for a letter." That was true enough! "And yes, I imagine they will be a bit surprised." With a sudden wrench, he thought of Caroline, his fiancée. Odd that he hadn't considered her before now—though certainly he'd had ample excuse for distraction.

"Pleasantly so, I presume," put in Addie, with a smile for Della.

He managed a halfhearted smile in response. *Surprised* wouldn't even begin to cover it! But surely he could disentangle himself from Miss Gilley before actually reaching his home. What an idiot he'd been to insist that they maintain this deception! He should have tried harder to find some alternative. Now there was no turning back.

Della was exhausted by the time they left the table. She'd never, in her whole checkered life, had to improvise so thoroughly or so quickly. Mr. Bradford had been no help, other than filling in a few details about his shipping business. He'd left the entire burden of describing their meeting and courtship to her.

"An occasional comment from you might have made the story more convincing," she murmured as they moved away from the others to climb the stairs to the promenade deck.

"You seemed to have the whole matter well in hand," he replied. "I was agog to hear what you would come up with next." He carefully did not touch her, she noticed as they moved to the railing—as though she were slimy or contagious.

Suddenly angry, she turned to face him. "It was your idea—no, your *command*—that I continue in this role, if you recall. What else was I to do when they began asking questions? I only did what you demanded, and now you despise me for it."

Surprisingly, he smiled. "I'm being most unfair, am I not? You're right, of course, but I'd have been little help even if I had tried. I fear I have nowhere near your skill in, ah, such matters. It's not something I've been used to."

He was still mocking her, condemning her. "You'd best develop such skills, then," she snapped, "if you insist we play these parts for the next two weeks."

"Don't forget—don't ever forget—that you brought this upon yourself, Miss Gilley." The smile was gone now, his voice low and dangerous. "I'm merely trying to minimize the damage you've already wrought."

It was true, she knew, but she tossed her head

and stared out at the sparkling water rather than meet his gaze. "Then you'll have to play your part as well. Behaving as if your new wife has the plague will hardly convince anyone that our story is true."

He was silent for such a long time that she finally risked a quick glance to make sure he hadn't left her standing there alone. But no, he also was staring at the sea, his brow furrowed.

"This whole thing is alien to my nature," he said at last. "But I see no other way now. I'll endeavor to do better."

It pricked her pride that he should so obviously regret being thrown together with her, but under the circumstances, she could hardly blame him. "If it helps at all, I'm truly sorry I've forced you into such a situation," she said softly.

He turned to look at her, his expression enigmatic. "Thank you. It does. But I imagine that before all is over, you'll be sorrier still."

She glared at him, her sympathy abruptly evaporating. "And you plan to make sure of that, don't you? It appears I made a poor choice after all. You, Kent Bradford, are a bully!" With that, Della stalked off to find another section of rail for her vantage point—one as far from that infuriating man as possible.

The weather was fine, warm but not uncomfortably so, and the promenade deck was crowded, but she managed to find a corner to herself near the bow of the ship. As she watched the ocean flowing away beneath them, the enormous twin paddle wheels compensating for the lack of wind, Della's anger seeped away.

So many things could have gone wrong, preventing her from being where she was right now! That accusation could easily have come on any other day, as the steamer sailed only every second Thursday. She could have been too late for the sailing, or the police could have caught her before she boarded. Or Mr. Bradford could have exposed her the moment she first spoke.

No, awkward as her situation was now, it could have been far, far worse! Lady Luck had been her ally yet again, and Della had much to be grateful for—even if she'd rather not be obligated to an insufferable man like Kenton Bradford.

A high, breathy voice broke into her musings. "Mrs. Bradford—or may I call you Della? Isn't this a lovely day?" Della turned to see Mary Patterson, brown-haired and bouncy, at her side.

"It certainly is," she agreed. "And please call me Della. I've never been one to stand on ceremony."

"Oh, good! Neither have I. I'm sure we're going to be great friends by the time we reach New York!"

Della had every intention of leaving the group long before that, but she smiled. Certainly she could use all the friends she could get just now. "I hope so," she said lightly. "You're originally from New York, aren't you?"

"New Jersey, actually. Close enough. I'm a bit

homesick, I confess. Of course, when I came to California with Papa last year, I never thought that I'd be going home a bride—though I rather *hoped* I might!" She tittered.

Mary was a bit silly, Della realized, but good-natured. And she'd hardly been a paragon of sober responsibility herself, she had to admit.

"Your Mr. Bradford is from New York, too, is he not?" Mary asked her. "One of the New York Bradfords? He seems terribly young—and handsome!—to be the owner of his own business, as my Robert says he is. That's not uncommon in California, of course, where fortunes are made and lost overnight, but things are more settled in the East, I know."

Della felt her smile become fixed, and strove for a more natural expression. "I . . . I believe he had the business from his father," she improvised, remembering a comment by Mr. Sharpe. "He really hasn't spoken much about it to me." Much? She knew nothing whatsoever about Kent's New York business concerns!

"No, I suppose not. Business is so dull, after all, and our feminine brains really aren't made to handle it. Robert often tells me so."

With an effort, Della refrained from contradicting her. She herself had always had an excellent head for business—far better than her father's, certainly! "Dull. Yes, of course."

"So Mr. Bradford's father is dead, then?" Mary continued. "How sad. And you an orphan, too! Is his mother alive, at least?"

Della tried to remember whether he had mentioned his family during the noon meal. He hadn't. "I, ah, believe she still lives in New York. I hope her surprise at our marriage won't keep her from welcoming me into the family!" What did it matter if she was wrong about his family or business in New York? She'd be gone long before the truth came out.

But no—Mr. Sharpe might know the details, and Kent himself would no doubt reveal various facts about himself to the others aboard. It wouldn't do at all for her stories to conflict with his. That might arouse suspicions, and she couldn't afford that—not yet. For one thing, there was that man with the walking stick. She'd caught a glimpse of him again in the dining saloon, though he hadn't looked her way. . . .

"Mary, if you don't mind, I believe I'll return to my room for a deeper-brimmed bonnet. This lovely sunshine will make me freckle terribly if I'm not careful."

Her companion completely understood such vain concern and waved her away cheerfully, promising to resume their conversation later. "If you're not back right away, I'll know you and Mr. Bradford are passing the time more agreeably," she added with a playful wink.

Della turned away quickly, before Mary could see her blush. That was another curse of her coloring, besides the tendency to freckle. She'd discovered long ago that she had to keep her emotions ruthlessly in check or her blushes would betray her—which could be disastrous in the middle of a business negotiation.

So why should Mary's teasing so easily overthrow her practiced control? She wasn't sure she wanted to know the answer.

A *bully*? Had that infuriating woman actually called him a bully? No one had ever called him a bully before! He was generally held to be among the most upright and reasonable of men, never making any decision before weighing all of the options, giving a respectable portion of his income to charities and the church. A *bully*?

With a snort, he turned to glare at the sea, frowning at the puffy white clouds meandering along the horizon. He would *not* let her rattle him or make him behave in any way out of character. No more than she already had, anyway.

He started when a hand unexpectedly clapped him on the shoulder. "So, Bradford, you were going to finish telling me how your negotiations in Sacramento turned out."

Just as glad to turn his mind to other matters, he faced Nelson Sharpe with a smile. "Indeed I was. Competition will be a bit stiffer than I'd hoped, but shipping still seems to be a rapidly growing business in California."

Nelson nodded. "It hasn't reached saturation point yet, not by a long shot. The days of overnight fortunes may be nearly over, but a man can still make quite a comfortable profit here. I know your main focus has been manufacturing in the past, but you've got some shipping contracts already, don't you?"

"Only in the immediate New York area, but that's about to change." Kenton went on to elaborate on his plans for expanding the shipping portion of the Bradford business, letting his enthusiasm color his voice.

What he didn't say, and preferred that Sharpe not discover, was that without this expansion, Bradford Shipping and Mercantile would be in danger of becoming obsolete. He had to land these California contracts to ensure the survival of the original business—the business that supported his mother and sisters, as well as his own future hopes.

Nelson's enthusiasm seemed to match his own. Of course, as a partner in the California shipping branch, the man stood to make a substantial profit himself. "And then there's the extra bonus you picked up on this trip, too," he commented after listening to Kenton's list of the Sacramento firms that had committed to him.

"Bonus?"

"The little lady, of course," Nelson clarified with a grin. "You managed to snag yourself a pretty armful there. Dare I hope she's an heiress to boot?"

Kenton felt vaguely repelled by the man's blatant avarice. Nor did he know the answer to his question, though he rather doubted it. "She's hardly destitute," he replied, remembering that she at least had the means to buy a steerage ticket—and that flattering dress she wore. "But an heiress? I'm afraid not."

"Ah, well, one can't have everything." Nelson chuckled. "So her father wasn't one of those who struck it rich in the gold fields, eh? She does seem rather too high-class to be the daughter of a prospector, I suppose."

They were getting into dangerous territory now, for Kenton knew absolutely nothing about Della's parents or background, beyond the little she'd fabricated over lunch. She could be the illegitimate daughter of a prostitute, for all he knew!

"I believe he tried his hand at mining but didn't make a career of it," he offered, hoping Miss Gilley wasn't even now telling a completely different story to someone else. "Speaking of my wife, however, reminds me that I was to meet her back at our stateroom five minutes ago. We'll talk more about the business later, if that's all right."

Nelson shot him a knowing grin. "Business can't compete with the joys of a new wife. I'll see you at supper if you can bring yourselves to leave your cabin."

With a curt nod that he hoped would be interpreted as impatience rather than irritation, Kenton turned and hurried toward his stateroom. He glanced about the deck as he went, hoping to spot

Della and subtly let her know he needed to speak with her, but she was nowhere to be seen.

He felt a sudden stab of anxiety. Whom was she with? What was she saying? Might he find himself in an even deeper quagmire of lies than before?

A fair number of people had retreated from the sun to converse or play cards in the dining saloon, but Della wasn't there, either. With an exasperated sigh, he opened the door to their stateroom.

"Oh, thank goodness!" Della greeted him. She was seated on the padded trunk, her green skirts billowing about her most fetchingly, though they took up nearly half the space in the cabin.

"We need to talk," they said simultaneously.

FOUR

Forthwith this frame of mine was wrenched
With a woeful agony,
Which forced me to begin my tale;
And then it left me free.

—SAMUEL TAYLOR COLERIDGE,
The Rime of the Ancient Mariner

A SPURT OF LAUGHTER ESCAPED DELLA, AND to her surprise, Kent joined in—for a moment. He leaned against the closed cabin door, and almost at once his expression sobered.

"I take it you've discovered, as I have, that we need to fill in a few gaps in our stories?"

Della nodded, shifting her seat slightly on the trunk, trying for a more comfortable position. "I know you think I'm the world's most experienced liar, but I'd really rather not make up an entire fictitious family for you if I can learn about your real one instead."

"Are you?" he asked.

"Am I what?"

"The world's most experienced liar." Though his expression was more amused than condemning, Della could not suppress a surge of irritation—and hurt.

"Of course not. I've had to talk my way out of a tight place or two over the years, but in general I'm a very honest person." And she was, though his eyes showed clearly that he doubted her. "I do realize your limited acquaintance with me might suggest otherwise," she allowed.

"It might indeed. But trust is something that only grows over time. For now, it is more important that we guard ourselves against any obvious slips that would undermine the trust of our fellow passengers."

Della nodded again. "Not to mention our own embarrassment, if we happen to contradict each other's stories. For example, Mary Patterson was asking me about your family back in New York. I told her your father was dead and your mother alive, but I have no idea if that's true."

His dark eyebrows rose, but she thought he looked almost approving. "Strangely enough, it is. I also have two sisters, both of whom live with her, and one brother, who does not."

"I didn't dare invent any siblings," she said with a grin. "I managed to change the subject before she could probe further."

"It appears that you have more than your fair

share of luck, Miss Gilley, as well as a facile tongue."

She felt herself turning pink again at his use of her alias, and ruthlessly subdued her emotional response to that steady golden brown gaze. "Yes, I do, actually. It must be the Irish in me."

"No doubt," he said dryly. "But rather than trust too blindly to it in the future, I'd prefer we learn enough about each other's background to avoid too many slips. Until we do, I fear it will be risky for either of us to go about the ship without the other, and I'm sure you have no more desire to be continually in my pocket than I have to be in yours."

Della swallowed, wondering if he realized how harsh that sounded—or if he cared. "I should say not!" she agreed quickly. "So, where shall we begin?"

"Since I am the poorer liar, perhaps you should first tell me about yourself," he suggested. She tried not to bristle at his implication, especially since it was somewhat justified. "Where were you born? Who were your parents? Any siblings?"

She twined her fingers together and leaned back against the cabin wall, the light from the porthole bathing her hair. "Right. I may as well start at the beginning. I was born, and spent the first twelve years of my life, in Cincinnati, Ohio, the daughter of Murphy and Aileen O'Dell . . . Gilley."

Yes, she would keep the alias for now, though she was beginning to believe she could trust this man. In token of that trust, she added, "My first name is actually Odella, to honor my mother's family, but I've always gone by Della."

"It sounds as though the Irish in you is all of you," Kent commented, breaking his forbidding stance by the door to seat himself on the bottom berth.

She glanced sharply at him, but his expression was as neutral as his tone, revealing no particular prejudice. "Well, yes, I suppose so—though my mother was born in America and my father came here in his early teens. I've never met my paternal grandparents. They lived—or perhaps still live—in Philadelphia."

He started slightly—or perhaps she only imagined it. "And your mother grew up in Cincinnati?"

"Yes. Her parents married there, and she lived with them until she married my father. They used to write to us, even after my mother passed away, but I haven't heard from them for well over a year now—though that's likely my fault rather than theirs," she admitted. "I've moved around a bit."

His gaze was definitely disapproving now. "Avoiding the law?"

"Of course not!" she said indignantly. "Just following the best business opportunities. I'm not a criminal and never have been. I told you that."

"Yes, you did." But his expression was still

wary. "So what brought your family to California?"

"What brought everyone to California? The gold, of course. My father was one of the first to head west when the news reached Cincinnati."

"And he brought the whole family?"

She nodded. "My mother refused to stay behind. In some ways my father was rather helpless, I suppose, though of course I couldn't see that at the time. She probably didn't think he could take care of himself properly—or perhaps she was afraid he'd never come back."

Glancing up, she surprised a shadowed, almost pained, look in Kent's eyes. "A legitimate fear, certainly," he said. "Many men never did."

"Was there someone—"

"Never mind. You're telling your story now. I'll tell mine later."

Della didn't allow his brusqueness to sting, since he clearly was using it to hide some past hurt. "Of course." He frowned at her gentle tone, so she became brisk again. "Anyway, we headed west, along with several other families, in the spring of 1849. I suspect if my father had realized how rough the trail would be, he'd never have left. Certainly he would never have brought the family along. It took us six months to reach Sacramento, though it seemed like years."

Now it was her turn to remember old pain, but she refused to dwell on it. "By the time we got there, in mid-October, thousands of prospectors had arrived from all over the world. It was exciting but rather frightening."

"I can imagine," Kent murmured. The sympathy in his eyes surprised her, making her wonder if he guessed at the part of her story she'd left out.

"We had very little money," she continued, "and everything was incredibly expensive. Still, we headed straight for the gold fields. My father was sure he'd make his fortune within the week, and then we'd never know another day's privation." She shook her head at such naïveté. Even at twelve, she'd had a far more realistic outlook than her dream-chasing father.

"So he never found any gold?" Kent prompted when she paused.

"Oh, he did find gold. But not right away, and not enough of it. In the mining towns and camps, things cost even more than they did in Sacramento. Luckily, my mother was an accomplished seamstress and was able to mend and sew in exchange for some of what we needed."

She paused again, and he probed her with his eyes. "And you? Did you pan for gold, or help your mother sew?"

"Neither," she said with a sudden grin that made him blink. "I convinced my father to let me buy a hen from a traveling peddler with some of our precious gold, then I sold eggs to the miners for a dollar apiece."

He stared at her, one brow raised. "Quite the youthful entrepreneur, I perceive."

"It was only sense." She shrugged, refusing to be nettled by his sarcasm. "There were people finding fortunes in gold, but not many. Maybe one miner in a hundred at first, then progressively fewer. The ones making a consistent living were those selling goods to the prospectors."

He leaned back in the berth and stretched out his long legs until they brushed the spreading hem of her skirt. "So you contributed to the family income by selling eggs at exorbitant prices."

"In the mining camps, everything sold for exorbitant prices. A dollar an egg was the going rate," she said tartly. "Actually, I started off selling them at seventy-five cents, to undercut the camp store. Then we moved to another camp, where the store owner had no chickens, so I raised my prices."

His expression was unreadable, so she hurried on. "I helped my mother get the best prices for her sewing as well. And my sister and I became quite adept at retrieving anything the miners threw away, then repairing what we could so that we could sell the items back to them. After a couple of years, Papa finally did find a big enough lode to allow him to stop mining. We returned to Sacramento and settled there. And now, suppose you tell me a bit about yourself?"

"You haven't brought your own story up to the present yet," he pointed out. "What happened to your parents? How did you come to be in San Francisco?"

"My mother died in the cholera epidemic of '52, less than a year after we left the gold fields. Papa died last year, of diphtheria. And we're telling everyone we met in Sacramento, remember?" She was reluctant to describe her most recent business venture, of which he would certainly disapprove.

His eyes narrowed, and for a moment she thought he would insist on further details, but then he shrugged. "I suppose that will do—for now. I'll take my turn and let you rest your voice."

Della wondered whether the man was capable of making a statement that didn't sound sarcastic. She leaned forward, propping her chin on her hand, her elbow on her knee, and gave him her undivided—and exaggerated—attention.

One mocking glance told her he saw what she was about, but he began his own narrative without further delay. "My name is *Kenton* Bradford, of the New York Bradfords. Only my sisters call me Kent."

No doubt she was supposed to feel rebuked, but she had to suppress her amusement. Could the man truly be this pompous, or did she bring out the worst in him?

"I was born and raised in New York City," he continued, "where my parents were both prominent citizens. My father founded Bradford Shipping and Mercantile with his father, and I inherited the business when he died."

As she'd suspected, he hailed from one of New York's high-society families, the kind she'd only heard stories about. No wonder he seemed so full of himself. She leaned back again, though still giving him her full attention.

"I've done my best to keep the business going," he went on, "but it has recently become necessary to expand. A year ago, I met Nelson Sharpe in New York, and he told me there was still great demand for shipping in California. I came to Sacramento six months ago to research the possibilities for a West Coast branch of my business, and now I am headed back home to complete the arrangements." He stood up and stretched, his hands touching the low ceiling of the cabin.

"And that's all?" she asked in disbelief.

He looked confused. "What else is there to tell?"

She stared at him, exasperated. "Why, the sorts of things people are likely to ask me about, of course. You mentioned a mother, two sisters, a brother. What are their names? Do you have friends? How old were you when your father died?"

"Oh." He blinked and sat back down. "Let's see. I was seventeen when my father died. His name was also Kenton Bradford. I am the third of that name. My mother was born Willa Maples, of Philadelphia." That explained his start earlier, when she'd mentioned that city. "My sisters are Barbara and Judith, my brother Charles. I do have friends, of course, but as you wouldn't have met them anyway, I see no need to list them."

He seemed oddly reluctant to reveal further details. "Seventeen. That was fairly young to take over responsibility for the family business," she commented, hoping to draw him out further. "How old was your brother at the time?"

Her question clearly irritated him, and for a moment she didn't think he was going to answer.

"A year younger," he finally said. "We managed well enough. We had the advice of family friends, of course, and our longtime managers knew the business. They were able to keep things going until I—we made the adjustment."

It *had* been hard for him, and there was something—something about his brother—he wasn't telling. She read it in his face, in his voice, in his hesitation. But she wouldn't push. Not now, anyway. "And your sisters?"

"Barbara was twelve, and Judy . . . let me see. She would have been eight."

"I hope you won't find my next question impertinent," she said then, trying to keep any trace of amusement from her voice, "but exactly how old are you now?"

To her surprise, he grinned, his face briefly transformed into something approachable, friendly, and disturbingly handsome. "I guess you would need to know that to pose as my wife. I was thirty in June. And if I've done my arithmetic properly, you're ten years younger."

"Yes, I was twenty on February fifteenth."

Leaning forward from his seat on the bunk, he examined her face closely—so closely that she had to fight against the blush she felt threatening. Would he tell her she looked older than twenty, or younger? she wondered. He did neither.

"It occurs to me that you've experienced far more in twenty years than I have in half again as many. I find it a bit surprising that your past hasn't left its mark visibly upon your face. If I knew nothing about you at all, I'd assume you were as innocent as any other girl your age."

She lost control of the blush. "What exactly are you implying?" she demanded. "I *am* innocent. I told you earlier that my virtue is perfectly intact."

He smiled again, but not as pleasantly as before. "Oh, I'm not doubting your virginity. But innocent, Miss Gilley, you definitely are not."

Clearly he didn't mean that as a compliment. "I won't apologize for the way I've lived my life. I am accountable only to myself, and I have no regrets."

"Even now?" He was openly mocking her, but she refused to rise to the bait.

"I have had unpleasant experiences before, and this will doubtless be another. That's not the same as regretting my own decisions. Had I not come aboard and begun this ruse, I imagine I would now be having a far less enjoyable time than even this." She hoped her tone was cutting enough to put him in his place.

"So I'm preferable to a gallows. I'm flattered."

"Marginally preferable." She would *not* smile. "I'll simply keep reminding myself that it's only for two weeks."

Now he frowned. "That's the third time you've said that. I thought I made it clear that we would have to maintain this deception until we reach New York."

"But I'm not going to New York," she exclaimed, taken aback. "I'm only going as far as Panama. I'll catch the next ship headed north, and then go on to Sacramento."

"Leaving me to explain away your disappearance as best I may? No."

The angular planes of his face were uncompromising, but she tried again.

"We can manufacture an argument—that certainly shouldn't be too difficult! I'll say I'm leaving you and going back home." It seemed a perfect solution, but he was already shaking his head.

"What kind of man would leave his new wife all alone in Panama, whatever the provocation? You clearly don't care in the least what people think of you, but I have a bit more concern for my own reputation and family name. Some of the people aboard may very well know acquaintances of mine in New York. I don't care to have a tale like that spread about."

Della took her time answering, a slow smile playing about her lips. He accused her of being impulsive, but he hadn't planned any further ahead than she had. "And how do you intend to explain me away once we reach New York, Mr. Bradford? Even if I could arrange to vanish into thin air as I step ashore, you'll have an interesting time ahead of you."

He opened his mouth and then closed it, his long hesitation proving she was right. "I'll . . . we'll come up with something," he said lamely. Just then, the bell signaling supper rang. "We'll discuss this later," he promised.

"Yes, I think we'd better," she replied, still smiling. She'd won this round—but the next was yet to come.

What on earth was the matter with him? Kenton fumed silently as they left the cabin. Of course the same arguments he'd just used against her departing in Panama would apply equally in New York. He didn't have the faintest idea what he was going to do about it, either.

At lunch he'd told himself that he would somehow get out of this tangle before reaching home—and his family and fiancée—but how? By then, he and Della would have been pretending for nearly a month. It would look stranger than ever if they were to part company abruptly.

A tiny voice also told him that a lot could happen in a month. Much as he disapproved of her, he couldn't deny that Della Gilley was both attractive and charming. After weeks in her close company, would he *want* to let her go?

"You're being awfully quiet," she commented as they took the same seats they'd occupied for luncheon. They were among the first to arrive, with most of the others still on deck enjoying the fine weather.

"I have a lot to think about," he said tersely. Of course he would be willing to let her go! She wasn't his sort of woman at all—and Caroline most definitely was. His fiancée shared his background, his social sphere, his views. Her mother and his had been lifelong friends, and their engagement had been presumed for years before he finally proposed—at his mother's urging—before leaving for California. Caroline would be exactly the sort of wife a man in his position needed.

But how would he ever explain Della to her, should this matter come to her attention? Reluctantly he realized Della's original plan had made more sense from the start. He should have let her find a spot in steerage and explained her away as a hoax at the outset. No doubt she'd have helped him come up with a plausible story, one that would have satisfied Sharpe and the other investors. Perhaps it was still not too late. . . .

"Have you finally realized that I've been right all along?"

He turned in surprise to find her regarding him with barely concealed amusement. Had she read his mind, or just his expression?

"Of course not," he snapped, his only thought

to wipe the amusement from her face. He succeeded—but at what cost? Still, he couldn't bring himself to give her that satisfaction. "I won't allow you to make me look like a fool—here or in New York."

"I suspect you'll do a fair job of that all by yourself if you persist in being so stubborn." Her green eyes glinted with sudden anger.

"If I do, that's my affair—not yours." What was he saying? He was behaving completely out of character. Where was the calm, unemotional reasoning on which he prided himself? The events of this day seemed to have robbed him of rationality.

The logical thing to do was to confess that she'd been right and to explain to everyone what they'd done—now, before they got in any deeper. Before they spent a night alone in his cabin. He had opened his mouth to do just that when Della rose to greet the Eastons, just joining them at the table. He'd missed his chance—again.

Supper was an even livelier meal than luncheon had been, with the passengers eager to share their impressions of the ship and their first day at sea. As before, Kent and Della were surrounded by newlywed couples.

"I declare, being at sea has given me such an appetite," exclaimed Virginia Birch. "Is it the salt air, do you think?"

"Whatever it is, I'm glad to hear it," said her husband, Billy, suggestively. "For I've quite an appetite myself—one I'll sate after the meal." He waggled his brows up and down so comically that everyone at the table laughed. He sketched a mock bow from his seat while Virginia blushed prettily.

That began a series of humorously veiled comments by the gentlemen, designed to elicit blushes from the ladies. Kenton chuckled along with the rest but felt distinctly uncomfortable. If Della felt the same, she hid it remarkably well, he noticed irritably.

"I'd guess none of us will be staying up very late playing cards tonight," said Robert Patterson with a broad wink as the dessert dishes were cleared. His wife tittered, as did Addie and Virginia.

Della, Kenton noticed, only smiled. He was glad she wasn't a giggler, at any rate. "It's a bit early to turn in yet," he said as casually as he could manage. "The sun hasn't even set. Will you three gentlemen join me in some whist?"

To his relief, they agreed, and the ladies retired to the sofas along the side of the saloon to chat. It was only a brief reprieve, he knew, but he would take it.

"You met your bride in Sacramento, I believe you said, Bradford?" asked Ansel Easton as he dealt the second hand fifteen minutes later. "I've met several of the prominent families of that town. What was her father's name?"

For a split second, Kenton panicked, then

remembered that he knew the answer to this question now. "Gilley. Murphy Gilley. But her family is originally from Ohio. They only came to California in late forty-nine."

Easton grinned. "As did I—as did most of the population of California, in fact! I'm originally from New York, like yourself. Your family has always been one of the more prominent in the city, as I recall."

To Kenton's relief, the conversation then turned to his more recent recollections of New York, and his momentary anxiety abated. Only later, when Robert Patterson and Billy Birch were arguing over a point, did it suddenly occur to him that if Della was wanted for murder, he shouldn't have revealed her last name. He really wasn't good at this sort of thing at all.

Several times, as the sun sank toward the horizon, he glanced over to where Della sat talking with the other women. She seemed as vocal as any of them, and he had no doubt she'd made good use of the little bit of information he had given her that afternoon. He sighed. No, there really was no turning back now, however much he might wish otherwise.

"Well, that's the rubber," Robert Patterson declared, totaling up the points from the last hand. "And I'm for bed. How about you gents?"

Kenton was the only one who didn't agree with enthusiasm, and Billy Birch quirked an eyebrow at him. "We're forgetting, Bradford here is an old married man—of two whole days! No wonder he's not quite as eager as the rest of us." That drew a general chuckle, which Kenton was wise enough to join in. Then they all rose.

The ladies were no less eager than their husbands, it seemed, for they came forward at once, whispering and giggling to each other behind their hands. Della, bringing up the rear, glanced up and caught his eye and, to his amazement, blushed bright pink.

This promised to be the most awkward—and perhaps the most interesting—night of his life.

FIVE

The western wave was all a-flame.
The day was well nigh done!
Almost upon the western wave
Rested the broad bright Sun.

—Samuel Taylor Coleridge,
The Rime of the Ancient Mariner

She'd lost control—again. Della could feel the heat in her face, could see Kenton's surprise that a hardened adventuress, which was what he clearly considered her to be, could blush. But she couldn't help it. She kept her face averted from him as he opened the door to their cabin, hoping none of the others had noticed. Not that blushes were remarkable in a supposed new bride, of course—but she *hated* to betray herself this way!

"Are you all right?" he asked her once he'd closed the door behind them.

Reluctantly she turned to face him, fully aware that her cheeks were still flaming. No doubt the lingering crimson of the sunset, pouring in through the porthole, served to emphasize her embarrassment. "If I didn't know better, I might almost believe you were concerned." Immediately regretting her waspishness, she quickly added, "Yes, I'm fine."

But already his expression had hardened. "You can't resist baiting me, can you, Miss Gilley? It might interest you to know that I was on the verge of agreeing to your plan earlier, of admitting our deception and going our separate ways, but your insufferably smug attitude prevented me."

Della could not contain a gasp of laughter. "Prevented you? Is your pride so enormous, then, that the thought of admitting a woman is right should overset your reason?" She shook her head, still chuckling. "Tell me, Mr. Bradford, how *did* you come to be such a successful businessman with such a closed mind?"

"Closed—" He bit off whatever he had been about to say and turned abruptly away from her. After a moment he continued more calmly. "I do not have a closed mind. I'm generally considered very forward-thinking, in fact. I've had to be, to keep the business afloat."

She seized on that scrap of information. "Afloat? Your business has been struggling, then? Is that why you're so reluctant to risk anyone's poor opinion?"

He turned to give her a long, appraising look. "I may not care for your ethics, but there's no denying your perceptiveness. Yes, Bradford Shipping is in some trouble—or nearly so. This California venture is essential to its survival. Alienating the gentlemen aboard, several of whom promise to become important investors, could eventually ruin me."

"Then at this juncture, it might be fair to say that you need me more than I need you," she remarked, the sudden outrage on his face spurring her to chuckle anew. "I recall how delighted Mr. Sharpe was to discover you had acquired a wife."

He glared at her. "I do not need you. You orchestrated this whole situation for your own ends, not mine. I simply wish to get out of it with a minimum of damage to my reputation."

"Which means you need me." She gave him her best impish grin, the one she always used to drive home a winning argument without mortally offending her opponent.

For a moment, she thought she'd failed in her aim, as he continued to glare at her. Then, as she continued to smile, her head cocked questioningly to one side, a glimmer of amusement began to flicker in his eyes.

"Very well, then, have it your way," he said, the tiniest hint of a chuckle coloring his voice. "What a stubborn woman you are, Miss Gilley. Have you ever lost an argument in your life?"

"Oh, no doubt, though at the moment I can't

remember one," she replied lightly, ignoring the flutter his intent gaze produced in her belly. Her cheeks had finally cooled, and she would *not* allow her color to flare out of control again. "Winning this one gives me little satisfaction, however, as it means you are less likely than ever to allow me to depart in Panama."

He nodded, his brief levity gone. "Quite true. But perhaps if we put our heads together, we can come up with a plausible way to separate upon reaching New York. We have weeks to come up with something, after all."

Della swallowed, suddenly brought back to their immediate situation, trapped together in this tiny stateroom for the night—and for a few dozen nights to come. "Yes, I'm sure we'll think of something." To her dismay, the words came out high and breathless. He quirked an eyebrow at her, and she felt yet another blush creeping up her throat toward her face.

To her relief, he turned his back on her then. "Tempting as it is to simply talk all night, we shall both have to sleep sometime. We may as well work out the arrangements now."

Did she imagine it, or had the back of his neck darkened as he spoke? Somehow it heartened her to think he might be as embarrassed as she was.

"There are three berths," she pointed out, her voice more level. "As the cabin is yours, it seems only fair that you get first choice."

He nodded, not quite looking at her. "I'll take

the top, and you may have the bottom. We'll leave the middle one free for our excess luggage."

She exhaled in relief. That would mean she need not climb, nor be assisted by him, to her bunk. Modesty would be much easier to preserve this way.

Abruptly her relief evaporated. Modesty! She could scarcely sleep in her best dress, even if she could discreetly remove the hoops. That meant—

"Er, I-I'll just get my night things out of my valise," she stammered, hoping a solution might present itself. She could ask him to leave the cabin while she changed, she supposed, but as she had just pointed out, this was *his* cabin. Surely, though, he would offer to do the decent thing?

He did not. "I'll sit on my berth and close the curtains while you change," he said instead.

Della was unable to completely stifle a gasp—not quite of outrage, but certainly of surprise and dismay. The look he shot her was far too perceptive.

"Yes, I'm certain you'd prefer that I leave the room entirely, but think for a moment. If anyone were to see me, it would look exceedingly odd. In any event, it seems we may as well begin as we mean to go on. Even if I were unobserved tonight, I can scarcely leave you alone in here every evening without giving rise to speculation both of us would prefer to avoid."

She managed a shaky—very shaky—laugh. "Yes, we *are* supposed to be newlyweds. I suppose you're right." She hated to admit it, though—and hated even more that he'd seen her nervousness. At least it should convince him that she'd told the truth about being virtuous! "I'll . . . wait until you're in your bunk." Not calling the berths "beds" helped a little.

"Just a moment." He sat on the trunk and removed his boots while Della did her best to control the ridiculous trembling in her midsection. She would *not* betray any more nervousness than she already had. A minute later, in his stocking feet, he climbed up to the third berth and, true to his word, closed the heavy curtains behind him.

Della examined the juncture of the two curtains. Was there the tiniest gap there, or was she imagining it? She opened her mouth to ask him to turn his back as well, but stopped herself in time. She was behaving foolishly enough already. Turning her own back, she began undoing the long row of buttons down her bodice. Her fingers shook, making a clumsy business of it.

She was on the last button when his voice came from behind the curtain. "You will let me know when you've finished, won't you?"

Her head whipped around, but she kept her body turned away from him. "Yes, of course. Ladies' clothing takes a bit of time to remove, I'm afraid." Even as she said the words, she felt the rush of blood to her face at the thought that they might seem suggestive. "Th-That is to say," she stammered, "um, I'll hurry."

"No, no, take your time. I'll endeavor to stay awake until it's my turn."

She heard his body shifting on the bunk as he presumably stretched himself out upon it. No, she would not imagine— Quickly she undid the last button and unhooked her hoops. A few moments later, she was able to step free of the dress.

Glancing nervously over her shoulder, she unlaced her corset as quickly as her fumbling fingers would allow. Like her gowns, it fastened in the front for convenience, which was a blessing right now. In a moment, she was free of its restriction. Thank goodness she'd thought to pack her flannel wrapper! She would sleep in it.

Hurriedly she dug the robe from her valise and scrambled into it, belting it tightly over her thin shift. Tossing her petticoats and collapsed hoops onto the trunk, she smoothed out her green dress and laid it on top, then tucked her corset underneath, out of sight. Finally she splashed some water from the ewer onto her face, and dove through the curtains onto the bottom bunk, pulling them tight behind her.

"All right, I'm finished."

She heard his weight shifting above her, and then the heavy damask draperies parted—as they must, since they extended the height of all three berths. With a gasp, she pulled the inner cambric curtains, the ones shielding her berth individually, closer. But then his feet hit the floor with a soft thud and the heavier drapes fell back into place.

"Thank you," was all he said before beginning his own toilette.

Though she tried very hard not to listen, Della could not help hearing the sounds of his undressing, and she was unable to stop herself from analyzing each one. Vainly she tried to block from her mind the picture of his coat and shirt parting to reveal his chest and arms, his trousers peeling away from his powerful legs. What would he sleep in? No, no, she mustn't wonder.

At the same time, she was embarrassed to think that her hoops, petticoats, and corset were out there on the trunk, shielded only by her dress. What imaginations might those stir? Kenton Bradford was a gentleman, it seemed—but he was also male and healthy. Very healthy.

Unwillingly occupied with such thoughts, it seemed no time at all to her before he was climbing back up to his berth, briefly parting the outer drapes and then closing them again. The sun had finally set, so now the welcome darkness offered additional concealment. Della breathed a sigh of relief. That had not been so terrible after all.

Above her, his bunk creaked as he lay back down. A rustle indicated he had pulled his blanket over himself. Again the bunk creaked as he settled himself, and then again.

"Not very comfortable, for the exorbitant price they charge," he commented.

She smiled into the darkness. "I've made do with far worse, I assure you."

"I suppose so." He was silent for a moment. "You're probably thinking that I've led a very pampered life."

"Actually, I was thinking how much less comfortable a berth in steerage would be," she replied. She had thought what he said as well, but admitting it seemed unkind.

"Or in jail."

Kindness be damned, she thought. "Even jail would no doubt be more comfortable—physically—than many places I've had to sleep in my lifetime. Your existence may have been luxurious, Mr. Bradford, but it has also been very sheltered—and probably boring. I can't truly say I envy it."

Now the silence stretched for so long that she wondered whether she'd mortally offended him—or if he'd simply fallen asleep. But then he said, "I'm sorry, Miss Gilley. That remark about jail was uncalled-for. Perhaps tomorrow you can tell me more of your experiences, that I might broaden mine vicariously. For now, though, I suggest we both get some sleep."

She was just as glad to discontinue the conversation. Talking into the darkness like this, while she lay on her bed, seemed terribly intimate—particularly when his voice softened, as it had just now. "A wise suggestion," she said. "Good night, Mr. Bradford."

But even rocked by the gentle motion of the ship and lulled by the hum of the engines, it was a long time before she fell asleep.

* * *

The next morning, Kenton awakened before Della did. As quietly as possible, he climbed down from his berth and dressed, not without frequent glances to assure himself that the curtain in front of her bunk was still tightly closed. Then he left the cabin. She'd no doubt be most grateful to have it to herself when she awoke—and he needed some time to think before he faced her again.

A glance at his watch told him it would be a full hour before breakfast was served. Just as well. He headed out into the early sunshine, turning up his collar at the breeze that doubtless would become warm later but was now almost uncomfortably cool. The sails were spread to take advantage of the following wind and ease the burden on the engines. He took a few turns about the deck, then found a private spot near the bow from which to watch the slightly choppy sea, and to think.

Before falling asleep last night, he'd replayed their brief conversation over and over in his mind, wanting to curse himself each time he came to his quip about Della in jail. She'd said nothing to antagonize him—until after that unforgivable remark. And then . . . *Had* his life been boring? The thought bothered him nearly as much as her calling him a bully had yesterday.

Certainly the years immediately after his father's death had been interesting enough, though he hadn't had to struggle too hard to learn the business, for the managers had readily provided assistance. Then there'd been the mad scramble after Charles sold out his share of the business and left. He had worked long and hard to rebuild after that. Boring? No. But not exactly exciting, either, he had to admit.

And what about the past few years? He'd fallen into a routine, no doubt about it. It had involved hard work still, but little risk, little imagination—until this trip to California. The past six months had been the most exciting of his life, he realized. Even so, he'd faced no hardship, no danger—merely the unfamiliar. Compared to what he knew of Della's life, his own *had* been sheltered.

The bell signaling breakfast cut into his ruminations, but he welcomed the interruption. Turning from the rail, he saw Della coming toward him from the dining saloon. She was wearing a pale lilac dress that set off her coloring nearly as well as yesterday's green one had, and made her look extremely feminine. And innocent.

"Thank you for leaving me the cabin to myself," she said with a smile as soon as she was close enough to speak without being overheard. The promenade deck was a good deal more crowded than it had been an hour ago.

"I didn't believe my rising early would cause comment," he replied. "This will probably be the easiest way to handle the mornings." Then, because he felt the need to put things on a more cordial footing, he added, "That's a very pretty dress."

Her green eyes widened with surprise, and her

smile broadened. "Why, thank you. I'm glad you approve, as this and the one I wore yesterday are the only ones I have with me. I'm afraid I'll have to alternate them for the rest of the voyage."

"We'll come up with a plausible explanation," he said, almost without thinking. "Perhaps we can say that your trunk fell overboard when the riverboat we took from Sacramento hit that snag—which did delay me."

"I think I must be a corrupting influence." She grinned at him. "You're getting better at this sort of thing already. Or perhaps you have a talent for it that you've never developed."

Abruptly all humor left him. "Perhaps," he said shortly. "We'd best go in to breakfast."

He knew she was watching him curiously, wondering about his sudden mood shift, but he did not feel disposed to explain. He wasn't even sure he *could* explain. All he knew was that her remark had reminded him forcibly of his brother, Charles, and he didn't want to discover any likeness there.

"Good morning, Bradford!" Nelson Sharpe greeted him as they entered the saloon. Though the skylights let in ample sunshine, it seemed dimly lit after the morning brightness of the deck. "Sorry I didn't have a chance to speak with you last night. Invited to the captain's table, you know, with all the bigwigs. Couldn't pass that up." A broad wink punctuated his words.

"No, of course not," Kenton agreed. Sharpe

would always have an eye to the main chance, he reminded himself. No claims of friendship would ever take precedence over the man's ambition.

"Mind if I join you and your lovely bride for breakfast?" he asked then. Kenton nodded his assent.

Of the other newlywed couples, only the Pattersons appeared for breakfast, and they sat apart from the group, totally absorbed in each other. After an initial greeting, Sharpe largely ignored Della, plunging directly into business concerns.

"As you probably discovered yourself during your stint in Sacramento, California is overrun by knaves and grifters, becoming ever more clever at bilking honest men out of their money with so-called business opportunities." He paused to take a bite of toast and jam and a swig of coffee. "It's made investors chary of trusting newcomers."

Kenton nodded. "Yes, I noticed. More than one merchant took quite a bit of convincing. Of course, I brought references with me, testifying to the longevity and stability of Bradford Shipping. It also helped that I met more than one highly placed gentleman who hailed from New York and remembered my father."

"Your father was well respected," Sharpe agreed. "But some of those who are aware of his reputation have also heard about your brother's."

Kenton glanced quickly at Della. She was demurely eating her salt ham and eggs, but her eyes were alight with curiosity. *Damn.*

"I've had no contact with my brother for more than seven years," he informed Sharpe, hoping his tone would discourage further comments along this line. He was disappointed.

"That's all to the good, of course, but now that gold's not so thick on the ground, so to speak, investors aren't so free with it. They want assurances—especially when there's any sort of financial scandal in the background." Sharpe emphasized his point with a wave of his fork.

Kenton frowned. "What sort of assurances?"

"That their money will go where they've been told it will go, to build profits. That this isn't just another scam."

"I'll give my personal word of honor, of course." He still wasn't sure what the man was driving at. "As for building profits, I suppose only time will give the definitive proof. Is there something else you feel I should be doing to ensure their trust and goodwill?"

Sharpe shrugged, then wiped his mouth with his napkin and rose. "It's more a matter of what you shouldn't do. Even a hint that all is not completely on the up-and-up, and your investors will run for cover." His gaze swept from Kenton to Della and back. "I simply wanted to put you on your guard."

SIX

But tell me, tell me! speak again,
Thy soft response renewing—

—SAMUEL TAYLOR COLERIDGE,
The Rime of the Ancient Mariner

DELLA STARED AT MR. SHARPE'S RETREATing back, then turned wide eyes to Kenton. "It sounds like he suspects something," she whispered. "What have you been telling him?"

But he looked as startled as she felt—perhaps more so. "Nothing. Absolutely nothing. Of course, he may mean nothing about our marriage at all." But his expression showed he didn't believe that.

Neither did Della. "No, he made it clear that he thinks we're hiding something—we, not you. He must have some reason to mistrust us, or your motives." Or perhaps he'd heard something about her—from the man with the walking stick? She refused to consider that possibility. "What was that about your brother?" she asked, as much to distract herself as because she was curious.

Though he'd scarcely touched his breakfast, he rose abruptly. "Not here. I'm going out onto the deck. You may join me when you've finished."

"I'm done now." Hastily she rose to accompany him. Not for the world would she miss whatever he was about to reveal.

He remained silent as they paced along the promenade deck, up one side of the ship, then back along the other. Already the day was becoming warm and fine, as sparkling as yesterday had been. Della found herself irrelevantly comparing this exquisite weather with the incessant fogs and rains of San Francisco, which was but one day behind them.

"Well?" she prompted as they began their second circuit of the deck without a word spoken. At any moment someone might intercept them and the chance would be lost.

With a sigh, he nodded, slowing his pace somewhat. Daringly she took his arm, realizing belatedly that it might look odd if she did not. He frowned down at her hand, then gave an almost imperceptible shrug. "Very well. I suppose it's better that you hear it from me than from someone else."

Della remained silent, waiting, matching his pace.

"I told you that my brother, Charles, was only one year my junior." She nodded. "After our father died, it was generally assumed that we would run the business together, as partners, with the help of our advisors, sharing the responsibilities equally. That's not exactly how it turned out."

He guided her to a relatively deserted section of the railing before continuing, staring out at the sea as he spoke. "Charles showed himself to be less than responsible. Within a few months, our advisors didn't even bother to seek him out, as he so frequently forgot or ignored their counsel. Within a year, he had abdicated his role as partner, leaving virtually all of the business decisions to me."

"And you were but eighteen." Della knew all too well what it was like to have responsibility thrust upon one so early.

He shrugged. "I was old for my age, even then. And I did have my advisors. Over the next few years, Charles grew progressively wilder, less willing to take advice from me or anyone else. I saw less and less of him, though he attended a university within a few miles of home. When he did confide in me, it was only to speak of his dreams of adventure, and of his resentment of his heritage—of Bradford Shipping—which he saw as robbing him of those dreams."

"He was still very young," Della pointed out. "Most young men yearn for more freedom than they have, I would think."

"You needn't defend him," snapped Kent—as she more and more often found herself calling him in her thoughts. "Charles was always one to chafe at *any* restrictions, never able to accept a bit of responsibility, for himself or for others." His bitterness came through clearly.

He fell silent, staring moodily into the distance. Following his gaze, Della saw a set of sails near the horizon—another ship. The whiteness of the sails against the deep blue of ocean and sky was startlingly beautiful, but she turned her eyes back to the man at her side.

"And then he left?" she prompted.

He started slightly, as though he'd forgotten her presence, then nodded. "When the rumors of gold in California reached New York, he saw it as his call to adventure—a chance to finally realize his dreams. Within a month he had taken ship for the gold fields, along with all the other wastrels. I never saw him again." Though he was doubtless trying to hide it, resentment was plain upon his face.

Remembering her own father and countless other prospectors whom she'd counted as friends, Della felt obliged to say, "Your brother was but one of thousands. The lure of gold led a great many men, good men, to abandon home and career in hopes of returning with wealth and influence—and many were able to do just that."

"I doubt he ever intended to return," said Kent dryly, "considering that he all but ruined the firm to finance his trip."

"Ruined—? Oh, my." Now Della began to understand the depth of Kent's resentment—and his investors' wariness. "Did he embezzle the funds? That must have been terrible for you."

"It was not embezzlement—not quite—though he knew that by cashing out his share of the company so precipitously, it would push us to the brink of disaster. It took me several years to rebuild Bradford Shipping's capital and reputation. It's no wonder that savvy businessmen would want some assurance that such a disaster will not occur again."

Della's eyebrows rose. "But how likely is that? Your character is clearly different, I might even say opposite, from your brother's, and a gold rush is a unique event—something that happens perhaps once in a lifetime, if that."

For the first time since leaving the breakfast table, Kent smiled, leaving her oddly warmed. "I'm pleased that you are so ready to vouch for my character after only a day's acquaintance."

"I've generally been held to be a good judge of character," she explained. "It's a skill that has stood me in good stead on numerous occasions."

He nodded, unsurprised. "I'm sure it has. And yes, if anything, I have striven to be as unlike my brother as possible. But serious investors can hardly be blamed for wanting more tangible proof of my good intentions and business acumen—or for withdrawing their support should they have reason to believe I might follow in my brother's footsteps."

"Where is he now? Have you heard from him since he left?"

His expression again became grim. "From him? No. But *of* him? Far too often. It would seem that he made just enough in the gold fields to finance one mad get-rich-quick scheme after another. Tales of fortunes gained and lost, debts dodged, and excesses of every kind made their way back to me, most eagerly related by those with an interest in seeing me fail."

Suddenly Della understood his insistence on maintaining the charade of their marriage. If these investors felt he had fooled them, even about something as harmless as this, they would take it as proof of his instability—something they were half prepared to believe already, because of his brother's exploits. It would be all the excuse they needed to invest their money elsewhere. She had trapped both of them far more thoroughly than she'd realized when she'd opened her mouth yesterday.

Though she'd already apologized, she felt obliged to do so yet again, now that she fully understood the position in which she'd placed him. "I . . . I didn't realize. If I had, of course, I would never have—that is, I'm terribly sorry that—"

"Never mind." He cut her off abruptly, but not as angrily as she'd expected. "That damage is done now. If we play our parts well, perhaps no more will occur. Shall we walk some more? It's the only exercise we're likely to have for the next few weeks."

Della assented and took his arm again, her mind busy with everything she had just learned.

Kenton breathed deeply of the fresh salt breeze, trying to dispel the old feelings of betrayal his story had revived. He thought he'd managed to put all of that behind him, forgiving Charles as a Christian should forgive his brother, but clearly he had not. As he recounted the events to Della, his emotions had rushed to the surface, every bit as fresh and painful as they'd been seven years earlier.

Seeking to distract himself, he turned to Della again. "I've paraded my family skeletons and given a hint of how they shaped me. Now it's your turn. Why were you accused of murder?" He was careful to keep his voice low. "What was growing up among the mining camps like, and how did it affect your outlook on life?"

She raised startled eyes, wide and green, to his. He was struck by the depth and beauty of that gaze before she hid it with her long lashes and faced forward again.

"Life in the mining camps was . . . challenging," she said softly, choosing the lesser question first. "I'm sure it forced me, and my sister, to grow up more quickly than we would have had we stayed in Ohio. Rather as you were forced to do by your father's death and your brother's abandonment."

Abandonment. An interesting word choice, he

thought, with a double meaning—both of them appropriate. "You sold things, you said, to help support your family," he prompted, unwilling to dwell on his own story.

"Yes." Her lips curved in a slight smile. Clearly her memories were less painful than his own. "We became quite resourceful, in fact, though had our mother suspected half of what we were doing, I'm certain she'd have put a stop to it. In retrospect, I suppose we did take some foolish risks."

"But your Irish luck saw you through?"

She shot him one of her quick, breathtaking grins. "It must have. Maire and I explored abandoned diggings and panning sites, salvaging broken picks, pans, combs, whatever we could find. Many things were too damaged to repair with our limited tools, of course, but what we did manage to sell brought pure profit, as we'd paid out nothing."

He tried to imagine two young girls wandering alone in the wild countryside, at the mercy of wandering outlaws or drunken, disappointed prospectors. "You were what, twelve or thirteen? And your sister even younger?"

"Thirteen. We weren't really settled anywhere until the spring of 1850. Maire turned twelve late that summer."

Unwillingly he thought of his own sisters at that age. Both had still been very much children, sheltered from birth, with no knowledge of the world. They'd have been easy prey. He shuddered. Somehow, though, he knew that Della had never been that innocent—or foolish.

She adjusted her white straw bonnet to better shield her face from the sun—and his gaze. "By the following year, some of the miners were beginning to notice us in a way I didn't care for. Particularly Maire, who was already becoming quite a beauty. I cut off our hair—over her protests, and my mother's—so we could disguise ourselves as boys. Maire agreed, once I explained things to her."

"And your mother allowed this?" Kenton began to doubt the fitness of her parents.

"Oh, I told her it was because of the heat. She never had any idea of how far afield we went in our scavenging. And of course we took care to transform ourselves back into girls before returning home."

He quirked an eyebrow at her. "So you lied to her."

Della looked slightly uncomfortable. "We—I—didn't always tell the entire truth, I suppose. I told Maire it was for Mama's own good, so that she would not worry. She had enough to worry about with Papa already, you see."

"No, I'm not sure I do see. Tell me about him."

She frowned up at him for a long moment, but he simply waited. He'd told her more than he'd intended about his own past, and now it was her turn.

"Before we left Ohio, I remember him as very merry, always with a song or a jest on his lips," she said at last. "But then he changed. I suspect he never forgave himself for Tommy's death."

This was new. "Tommy?"

"My little brother. He was not quite two when we headed west, and he didn't survive the trail. I cared for him as best I could, as did my mother, but he just . . . wasted away." Her chin trembled, and though her eyes were shielded by the wide brim of her bonnet, he suspected she was on the verge of tears.

"I'm sorry," he said softly. "I'm sure you did all you could."

She sniffed once, then raised her chin almost defiantly, repudiating her momentary weakness. "Yes, I know I did. And it was a very long time ago."

Her tone became brisk again. "But Papa took Tommy's death personally, and seemed to feel that if he could just find his lode and give the rest of us a life of luxury, it would compensate somehow. A penance, I suppose. So he worked longer hours than any of the other prospectors, even though he was by no means one of the stronger men. He broke his health, in the end, but he did find what he sought."

"And settled you all in Sacramento," Kenton recalled from what she'd told him yesterday. "You were rich, then?"

She smiled again, but this time it held more

than a hint of bitterness. "Briefly. Very briefly. Papa bought us a fine house and fine clothes, hired servants—all the trappings. He seemed almost his old self again, cheerful and carefree. But only a few months later, cholera swept through Sacramento. Maire recovered, but . . . Mama died." She sighed.

He might not trust Della, but he felt nothing but sympathy for her now—or, at least, sympathy for the girl she had been five years ago. Of course, that could be her whole motive in telling him this story . . . but he didn't think so. "And your father?"

The deck was growing crowded now, so again they retired to the railing, as far from other people as they could manage. Della stared at the waves, much as Kenton had done earlier.

"He changed—again. This time, though, he seemed to have no real goal beyond drowning his sorrow. He took to drink, then to gambling. All too soon, Maire and I were forced to find work. She found a position in a florist's shop, and I served drinks at one of the finer restaurants until I had saved enough to start my own business."

Kenton could not suppress a grudging admiration for her resourcefulness and courage. "You were what, fifteen, sixteen?"

"Sixteen. I would pull my hair into a bun to look older and more responsible." She flashed a grin at him that for a fleeting moment made her look not much more than sixteen.

"And what was the nature of your business?" he asked when she turned back to the sea.

She hesitated. "Actually, I tried several things before I found something profitable. I started with vegetables and poultry from our own small garden and henhouse, but with the competition in Sacramento, I couldn't undercut prices and still make enough money to live on. So I shifted to more gourmet items, but those took a long time to prepare. Again the return was too small. The same was true of sewing."

He nodded. He knew what it was like to struggle to keep a business afloat, to have family depending on oneself. "So your sister was largely supporting you all?"

Della turned wide, startled eyes on him. "Oh, no. I was bringing in far more than her meager salary, but I knew there was much more money to be made if I could just find the right product. Finally, just about the time my father died, I did. The market in San Francisco was even more lucrative, so as soon as Maire had wed and left, I went there."

"And that product would be . . . ?" She seemed extraordinarily cagey on this point, he thought, his earlier suspicions reviving.

And still she hesitated. "Patent medicines," she said at last, not looking at him. "I bought up a traveling salesman's remaining stock and literature, did a bit of research, and set up shop myself."

"You mean—" But the noon bell cut across his words. Glancing up, he realized in amazement that the sun had climbed to the meridian while they talked. Immediately, though, his thoughts returned to what she'd just said. Patent medicines? Della Gilley was nothing more than a snake-oil saleswoman!

"Shall we return to the dining room?" she asked, still not meeting his eye. Evidently she had no more respect for her profession than he did. If anything, that lowered his opinion of her even further.

He wanted to demand to know how she could justify making her living in such a way, preying on the hopes and fears of her fellow creatures, but now people were pressing close to them. Their brief idyll of solitude, rather remarkable in retrospect, was broken.

And now it would be harder than ever to play his role, knowing that, in essence, Della was little different from his brother, Charles.

Della didn't quite dare to take Kent's arm as they headed back to the dining saloon. She was afraid he might pull away from her if she tried, which would be mortifying—not to mention hard to explain to the others. Why had he dragged the truth of her most recent enterprise from her? Why had she let him?

"You two have been in such close conversation all the morning!" Mary Patterson exclaimed from her left just then. "I had always heard that once a man and woman married, they no longer found anything to talk about. It's terribly romantic to see you proving that old saw wrong! Is it not, Robert?" She nudged her husband.

He chuckled. "See what you've done, Bradford? Now the rest of our wives will expect us to devote that kind of undivided attention to them all the day long. We'll have to trade cards, cigars, and masculine conversation for feminine chatter 'round the clock."

"What's that, Patterson?" asked Billy Birch, coming up just then. "Do you mean to say you haven't discovered the way to make your bride forget about talk for at least part of the day?"

Virginia Birch tittered and swatted him with her furled parasol, drawing a general laugh from the others as they seated themselves at the long tables. Soon the tone was much as it had been at supper last night, with Billy leading the other gentlemen in ribald jests.

Della tried to smile in all the appropriate places, but her thoughts were still on her earlier conversation. She had not missed the way Kent had withdrawn when she mentioned her patent medicines, and she could hardly blame him. Most such peddlers were hucksters and swindlers, and the worst were a menace to mankind. In fact, she'd discovered a fair number of noxious compounds among the ones she'd originally purchased, and she had quickly disposed of them.

Earlier, while she'd told of her childhood and adolescence, she was almost certain she'd surprised an expression of respect on his face, perhaps even admiration. But now she had destroyed that, perhaps permanently. She wasn't sure why gaining his admiration was so important to her, but it was. And even more than his admiration, she desired his trust—something that was surely lost to her now.

"Della, you mentioned a sister who recently married," Addie Easton said when the group quieted somewhat to turn their attention to their meal. "Was she younger or older than you?"

Welcoming the distraction, Della replied, "Younger by a year and a half. Quite the beauty of the family, Maire is, with long golden curls and eyes like turquoise. It's no wonder one of the most prominent young men in Sacramento snapped her up."

"Maire. What a pretty name. Is your family Irish, then?"

Della nodded.

"Well, we'll try not to hold that against her, eh?" called Mr. Sharpe from a few places down the table.

Glancing his way, Della caught a glimpse of something in his expression that repelled her—something she'd seen too many times before. Prejudice. She tried not to bristle, mindful of the importance of Kent's business dealings with this man.

"How kind of you, Mr. Sharpe," she said with exaggerated gratitude, earning a chuckle from those around her. "I'll do my very best not to embarrass my husband by my ancestry."

"I'm sure we're all prepared to make allowances," replied Sharpe with a smile she didn't much care for.

Della opened her mouth to tell him what she thought of his "allowances," but Kent spoke before she could.

"I assure you, Sharpe, my wife can hold her own with the bluest-blooded among us—in both wit and manners." He kept his voice light and bantering, but there was no mistaking the steel underneath.

For a moment, an awkward silence descended over the table, but then Billy Birch piped up. "Nicely said, Bradford, and an example to all of us new husbands on how we're called upon to defend our women, eh?" He raised his fists and simulated a boxer's stance, which was quite comical as he was still seated.

Laughter effectively broke the tension, though Della noticed more than one accusatory glance directed at Mr. Sharpe for his rudeness. Sharpe noticed it, too, for he lapsed into embarrassed silence for the remainder of the meal. When at length they all rose, Sharpe remained seated. Glancing back, Della intercepted a glowering stare before he quickly schooled his expression into one of nonchalance.

Pretending not to notice, she turned away and took Kent's arm to accompany the others out onto the deck, where they played a game of counting the knots in the rigging. There was no real opportunity for private conversation, but Della did manage a quick word to Kent while the others were distracted.

"Thank you for defending me earlier." She hoped her sincerity was evident in her voice and expression. "I know you would have preferred to avoid antagonizing Mr. Sharpe."

He slanted an unreadable glance down at her. "I've never been able to stomach prejudice in any form—even when it may be deserved."

She bristled, but he continued before she could speak.

"In any event, I meant what I said to him. But I fear he will be even more on the alert now for anything that might discredit me—or the pair of us."

Mary Patterson called their attention back to the game then, allowing Della to hide her sudden thrill of alarm. The easy camaraderie of the group was a welcome distraction. Still, Della spent every idle moment for the remainder of the day trying to decide which frightened her more—her risk of capture, or her feelings for Kent.

SEVEN

The Sun came up upon the left,
Out of the sea came he!
And he shone bright, and on the right
Went down into the sea.

—SAMUEL TAYLOR COLERIDGE,
The Rime of the Ancient Mariner

KENTON'S THOUGHTS WERE IN EQUAL TURmoil as the day wore on toward evening. His feelings toward Della seemed to careen wildly back and forth between revulsion and distrust and admiration mixed with no little bit of attraction. He glanced over to where she stood near the starboard rail, laughing and pointing up at the rigging, silhouetted by the sinking sun. Never had he known anyone more vital, more alive.

More beautiful.

Oh, Della wasn't a beauty in the classic sense, as was his fiancée, Caroline, with her sculpted features and smooth blond locks. But her vivid coloring, combined with the intelligence and spirit that animated her features, created a whole that was incredibly alluring.

He shook himself. This was absurd! He could not afford to think along these lines—particularly when they still had tonight to get through, and all the other nights to come, alone in their tiny cabin. Besides, he didn't really even *like* the woman. Did he?

"Come, Bradford, we need you to settle this argument before the dinner bell rings," exclaimed Robert Patterson, breaking in upon his thoughts. "Does that tangle up there, just to the right of the topsail, count as two knots or three?"

The distraction was welcome, and Kenton turned his attention to the knots in question, pronouncing his opinion that there were, in fact, four, just before the bells rang out to signal the evening meal.

Della joined him as they made their way back to the saloon, looking flushed, windblown, and happy. He couldn't resist smiling back at her and wondering how much happiness she'd actually had in her short, difficult life.

Sharpe had not been in evidence all afternoon, nor did he join the newlywed couples at dinner. A glance down the long room showed that he was again seated at the captain's table. Kenton was just as glad, though he knew he'd eventually have to make his peace with the man. Sharpe had too many important connections to ignore. Still, he could not help being unsettled by the glimpse he'd had earlier of the uglier side of the man's nature.

"Yes, the Carolinas," Della was saying to Virginia Birch, who sat across from her. "Charlotte, I believe. Her husband's family is there, and he is to be heir to their plantation."

"So your sister has gone to be a southern belle," Virginia commented. "That will be quite a change from California, I imagine."

Kenton listened for a moment, learning a bit more about Della's family in the process. But he'd have to wait until they were alone to discover the things he really needed to know—such as how she had come to be accused of murder. And how likely it was that Sharpe might discover that disturbing little fact.

"I thought you were going to give me a head start, so that I could change before you came in," said Della the moment the cabin door closed behind them a couple of hours later.

In his eagerness to hear the rest of her story, Kenton had forgotten their plan to allow her additional privacy. But now that they were both inside the little room, it was too late for him to back out without causing comment.

"I, ah, I'm sorry. You go ahead and change first again." Feeling foolish, he climbed up to his berth and pulled the draperies closed behind him before stretching out to wait his turn. *Damn*. He'd forgotten to take off his boots, he realized. Where was his mind tonight?

As if in answer, a soft rustling began outside the curtains as Della undressed. Just as he had last night, he found it far too easy to visualize what was going on out there in the cabin. Now, knowing Della even better and having admitted to at least some degree of admiration for her, it was worse.

One shoe, and then the other—dainty little half boots, he remembered—thunked softly against the floor as she removed them. And that—that would be the sound of her unfastening her hoops. He imagined her slipping them from beneath her skirts, perhaps revealing ankles and calves as she did so.

That rustling—would that be her petticoats? Had she unbuttoned her dress yet? He knew he should not be allowing himself such thoughts, but he had to pass the time somehow. The sound of her valise opening and then closing indicated that she had taken out her nightgown. What did women wear under their nightgowns? Anything at all? Was hers of cotton or satin, and what color was it likely to be? Would it outline her breasts?

No! This was absurd. He could *not* afford to think about Della like that, or this voyage would become impossible. He tried valiantly to bring a picture of Caroline before his mind's eye instead. Blond. She was blond, and tall—much taller than Della. Della would come only to Caroline's nose.

Her petiteness brought out an odd protectiveness in him. . . .

Even as he realized his thoughts had strayed again into forbidden channels, the drapes parted, then closed. "I'm finished," Della informed him from below.

Not a moment too soon, he told himself. It dawned on him that the greatest risk from this charade was not to his business reputation, or family name, but to his own integrity. To distract himself from such an unsettling revelation, he began speaking as he removed his boots, leaning against the wall for support, as Della's hoops again occupied the trunk.

"You never did have a chance to finish your tale this morning," he said. "We were interrupted just as you told me the nature of your most recent business." Remembering what that business was helped to steady his unruly inclinations.

Muffled by the draperies, Della's voice was hesitant. "I know you cannot approve of what I was doing, and it was not what I set out to do, of course. But my remedies were no worse than those sold by the various apothecaries and druggists in town, I assure you."

Kenton shrugged out of his jacket, frowning. "But those men have training, experience—"

"In the East, perhaps." She spoke more forcefully now. "In San Francisco, I assure you, not one apothecary in ten is qualified for the profession. Nor most physicians, either."

He realized her words were probably true. His frame of reference was different. Perhaps he shouldn't judge the situation by New York standards. "So you were selling real cures? Concoctions that actually helped more than they harmed people?" He was still skeptical.

"I believe a few of my remedies were genuine, yes. I gathered several testimonials about the efficacy of my sovereign indigestion and sleep potions. And many of my medicines were fortified with nutrients, so they were bound to do some good, even if they weren't able to treat the condition for which they were intended."

Did she really believe this, or was she simply reciting a litany she'd used to convince herself and her customers over the years? "Are you saying that you mixed up these remedies yourself?"

"For the most part, yes. I tested much of Dr. Mirabula's original stock on myself, and disposed of anything that caused even the least adverse reaction."

"That was daring," he exclaimed, turning his back to the berths to remove his trousers. Not that he really believed she would peek, of course. "You might easily have poisoned yourself."

"I was careful, starting with minute amounts, then increasing to the recommended dosages if I observed no ill effects. Maire offered to help me test them, but her health was delicate after a bout of dysentery, so I was unwilling to allow that."

Stripped to his drawers, he doused the light

and quickly climbed back into his bunk. Settling himself, he finally asked the question he'd been putting off. "The murder accusation—did it come about as a result of your remedies?"

"Yes. But not because they harmed anyone," she added quickly. "My ague remedy was perfectly harmless, and Mrs. Potts was already exceedingly ill. I didn't expect my medicine would cure her, but I'm absolutely certain it did not hasten her demise. Her husband was anxious to ascribe blame, however, and a certain rival apothecary was only too eager to direct suspicion my way."

Finally he began to understand. "Was this apothecary also treating the unfortunate Mrs. Potts?"

"You're very astute." He could hear the approval in her voice. "He was, and no doubt feared for his own reputation if he was unable to fix the blame elsewhere. Particularly since questions had already been raised about his asthma cure. I sampled some myself once, out of curiosity, and I'm almost certain it contained significant quantities of opium."

"Then why should you fear his accusations? It sounds as though you had ample evidence to defend yourself." He wanted—needed—to have reason to doubt her, but it was becoming more and more difficult to do so.

"I did." She sighed. "But as I believe I may have mentioned before, Mr. Willis was more respected—and far wealthier—than I. He founded his shop just after the gold rush began, more than seven years ago. He had numerous associates who served on the last Vigilance Committee. I had no one in San Francisco, no family and no friends, who would come to my defense, save my landlady. I admit my flight was impetuous, but I believe I had ample cause to fear for my safety under the circumstances."

Unwillingly he considered what it must have been like for her, alone in that lawless city, her parents dead, her sister married and gone. What had her life been but one abandonment after another? No, he really couldn't blame her. "I suppose you did. I'm sorry if I was harsh before."

Silence. Then, softly, floating up through the darkness, "Thank you."

This had been easier when Kent Bradford irritated her, when she still resented him for holding her to this bargain, Della decided. She strolled along the promenade deck with Mary Patterson and Addie Easton, their sprightly chatter washing over her as her thoughts returned yet again to the subject that had plagued her for the past few days.

She had been certain that Kent would withdraw completely once he knew the truth about her recent life. In fact, she wouldn't have been surprised if he'd decided at that point to risk his business and reputation rather than spend another moment in her presence. Instead he'd softened toward her. He'd even apologized. Guiltily she realized she still hadn't told him her real name. And now she didn't know what—or how—to think about him.

"How about you, Della?" asked Mary just then, breaking into her ruminations.

"Me? What?" She hadn't a clue what they'd been talking about. "I'm sorry—I'm afraid I was daydreaming."

Mary giggled. "No wonder! We were comparing the reality of marriage, after a whole week of it, to our expectations." She pinkened, but her eyes danced with laughter. "With a handsome husband like Mr. Bradford, though, I can't imagine you've been disappointed."

Now it was Della's turn to flush—which both of her companions took as confirmation of Mary's surmise. Her stammered reply only added to the impression, she suspected. "Disappointed? Ah, n-no, not . . . that is to say—"

"No need to go into specifics, dear." Addie placed a hand on her sleeve. "Mary, shame on you for embarrassing her so! Surely time doesn't hang so heavily on our hands that we need to discuss such very private matters to alleviate our boredom."

Mary quickly agreed, and Della absently murmured something about not being at all offended, but already her mind was elsewhere. Across the broad deck, Kent stood talking to several other gentlemen, the ocean breeze riffling his dark hair.

A week of sunshine had given his face a bronze glow, reminiscent of a Greek god.

Della blinked. What was she thinking? Kent Bradford might be handsome and a pleasant gentleman, but he was no god. Still, she could not suppress a quiver of appreciation at the way his muscular legs planted themselves on the deck, swaying slightly with the movement of the ship. Or the way the strong column of his neck emerged from his snowy white shirt, the breadth of his shoulders beneath the fabric . . . She stifled a sigh.

The routine they'd worked out, with her retiring first in the evenings and him leaving the cabin first in the mornings, gave her welcome privacy for her own toilette. No longer did she have to worry about what he might see—or imagine—as she dressed or undressed. But what of her own imaginings? Each night she had to pretend she slept while listening to the increasingly seductive sounds of his clothing being peeled from his body, while her imagination grew bolder and bolder.

It wasn't fair, she decided. Why should she be tormented so by the first man who had ever truly attracted her, while he remained unmoved? Not that she *wanted* him to desire her, of course. Did she?

"So, my dear, are you ladies keeping yourselves amused?" Kent's own voice broke into her musings, making her jump.

Turning, she saw that he, Ansel Easton, and Robert Patterson had joined them. "Of course," she replied with a smile. "After the gloomy San Francisco weather, I can't seem to get enough of this sunshine, though I fear all the bonnets and parasols in the world aren't enough to keep my freckles at bay."

He grinned down at her. "I rather like your freckles. Haven't I told you that before?"

She shook her head, captured by his amber gaze for a long moment before nervously looking away, afraid of what her own eyes might reveal. Since their first two days aboard, they had avoided private conversation, Della spending most of her time with the other ladies and Kent with the gentlemen, meeting mainly at mealtimes. Even now they were in a group of six, though the others paid them little attention at the moment.

"I've been negligent, then," he said, making her blink until she realized he was referring back to his comment about her freckles. "They give you character—though goodness knows you have enough of that even without them."

Surprised, she met his eyes again, to find a warmth there that sent odd tremors through her midsection. Her own eyes widened. Was it possible that she was not alone in her attraction? But even as the thought entered her incredulous brain, he glanced away, his tone suddenly lighter, making her wonder if she'd only imagined what she wished to see.

"I notice there are clouds on the horizon, off to the east. Perhaps you're right to enjoy the sun while you can."

She followed his gaze. "I doubt those clouds will affect us. I've long observed that storms in this part of the world generally come in from the west and move off to the east. That one will likely trouble the Mexican coast rather than head this way."

His eyebrows rose. "How observant of you. And, of course, you're quite right. I wasn't thinking."

Dared she hope she might be the cause of his distraction? But his next words seemed to dispel that idea.

"I've cemented deals with two more investors over the past two days," he informed her, his voice now low. Doubtless he'd noticed, as she had, that the other men didn't discuss business with their wives. "It seems Sharpe was right about the opportunities to be found aboard ship."

She took a few steps away from the others so that they might speak more privately. "Does that make your position more secure? Or do we need to be as much on our guard as ever?" The man with the walking stick had still not approached her, making her hope she'd been mistaken about that threat.

Kent shrugged. "It's hard to say. But I'm not finding our current situation too onerous in any event." Again he held her with that golden brown gaze. "Are you?"

Della shook her head slowly. It would be fatally easy to develop a real attachment to this man, she realized. For the first time, she allowed herself to wonder whether that would be such a bad thing.

"Oh, here comes Mr. Birch!" Mary Patterson exclaimed just then, reminding Della abruptly that they weren't alone. "Virginia said he was composing a new song, even funnier than the last. Perhaps he has finished it."

They rejoined the group in time to hear Billy Birch promising to perform his newest bit of cleverness that evening after supper. Everyone expressed their eagerness to hear it at once, but he waved them away. "Anticipation will ensure me a more appreciative audience," he joked. "Besides, any performance is better received on a full stomach, I've discovered, particularly if plenty of wine is served with the meal."

After a bit more banter of the same sort, the group again segregated by sex, the men to talk business and politics, the women to discuss fashion and gossip. Della's story of losing her luggage had been accepted without question, and now Virginia offered her tips on ways to make her remaining wardrobe appear more varied than it was.

"It's amazing what a bit of trim, a shawl, and a scarf or two can accomplish," she declared. "And I daresay you'll be able to buy another frock or two in Panama City, or if not there, then certainly in Havana."

Della had done her best not to think that far ahead, but now she had to wonder what her situation might be by then. Would she still be fighting her attraction to Kent, or might things have changed substantially between them? A delicious shiver of anticipation coursed through her at the thought. But Virginia claimed her attention again, and she had no further chance to dwell on such possibilities before the dinner bell rang.

"I see my remarks weren't enough to induce you to abandon your sunshades," Kent said teasingly as he joined her at the dinner table a couple of hours later.

Though her heightened awareness of him after her earlier musings was distracting, Della managed to reply lightly enough. "You have no idea what this southern sun can do to a complexion as fair as mine. While you might find my freckles appealing, I rather doubt scarlet, peeling skin would be equally so."

"No, I wouldn't want you to burn," he agreed. "I'm sure that would be quite painful."

She nodded. "It is—and I speak from experience. I learned years ago that even the misty northern California sun can wreak havoc with my complexion in summertime if I'm not careful. And some of the other passengers are no doubt wishing by now that they'd been more careful."

Addie Easton leaned forward from across the table. "Yes, did you see poor Mrs. Paddington? She's nearly as red as a lobster! She had a lotion of some traveling peddler that claimed to protect her from the sun, and so she relied upon that rather than more substantial shade."

"Not that she'll ever see the fellow again to demand her money back," commented Mr. Easton. He shook his head. "There should be laws to prevent those fellows from making their outrageous, unsubstantiated claims."

Della knew her smile had become fixed. Not for the world would she glance Kent's way just now. "Perhaps there will be one day," she said, surprised to hear how normal her voice sounded. "I'm sure those selling more legitimate remedies would welcome anything that reined in the charlatans who make a bad name for them all."

The others agreed with so sensible a comment, and then the conversation moved on to other topics, to Della's relief. Kent had remained silent during the exchange, and after a moment she gathered courage enough to look his way. He met her glance with an enigmatic smile.

"Very well said," he murmured, his eyes twinkling with amusement and . . . admiration?

Again she felt herself drawn into that gaze, finding depths there she had never noticed before. His smile faded slowly, making her aware of the shape of his lips, the lines of his face. With an effort, she pulled her eyes away and focused on the plate of beef-and-barley stew that had just been set before her.

As the voyage progressed, the quality of the

food had deteriorated a bit, though it was still far better than what she'd been used to for much of her life. Though sustaining and reasonably tasty, it could no longer command her complete attention—particularly with Kent sitting so close beside her on the bench.

He was speaking with a Mr. Gibson now, seated on his other side—one of the investors he'd lined up since boarding the ship, she recalled. With his attention elsewhere, she had a chance to examine him again, appreciating anew the strong lines of his body and his clean, masculine scent. He must have gone back to the cabin at some point today to bathe himself with water from the basin, just as she had done yesterday. What if she had walked in upon him, or he upon her?

She swallowed convulsively at the image such speculation conjured up. Just then he turned his head, and she had to lower her eyes quickly, lest he see the longing that no doubt was reflected in them. No longer could she deny her feelings—she wanted him. It had taken her so long to realize it simply because she'd never felt that way about any man before.

But did he want her?

There was only one way to find out, she decided impulsively. She'd ask him. Not outright, of course—even she wasn't bold enough for that. First she'd give him hints and watch to see how he responded. If he was interested, surely he would let her know. Then she could ask roundabout questions and figure out where she stood.

Lifting her head, she sent him her most charming smile and allowed her thigh to brush his under the table, where no one else could see. Not that it should matter if they did, she reminded herself, as they were supposed to be married.

His golden brown eyes widened. He fixed them on her, a new question in his expression. She faltered for a moment and glanced down, unsure what her next move should be.

Courage, she told herself. How else could she know what her chances with him might be?

Boldly she again lifted her gaze to his. A smile flickered at the corner of his mouth, and she was almost certain something smoldered deep in his eyes—

"Billy! Billy!" A sudden shout, quickly taken up by a dozen people, broke the moment abruptly. "The song! The song!"

Billy Birch stood with a smile and bowed before beginning his new masterpiece. It was hilarious, but Della sighed, her chance delayed. Would she ever be able to muster the nerve to pick up where she had just left off?

EIGHT

It raised my hair, it fanned my cheek
Like a meadow-gale of spring—
It mingled strangely with my fears,
Yet it felt like a welcoming.

—SAMUEL TAYLOR COLERIDGE,
The Rime of the Ancient Mariner

BY THE SECOND STANZA OF BILLY'S SONG, Kenton realized he had reason to be grateful for the interruption. Something had begun to kindle between Della and himself, something exciting, something he had very much wanted to pursue. But it was madness. He respected her too much now to consider her for a brief fling—but what else was possible?

Nothing, he realized. Odd that the knowledge should depress him so. He'd known from the start that she wasn't the type of woman who would make a man in his position a good wife. He understood her better now and, yes, liked her better—much better—than he had a week ago, but nothing had really changed.

Had it?

He slid a sideways glance at her. She sat watching Billy's antics, her full lips curved softly upward with amusement, her eyes animated, her cheeks flushed with a healthy glow. He had been quite honest when he'd admired even her freckles. They gave her face yet more character, and added to her illusion of innocence.

And in the most important way, he knew, she really was innocent. Her modesty and blushes made it perfectly obvious she'd never taken a lover, and he suspected, now that he knew her life story, that she'd never even been seriously courted. Amazing, considering her loveliness and the shortage of women in California, but she had moved around a lot, and could certainly be prickly at times. He had no doubt she could discourage any man who didn't interest her.

Or encourage any man who did.

As though feeling his eyes upon her, Della turned her head. Though sorely tempted to plumb the green depths of her eyes again—eyes that reminded him of the very Pacific on which they sailed—he had enough wisdom left to avert his gaze, focusing on the conclusion of Billy's performance before she could catch him watching her.

Though he laughed and applauded with the others as Billy finished his ditty, his attention was on the periphery of his vision, where he was able to observe Della with the tail of his eye. The moment she turned to chat about the performance with Addie Easton, he allowed himself to examine her again.

She was wearing the green dress today, the one that set off her coloring so well. Her curls, cascading down her back, seemed redder than ever, reminding him of dancing flames, alight with life, with passion.

No! He could not afford to think of her in that way. Deliberately he turned away to discuss finances with Mr. Gibson again, determined to pull his wayward emotions rigidly under control before facing the most dangerous hours of the twenty-four—the hours that would begin once he entered their stateroom.

Three hours later, he could claim to have been only partially successful. Even though the other gentlemen had been more interested in cards and ribald jests, he had turned the talk to business repeatedly, in an effort to settle his mind. And now he had given Della a full hour alone in the cabin before joining her, in hopes that she would be sound asleep, removing the last vestige of temptation for the evening.

Silently he closed the cabin door behind him. The damask drapes before the berths were tightly closed, which he took as a good sign. As quietly as possible, he removed his boots, but the second one thunked softly against the trunk as he set it down.

"Kent?" came Della's voice drowsily from behind the curtain. He wasn't sure she'd ever used the nickname before when they were alone. The single syllable affected him profoundly, making him face quickly away from the berths.

"Yes, it's just me. Go back to sleep." He spoke in a near-whisper. Surely, that was why his voice sounded so odd to his own ears.

A soft rustling sounded behind the drapes. "Mmm," Della sighed as she shifted and settled herself to resume her slumber. The sound was incredibly erotic.

He shook his head sharply. No, it was no different from other sounds she'd made—and he'd made, too—since sharing this room. His perspective was all that had changed. He had to find some way to change it back. That was all there was to it.

But telling himself what to do and doing it were two entirely different things. He splashed cold water on his face in an effort to cool his thoughts, but to little avail. His body remained rigidly—all too rigidly!—attentive to even the tiniest murmur from behind the curtain. Finally, in embarrassment, he doused the light before removing his trousers, then quickly climbed up to the privacy of his own berth. It was a long time before he fell asleep.

When Della awoke, the sun shone brightly through the porthole. Had she slept through the breakfast call? Sitting up, she parted the curtains and saw that Kent's clothes and boots were gone. Dimly she recalled him coming in late last night. She'd intended to talk with him then, but she hadn't awakened sufficiently, and instead had drifted back to sleep.

Today was a new day, however, and she would make the most of it. She would confess her one remaining deception—her name—and would at least hint at her feelings. She dressed quickly, then ventured out while her courage was still high.

The morning bell must have awakened her, for quite a few passengers were still finishing their breakfasts when she emerged into the dining saloon. Too eager to eat much, she only paused for a roll and some coffee before heading for the promenade deck to find Kent.

She spotted him almost at once, but he was deep in conversation with five or six other gentlemen. Any declaration would have to wait—not that she was exactly sure what she intended to say, anyway. She regretted the delay, knowing that if she took too much time to consider, she might well think better of her plan to put her feelings into words.

Her best speeches had always been the ones she prepared the least, so she resisted the urge to rehearse what she intended to say. Instead, she went to join Addie, Mary, and Virginia near the bow of the ship, where they were leaning as far forward as the railing would allow.

"Are we looking at something in particular?" Della asked, leaning out herself to watch the water as they did.

"Dolphins!" exclaimed Mary, gesturing. "See? There—and there!"

Della watched the sleek gray bodies with delight as they leaped from the water again and again, keeping pace with the ship. What incredible grace, what freedom! "They're so fast! I had no idea."

Now their excitement had attracted the attention of several other passengers, particularly the children. Parents lifted the smaller ones up to see the dolphins, squealing at the sight as loudly as their offspring. It reminded Della that she was by no means the only one experiencing her first sea voyage.

"Dolphins?" asked Kent in her ear, sending a delicious shiver down the back of her neck. "I remember seeing them on my trip to California last spring. Amazing, aren't they?"

Distracted by his nearness—he was almost but not quite touching her as he stretched his own length over the rail—Della could only nod at first. Then she found her tongue. "I've seen whales at a distance, out in the San Francisco Bay, but never dolphins. Why do you suppose they're not afraid of the ship?"

She felt rather than saw his shrug. "I suppose they've learned that it won't hurt them. What surprises me is how sociable they are, and how playful. They seem to have no worries at all." She caught a wistful note in his words.

"Are you worried?" she asked, almost without thinking.

For a moment, she didn't think he would answer. Then he said, "We all have worries, I suppose. Mine are less significant than those of most people, no doubt, though of course they loom large to me. At a moment like this, however, I can't seem to dwell on them."

She turned from the rail to smile up at him. "Then we have something to thank these dolphins for, don't we?"

As he had last night at dinner, Kent met her eyes with an intensity that took her breath away. No, she had not imagined the heat in those golden brown depths. It fairly scorched her before he abruptly shifted his gaze back to the animals below.

"Escaping from one's cares for a time is well enough," he said now, not looking at her. "But it would be dangerous to forget them entirely, particularly if doing so might harm others besides oneself."

"Your mother and sisters," she guessed, remembering that they were dependent on the income from his business. After a brief hesitation, he nodded, his expression now unreadable.

"Oh, they're leaving!" came a general lament from the crowd around them. Indeed, the dolphins were dispersing, heading west to the open sea.

With a sigh, Della left the rail. Perhaps now she could have a few private words with Kent. But already he was turning away. "I was in the middle of a discussion of how the influx of gold to the eastern markets is affecting business there," he said. "I'd best return to it now that the excitement is over. I'll see you at luncheon, my dear."

His tone was polite, even cordial, but also distant, she thought, as though he had deliberately put things back on a more formal—and less intimate—footing. Still, her courage had been bolstered by that glimpse into his emotions through their exchanged gaze. She would find a chance to speak before the day was out, she promised herself.

That chance did not come until just before dinnertime, however. Della almost thought Kent was avoiding her. But why now? He had not done so yesterday or the day before. Or . . . had she simply not noticed? Perhaps only now that she was anxious for a word alone with him had it become obvious.

She considered simply waiting until tonight, when they would have hours to themselves, but for some reason she was reluctant to do that. If he did not return her regard, it would make for an awkwardness from which there would be no escape—and likely no sleep. And if he did . . . She shied away from that possibility, too. No, better to discover the truth while there were still some hours in company ahead, to allow her time to come to terms with whatever she learned.

Besides, he might do as he had last night, and wait until after she fell asleep to come to the cabin. She'd planned to stay awake then and hadn't managed it, so she didn't want to gamble that she would tonight.

The sun was hastening toward the horizon when the other ladies left her to go freshen up before dinner. She spotted Kent standing alone near the stairs leading down to the cabins and dining saloon, and hurried over to him before he could descend.

"Do you have a moment?" she asked, then chided herself for the clumsiness of her words.

He turned in some surprise. "I did not see you there. Did you wish to visit the cabin before dinner? If so, I can remain here."

She shook her head. "No. That is, I'd prefer to remain here with you, unless . . ." Della could not recall ever being so tongue-tied in her life. "I'd—I'd like to talk," she finally blurted out.

Now she thought he looked wary, though he merely nodded and moved toward the nearby railing. "Certainly. What about?"

He wasn't going to make this easy, she realized. Or perhaps he really had no clue about what she wished to say—or to ask. Frantically gathering her thoughts and her dignity, she followed him to the railing. He was watching her expectantly now. She *had* to speak!

"We've . . . gotten to know each other fairly well by now, wouldn't you say?" she began.

He raised an eyebrow. "I suppose we have, yes." He looked curious but not at all forbidding. She took it as a good sign.

"When we first met—that first day or two—I didn't think I liked you very much. You seemed pompous and dictatorial, and you quite clearly disapproved of me." That wasn't what she'd meant to say at all! She was making a botch of this, insulting him and reminding him of reasons *not* to care for her.

But then he smiled, easing her worries. "I hope your opinion of me has improved, as mine has of you," he said, buoying her hopes further.

Della nodded. "Yes, it has. That's what I wanted to speak with you about. I wanted to let you know that, and to apologize for my earlier attitude." She paused. "And I'm pleased to hear you no longer dislike me, either."

He was still smiling. "I don't dislike you at all, Della. I've found you provoking at times, and a bit of an enigma, but I don't believe I ever actually disliked you, though I'm sure I acted as though I did."

Now it was her turn to raise an eyebrow, her original purpose momentarily forgotten. "Oh, come! That first day we met, you found me the most irritating person you'd ever known, and a confounded nuisance. You'd have wished me out of existence if you could have done so. Admit it."

His smile became a bit sheepish, though his eyes still twinkled. "I can't deny that, no. I already said I found you provoking. But that's not precisely the same thing as dislike."

Was he hinting that even then he'd found her attractive? If so, certainly that boded well. "If you didn't dislike me even then, does that mean you actually like me now?" She kept her voice light, so that she didn't risk too much, but held her breath for his answer.

"Of course I like you, Della," he said without hesitation. "I'd have thought that was obvious by now. I enjoy your conversation, and you're quite easy to look at as well."

His voice was light, too, holding no real hint of his emotions, but his words made her nearly sag with relief. Still, she couldn't seem to bring herself to look at him as she asked the next question—the one that meant so much. Gripping the rail with both hands, she stared out at the red disk of the sinking sun and spoke the words she'd been building up to.

"I like you, too, Kent. In fact, I . . . I find I'm more attracted to you than I've ever been to any man. Which is why I feel I should confess—"

The supper bell cut across her words, immediately followed by Mary Patterson's voice. "There you are, you two! The tables are filling up quickly this evening, so you'd best hurry if you don't wish to sit with strangers. Come on!"

She clearly planned to wait for them, so they had no choice but to accompany her, Della mentally cursing the whole way down. If only she'd had five more minutes! Even two minutes would have been enough for her to finish her confession, both about her name and about her feelings, and to hear Kent's reply. Now they wouldn't have another chance for private conversation before bedtime after all.

The dining saloon was indeed crowded already, with several second-class passengers—or so Della assumed—encroaching on the section she and Kent normally occupied. The Eastons had saved them seats, however, so they were still able to sit at their usual table.

As the meal was served, Della tried unsuccessfully to catch Kent's eye. Surely she had said enough for him to understand her feelings—which meant she should be able to make a guess at his own from his expression, if he would only turn toward her. He was talking with the gentlemen, however, and she couldn't tell yet whether he was deliberately avoiding her glance.

"Virginia was just suggesting that we have a game of charades this evening after supper," Mary said to her then, forcing Della's attention away from Kent. "Won't that be a delightful change?"

"That is, if we can persuade the men to abandon their interminable card games to play with us," added Virginia with a fierce mock scowl at her husband, Billy. He was oblivious, however, talking with the other gentlemen.

"Do you think Mr. Bradford will play?" Mary asked Della.

Before she could hazard a guess, a voice from her other side exclaimed, "Bradford? Did someone say Bradford? That wouldn't be one of the New York Bradfords, would it?"

Della turned to see a plump matron in a bright orange gown seated at the next table. She'd seen the woman before during the voyage, of course, but hadn't had occasion to speak with her, as the older woman normally socialized with the other second-class passengers.

"Why, yes," she replied. "His family is in New York City."

The matron's small gray eyes lit up. "Would they be the Bradfords of Bradford Shipping and Mercantile?" At Della's nod, she then asked, "Then this Mr. Bradford would be . . . ?"

"Kenton Bradford," Della supplied, amused by the woman's eagerness, which now increased.

"How delightful!" she all but squealed, her puffy cheeks crinkling with pleasure. "I'm well acquainted with his mother, I'll have you know. I must introduce myself. Which gentleman is he?"

Thinking her acquaintance couldn't be terribly close if she had never met Kent, Della turned to tap him on the shoulder. "There's a woman here who would like to speak with you," she said when she had his attention.

His face displayed no recognition as he looked past Della to the brightly clad matron on her other side. "Kenton Bradford at your service, madam."

She stuck out her hand, forcing him to take it and nearly knocking Della off the bench. "How wonderful! I am Gladys Benbow. You wouldn't know me, but I'm acquainted with your mother, Mrs. Willa Maples Bradford."

Della thought Kent's smile looked rather forced. "I'm pleased to make your acquaintance, Mrs. Benbow. You are also from New York, then?"

"Oh, my, no! I can't abide the bustle of a port city like that. It's why I didn't stay long in San Francisco, even with my new grandbaby there. I'm from Philadelphia, myself."

"Ah." Kent's smile became even stiffer.

Mrs. Benbow nodded just as though he'd made a real comment, her improbably black curls bouncing by her ears. "Indeed, I live just one street away from the lovely Maples house, where your mother grew up. I knew her quite well when we were both girls."

"What a coincidence that we should be on the same ship, then." Kent began to turn away, obviously desiring to end the conversation. Though it was rude, Della could hardly blame him. Mrs. Benbow seemed a bit vulgar. She wondered how someone like this could have moved in the same social circle as the woman who had produced such a gentleman as Kenton Bradford.

Her next comment shed a bit of light on that mystery. "We attended the same primary school, in fact. Of course, Willa and I drifted apart as we grew older, particularly when she married your father and moved away to New York."

Kent turned back to her with obvious reluctance. "You still correspond, then?" he asked politely.

Mrs. Benbow looked slightly abashed. "Not in the strictest sense, no. But I do still hear of her and her family from mutual friends. Mrs. Cadbury, for one. My sister taught her daughters the piano, you see."

Della suppressed a smile. So that was how this brash woman claimed "friendship" with the old-money families. But Kent seemed not at all amused. In fact, his face had gone rather red, and he seemed to be suppressing some strong emotion. Again he tried to turn away from Mrs. Benbow, and again she recalled his attention.

"I was delighted, of course, to hear about you and dear Caroline late last winter, shortly before I left for California. Quite a coup for you both, I should think, with two such fine families and the strong friendship already in place between your mothers."

Kent glanced quickly at Della, and then away, but not before she had glimpsed the alarm in his eyes. She was seized by a sudden curiosity, bordering on suspicion, which was only intensified by Mrs. Benbow's next comment.

"It was in all of the papers, of course—quite the talk of the town for a week and more! She'll be so pleased at your return, I'm sure—and to think that I may be in a position to witness your reunion!"

Kent was now studiously ignoring the woman, apparently not caring in the least how rude he appeared. But Della had to know. She turned to Mrs. Benbow and asked, in a carefully disinterested tone, "And who might Caroline be?"

For the first time since speaking to Kent, the woman focused on her. "Why, Caroline Cadbury, of course, eldest daughter of Mr. and Mrs. George Cadbury, one of Philadelphia's finest, oldest families. Kenton Bradford's fiancée. Surely he has mentioned her?"

Della felt the dream world she had begun blithely constructing come crashing down around her ears. "No," she replied with an effort. "No, I don't believe he has."

NINE

The other was a softer voice,
As soft as honey-dew:
Quoth he, "The man hath penance done,
And penance more will do."

—SAMUEL TAYLOR COLERIDGE,
The Rime of the Ancient Mariner

THE BLOW HE'D BEEN TRYING TO AVOID HAD fallen with devastating suddenness. Kent hardly dared to look at Della, but he realized that half the table must have heard the obnoxious woman's words.

A nervous laugh swept through their shipboard friends, and Mary Patterson said, "Surely, madam, you must be mistaken. Della here is Mr. Bradford's wife!"

Della started, and for a moment Kent thought she meant to rush from the table. She quickly overcame whatever her initial impulse had been, however, and raised her chin almost defiantly. Some response from him was absolutely necessary.

He cleared his throat. "I'm not surprised you haven't heard, Mrs. Benbow, as you've been away from home." Now all eyes were riveted on him with varying degrees of curiosity and condemnation. Della's eyes held an urgent question he tried his best to ignore—for the moment.

"Caroline and I broke off our engagement just before I sailed. I doubt it would have made the papers before you left for San Francisco." He only hoped that there was no one within earshot who might be able to contradict his story.

Embarrassed in her turn, Mrs. Benbow sputtered, "Oh, I'm terribly sorry to hear that. That is"—she looked confusedly at Della—"I'm happy for you both, of course, but I . . . I'd have thought my sister would have written . . . so good at keeping me up with the gossip, you see . . ."

"Perhaps the Cadburys preferred to keep the news quiet," he suggested. "They did not inform me of their plans in the matter."

Mrs. Benbow seemed to accept this, as did all of the others at the table. Most of the others, anyway. Della's gaze was far too knowing for his comfort. He'd have to confess the entire truth to her later, when they were alone.

It was not something he looked forward to doing.

The conversation became general then, if rather stilted. To Kent's relief, Mrs. Benbow left the table immediately after finishing her dessert—and Della's, as she claimed she wasn't hungry. Once she was gone, the irrepressible Mary Patterson leaned across the table.

"Who *was* that woman, Mr. Bradford? How exceedingly rude of her to spread such gossip, embarrassing poor dear Della!"

He could only shrug. "I'd never met her before in my life, though it seems she once had a passing acquaintance with my mother. I suppose that at this distance, it's not surprising that she had her facts a bit muddled."

"But is it true that—" Mary broke off, apparently intercepting a glance from Della. "Well, I suppose it's none of my business anyway," she concluded awkwardly. The look she sent Della was sympathetic, which only added to Kent's irritation, though he could not have said why. Perhaps because it made him feel even more like a heel.

Vainly he tried to remind himself that Della had brought this whole situation on herself. But that couldn't excuse his glaring omission in not telling her about Caroline. No, the blame for this particular incident fell squarely upon him.

Virginia's scheme of charades was revived once the plates were cleared away, but now even the ladies seemed less inclined to play, claiming a collective desire to retire early. Kent couldn't help suspecting that they wished to discuss his possible perfidy with their own husbands in private—

though that was probably absurd. He could not so easily disregard the lingering suspicion in Della's eyes, however.

Nor that in Nelson Sharpe's when he approached a few minutes later. "What's this I hear about you jilting a Philadelphia socialite, Bradford?"

Though his tone was jesting, Kent could see he'd have some work to do to allay the man's renewed suspicions. "Stories have a way of becoming blown out of proportion when they travel halfway around the globe," he said, but did not elaborate. When—if—word got back to Caroline and her mother, they would certainly consider her jilted. *Damn.*

Sharpe nodded. "I assumed it was something like that. But a man can't be too careful of his reputation, eh? Especially when there's already one black sheep in the family."

"Of course." Everything seemed to be irritating Kent tonight. He had to stifle an urge to tell Sharpe to go to hell. Fortunately, the man had other business to attend to, so he took himself off, back to the captain's table.

Kent turned to find Della standing beside him. "I believe I'll turn in, if you don't mind," she said quietly. "I find myself unaccountably tired, for some reason."

Did he imagine it, or were those unshed tears swimming in her eyes? The sight tore at him. "Very well. I'll join you shortly." He tried to communicate with his eyes that he would then explain all, but she had already turned away.

The next half hour was agony, as he tried to maintain small talk with those gentlemen who had not yet joined their wives in their cabins, giving Della time to change for bed. Kent's mind kept straying to his own cabin, imagining what stage of undress she might be in—then sheering away in self-disgust. He had no right to think of her in that way. Especially not now.

Finally he felt enough time had passed that he could safely make his excuses to the others and head for the cabin himself. He found Della, wrapped tightly in her robe and seated on the edge of her berth, waiting for him.

"I'm . . . I'm glad you're still awake," he said, closing the door softly behind him.

"Are you?" she asked icily. "You surprise me. I imagined you'd been hoping to avoid this explanation, as you've avoided it for the past week and more. I assume it's true that you had, or have, a fiancée back East?" Her eyes bored into his, allowing for no prevarication.

With a sigh, Kent nodded. "I know I should have mentioned her before."

"That might have been nice," she agreed sarcastically.

Recalling his own recent inclinations, which she must have sensed, he couldn't blame her for feeling betrayed. Especially after what she'd said—tried to say—before dinner. Still, he attempted to defend himself in the face of her sudden coldness.

"At first it seemed irrelevant, as I thought surely I'd—we'd—think of a way out of our charade before reaching New York. And then, well, I forgot."

Her eyes widened in patent disbelief. "You forgot. That you were engaged to be married?"

Kent ran a hand through his hair and attempted to pace in the tiny room. As he could take only two steps in any direction, he quickly gave it up.

"All right. I didn't exactly forget, but discussing it wasn't foremost in my thoughts. I . . . had other concerns." He couldn't very well tell her that it was her own attractions that had driven Caroline from his mind. He had no right.

"I see." He wondered if she did. "I take it that your story to Mrs. Benbow about having broken off the engagement was one you fabricated on the spot?"

He nodded wretchedly.

"It appears, despite your claims to the contrary a week ago, that you are quite as facile a liar as ever I could be." Irony fairly dripped from her words. "Between us, it seems we can dupe everyone on the ship—to include each other."

Kent frowned uncertainly. "What do you mean?"

"I presume you still mean to carry off the fiction that we are married. As I have given my word, I will continue to play along. Though my ethics have previously been brought into question, they do not allow me to break a promise."

As she no doubt intended, Kent writhed inwardly at this reminder that he had been less honest with her than she with him. She continued.

"However, knowing what good liars we both are"—she seemed to delight in using that word, he thought—"we need to be certain we do not take our roles too seriously in private. We wouldn't want the lines between reality and fantasy to blur for *us*, would we?"

As she castigated him, he realized with despair that she looked more beautiful than ever—and completely unapproachable, despite being clad only in a wrapper.

"I'm sorry, Della. I—I realize now that I may have implied . . . that is, that my behavior—"

"That you led me on? Yes, you did. Perhaps I'll accept your apology at some point—that *was* an apology, wasn't it?"

He nodded.

"Good." The tiniest glimmer of humor returned to her eyes. "But not tonight. I'm too tired to think about it. Good night, Kenton Bradford of the New York Bradfords."

With that, she retreated behind the drapes and pulled them firmly shut behind her, leaving him standing in the middle of the cabin, feeling like a cad and a heel and a dozen kinds of fool. Sighing again, he bent to remove his boots.

He couldn't have botched things more thoroughly if he'd set out to do so—and she clearly meant to make him grovel. Whether he would oblige her or not, he hadn't yet decided.

Lying on his berth in the dark a few minutes later, he tried to sort out just what had happened and how he felt about it. In a way, it was a relief to have the truth about Caroline out in the open with Della. These past few days, when he'd felt the pull of attraction, the idea of telling her had seemed increasingly awkward. At least he no longer had to dread it.

Nor was she likely to pursue a relationship with him now, as she had so clearly been hinting earlier that she'd like to do. That should have relieved him, too.

But somehow it didn't.

He realized that after just eight short days, he knew Della better than he'd known any other woman in his life, including his own sisters. He knew her past, her likes and dislikes, her talents, her weaknesses, and her moods. And still he liked her. Perhaps more than liked her . . .

Vainly he tried to call Caroline before his mind's eye. Only a few days ago he'd told himself she was a classic beauty, but the vague image he was finally able to summon seemed but a pale imitation of Della—lifeless and insipid. His disloyalty gnawed at him. Was he really no better than Charles after all?

It suddenly occurred to him to wonder how

much loyalty he now owed to Della. She'd gamely gone along with his plan rather than risk his business standing with the other gentlemen aboard, and for what benefit to herself? None, other than avoiding the threat he himself held over her head. A threat they both knew by now he would never carry out.

He realized that to set her adrift after insisting she come to New York would be a far more villainous act than the mere breaking of an engagement—an engagement that owed everything to expedience and practicality and nothing to love. For the first time, Kent looked ahead to what such a marriage would be like, and found it unutterably dreary.

Even if Caroline would still have him—which was by no means certain—he wasn't at all sure he could go through with it. He'd had a glimpse, if only in imagination, of what pleasures a union based on real affection could hold. Would he now be willing to settle for less?

With that disturbing question circling in his mind, he finally fell into a fitful sleep.

Della woke feeling nearly as wretched as she had the night before. The long watches of the night had only allowed her to replay, over and over, her embarrassing admission to Kent the evening before—before she'd discovered his dirty little secret. To think she'd felt guilty about something as minor as concealing her name! Her only source of comfort now was that she'd stopped short of telling him she loved him.

And that, *that* was the shattering truth, the thing that had kept her awake for most of the night—the thing she had tried so hard to conceal from herself. Della Gilliland, humble Irish prospector's daughter, had fallen in love with Kenton Bradford of the New York Bradfords.

It was amazing and absurd that such a thing could happen, and in such a short time—but their enforced proximity had allowed them to get to know each other better in eight days than many couples managed in months of formal courtship. She could only hope that if she was able to fall in love so quickly, she might be able to fall out of love in a similar amount of time.

Her heart warned her, however, that her hope was vain.

Still, all she could do was try. The other way lay insanity and despair. With this resolution firmly in her mind, she sat up and listened. Slow, even breathing from above told her Kent still slept. Though their routine called for her to stay in bed until he left, she felt far too restive to lie still for what might be another hour or more. A glance through the curtains at the porthole told her it was barely dawn.

As quietly as possible, she slipped out of bed and dressed, keeping her back to the berths in case he should awaken before she was finished. He did not, however, and a few minutes later she was able to leave the cabin and make her way up onto the still largely deserted promenade deck.

This far south, even the early morning air was warm and humid, but she breathed deeply anyway, to clear her head. Over the past few days, she and Kent had not been in the habit of spending much time together. Perhaps the easiest way to get over her ridiculous infatuation with a man she could never have would be simply to avoid him.

She sighed. Easy? She knew it would be anything but. Leaning over the rail, she searched the calm sea for any sign of the dolphins that had yesterday shadowed the ship, but saw none. She did, however, see a school of some sort of brightly colored fish just beneath the surface, heading toward the ship as though to go under it. Trying to keep them in sight, she leaned out further.

Suddenly strong arms seized her from behind, startling her breathless.

"Della! What are you doing?" Kent pulled her away from the rail and swung her around to face him, his eyes wide with alarm.

His obvious concern touched something within her, but almost before she could register it, the aftermath of the sudden fright hit her, transforming into abrupt anger.

"Don't ever do that again! You scared me half to death!" she gasped.

"I was about to say those exact words." Now anger suffused his features, too. "What were you trying to do?"

She blinked at him, her anger fading as quickly as it had erupted. "I . . . I was just watching some fish." She pointed vaguely. "They were swimming under the ship. I had a firm grip on the rail. Did you think I was going to jump?" Her amusement must have shown on her face, for Kent's complexion darkened.

"I thought . . . I don't know what I thought," he said lamely. "You were leaning so far over, and . . ."

Della now became aware that he still held her, and that his closeness was doing odd things to her breathing and pulse. Tempted as she was to remain in his arms, she realized what danger she courted. "Your revelation last night wasn't quite enough to make me commit suicide," she said, her tone as dry as she could make it.

Her words had the desired effect: He released her at once. It *was* what she'd desired, wasn't it?

"I'm . . . I'm sorry. Of course not. I don't know what I was thinking," he repeated, rubbing a hand over his face in what appeared to be acute embarrassment.

Touched, Della unwillingly softened toward him. "And I'm an ungrateful wretch. If you thought I was in danger, you acted quite appropriately—and heroically. Thank you, Kent, for trying to save my life."

Finally an answering amusement lit deep in his amber eyes. "Even if I inadvertently frightened you half to death? I suppose it's a good thing I didn't startle you over the edge. But I'm glad you realize my intentions were good."

She gazed at him, wondering whether he referred to more than his rescue attempt. "You had such a firm grip on me, I was never in any danger," she assured him, then immediately regretted reminding him—reminding herself—of that sudden embrace. But she *had* felt safe in it. . . .

"Thank you for saying so." He gave her a rueful smile. "Now that I've saved your life, may I escort you in to breakfast? I believe the bell will be ringing any moment."

Right on cue the signal rang out, so she took his arm and accompanied him down the curving stairs. Not until they reached the dining saloon did they encounter any of those who'd witnessed last night's exchange with Mrs. Benbow, but now Mary Patterson hurried forward.

"I see you two have patched everything up. I'm *so* pleased! I know it can be unsettling when incidents from one's husband's past suddenly surface. It happened to me more than once while Robert and I were engaged, and on one occasion nearly caused me to cry off. But he had the right of it when he said that his activities before meeting me were none of my concern."

Della managed a smile, though again she wanted to shake Mary for so blindly accepting anything her husband told her. Still, Mary seemed happy enough, so it really wasn't her concern.

"Yes, as Kent and I had such a whirlwind

courtship, I suppose it was inevitable that we would discover things about each other that we hadn't suspected before we married."

A glance at Kent showed him watching her, but then he nodded. "We will just hope that no other such discoveries are as unsettling as that one was."

There was a question in his eyes, but Della pretended not to see it. She owed him nothing—but perhaps she would tell him about the little matter of her name after all. Not that it should matter, of course, as they clearly had no future together.

Suddenly depressed, she suggested they all take their seats at the table.

Della was avoiding him, Kent realized. He hadn't had a chance to speak with her since breakfast, and now it was nearly dinnertime. Not that he had anything in particular to say to her, of course. He glanced over to where she stood talking with the other ladies at the opposite end of the saloon, looking lovelier than ever with her curls gathered on top of her head.

". . . wouldn't you say, Bradford?"

But he had lost the thread of his discussion with Ansel Easton about loan rates. "Beg pardon, Easton? My mind wandered for a moment."

The other man grinned. "I noticed the direction of its wandering. Glad to see no permanent harm was done by that harpy last night."

Kent wished that were true. Until the encounter with Mrs. Benbow, he and Della had been moving toward some sort of understanding that went beyond simple friendship. He had even begun to hope that it might somehow be possible for them to explore a deeper relationship. But perhaps it was for the best.

"I can't really blame Mrs. Benbow. It was natural for her to wish to pursue a connection from her home, and it's scarcely her fault that she was in possession of outdated information."

The lie tasted bitter on his lips as he spoke the words. But he realized now that no relationship with Della would have been right if it were not based on honesty. He had finally come to a point where he trusted her, only to have her trust in him cruelly shattered. Why had he not told her the entire truth from the outset? Then perhaps—

"Ah," Easton exclaimed, breaking into his thoughts again, "Addie is gesturing for me to join her. Coming, Bradford?"

"In a moment."

No, if he'd told Della about Caroline at the start, it would have precluded even the degree of intimacy they *had* reached. Though that might have been better than what they both suffered now. Slowly he walked the length of the saloon, savoring Della's profile as he approached her. Might she now insist again on leaving him in Panama? And what right did he have—really—to stop her if she did?

"We were just choosing our teams for charades," Virginia Birch informed him as he reached the group. "It's decided that we'll play tonight after dinner. What do you think, Mr. Bradford? Shall we pit sets of couples against each other, or have the men compete against the women?"

"Oh, that would scarcely be fair," exclaimed Mary Patterson worriedly. "Such a disparity in mental prowess!"

Della cocked her head and smiled. "Perhaps we could make some sort of concession to the gentlemen, to help them to keep up with us," she suggested.

Mary looked confused, but the others burst into laughter. Kent grinned at Della's jest, even though it was directed at his own sex, but she would not meet his eyes. Yes, she was definitely avoiding him.

Finally it was agreed that the Pattersons and the Birches would make up one team, while the Eastons and Bradfords would make up the other. The dinner bell rang then, and they moved toward the tables, still discussing the rules by which they would play.

"May I sit with you?" Kent spoke softly in Della's ear as she passed him.

For the first time since his "rescue" of her this morning, she looked at him, her green eyes shadowed. "It would cause comment if you did not."

Not precisely the answer he had hoped for, but he would not quibble. He took his accustomed place beside her at the long table, her nearness reminding him vividly of how she had felt in his arms that morning. Her softness, the faint scent of rosewater that clung about her, the shine of her flaming hair in the early sunshine, ruffled by the breeze . . .

Why did he torture himself like this? Determinedly he joined in the conversation, dividing his attention between the discussion of games of charades played in the past and the food in front of him. Every time Della spoke, however, his awareness snapped back to her, memories of that morning assaulting him unbidden.

For he had faced a blinding revelation when he had stepped out upon the deck to see Della seemingly teetering over the rail. Her apparent danger had forced him to acknowledge the very thing he'd been dodging for days, a truth that had struck him fairly between the eyes in that moment when he thought he might lose her.

Kent was falling in love with Della Gilley, gold miner's daughter and sometime snake-oil saleswoman. And he had no right whatsoever to tell her so.

TEN

The fair breeze blew, the white foam flew,
The furrow followed free;
We were the first that ever burst
Into that silent sea.

—SAMUEL TAYLOR COLERIDGE,
The Rime of the Ancient Mariner

DELLA WAS FINDING IT INCREASINGLY DIFFIcult to maintain her distance, both physically and emotionally, from Kent. Over the past few days, since his confession about his fiancée, he had been unfailingly kind and attentive whenever she would allow him near her. She had more than once surprised an expression in his eyes that nearly melted her bones—an expression that said more clearly than words that he had grown to care for her.

But what difference did it make, truly? If she forgot her pride and confessed her own feelings, they might enjoy a brief dalliance for the remainder of the voyage. She had no doubt that it would seem worth whatever she sacrificed—for a time. But what would become of her when they reached New York?

Surely, once Kent was back among his own kind, he would quickly realize how out of place she was in his world. His mother and his fiancée would press their claims, and with the fantasy of the sea behind them, he would doubtless accede to them. How could he not? It was what he'd been raised to do—what generations of his family had been raised to do.

And did she have any right to demand he do otherwise? To risk the business that supported his mother and sisters? To turn his back on friends, family, and livelihood for the sake of an Irish prospector's penniless daughter? No, she could never do that to him.

She sighed, focusing again on the blur of the approaching coastline off the port bow. Tomorrow, barring unexpected weather, they would reach Panama City. Occasionally, as now, she toyed again with the idea of disappearing there. It would be the surest way to protect her safety, as well as her pride and her heart, and an easy thing to do in a crowded coastal town, she was sure.

The dinner bell sounded, but Della remained where she was, thinking.

No, she decided, she could not desert Kent in Panama. He'd be left to make up some kind of explanation, and despite what she'd said to him the night she learned about his fiancée, she knew he'd have a difficult time making his story believable. How much simpler this would all be if only she didn't care so much!

As it was, she doubted her ability to keep her distance for another two weeks, until they reached New York. Every moment in his presence was sheer torture—mealtimes and, worse, the nights, though she was always careful to pretend sleep when he came to bed and when he rose in the morning. But the games of charades they'd played for the past few evenings were the most difficult of all.

Then not only was she forced to interact closely with Kent in front of the others, but occasionally their roles called for them to touch for minutes at a time. Endless minutes, when she could not ignore the thrill of connection that arced between them. She was not certain whether Kent felt it, too, but again—what difference did it make, really?

"Are you coming, Della?" It was Addie Easton, who had become a good friend over the past two weeks, and particularly these last few days. "They'll begin serving at any moment."

She turned, just as glad to abandon her melancholy thoughts. "Yes, of course. I was just watching the coastline and daydreaming."

Addie looked at her in some concern. "Pray don't worry overmuch about how Mr. Bradford's family will receive you. I can see that it is preying on your mind, but I'm certain everything will come right, even if there is some initial resistance."

Della smiled at her. "Thank you, Addie. No doubt you're right." If only she had nothing worse to worry about! Linking arms with the other woman, she accompanied her new friend down to the dining saloon for another evening of sweet torture.

Kent was already there, standing by their accustomed place at the table. His face lit up when he saw her, and she rather suspected hers did the same. Perhaps this *was* nearly as hard for him as it was for her. She took a bittersweet comfort in the thought.

"The Panama coastline grows clearer by the hour," she commented as she joined him. She'd become adept at unemotional small talk of late.

He nodded. "Yes, I was watching it earlier this afternoon. We appear to be precisely on schedule." Did she imagine the trace of sadness in his tone? Could he suspect what she'd been contemplating?

Seeking to reassure him, she said, "I hope the weather is as perfect for the second half of our voyage as it has been for this half. And I confess I'm quite eager to see Havana—I've heard so much about it."

He locked his eyes with hers for a long moment, then nodded almost imperceptibly, as though satisfied with what he read there. "I look forward to showing it to you. It's more civilized than Panama City, you'll discover."

"Will we be allowed to disembark in Havana, then?" asked Mary Patterson from his other side. "Robert said he thought we might not, for fear of disrupting the schedule."

"I presume so, as I was allowed to go into that city on my way to California six months ago," replied Kent, "but I confess I have not discussed it with the captain."

"I have," offered Ansel Easton, across the table. "He said it would depend on the hour of the day or evening that we arrive there. A few passengers, those not bound for New York, will be disembarking, so there may be a chance of a few hours ashore for the rest of us, I should think."

With the prospect of spending most of the next day on land, crossing the Isthmus of Panama, several people then expressed their readiness to leave the ship, despite the delightful weather and company they had enjoyed thus far.

Della scarcely heard them, acutely aware—again—of Kent close by her side. The masculine scent of him, the lines of his body beneath his clothing, the very fall of his dark hair across his forehead—all called to her senses. It took every bit of her self-control not to slide closer to him, to "accidentally" brush his hand with hers as she reached for her wine glass.

Thus it was almost a relief when the meal ended and Virginia Birch called for the nightly game of charades. The tables were cleared and the group of players assembled, along with a sizeable audience of fellow passengers bored with card playing.

Della's relief evaporated abruptly when she read the first word she and Kent were to act out for their teammates: *kismet.*

She swallowed hard, not daring to look at Kent. There was only one conceivable way to act out that first syllable, and no way that she could see to avoid it. And now they would have to confer, if only to decide how to act out the second. Moving a bit apart, they turned their backs toward the others for their conference.

Kent cleared his throat, and Della risked a glance at him, marginally relieved to see that he looked as uncomfortable as she felt. "I suppose we can't very well ask for another word," he murmured.

"No, I suppose not," she replied softly. "But we're both adults. Surely we can manage a polite kiss in company without betraying our secret." She was far less certain that she could keep her own feelings secret from Kent during the process, however. "Only we will know it means nothing," she added, trying to convince herself even more than him.

He nodded almost mechanically. "Right. Of course. Now, what of the *-met* part? Come from opposite ends of the room and shake hands?"

"That seems the most obvious way to portray it. If we have to do the whole, we'll have to confer again. That could prove difficult." Her pulse was beginning to slow to normal now that the embarrassing part had been settled. "The word means 'fate,' does it not? How would one portray that?"

"We'll simply have to do well enough with the two syllables to make that academic," he suggested. His eyes sought hers, but after only the briefest glimpse of the question there, she averted her gaze.

"Let's get it over with, then," she said, not caring how brusque she sounded in her effort to conceal her emotions.

They returned to the group and took their places. Once they had everyone's attention, Kent signaled with his fingers that they were going to enact the first syllable of a two-syllable word. Della steeled herself, trying not to think, sternly willing herself not to blush.

Then, in full view of dozens of people, he grasped her shoulders and turned her toward him. Since she didn't want people to guess *fight* or *rape,* she forced herself to relax under his grip, tilting her face up to his.

After a split second's hesitation that probably no one but the two of them noticed, Kent lowered his lips to hers for what was to be their polite, perfunctory kiss. As their lips touched, however, something profound happened, changing the plan.

Brief touches of hands or shoulders had been unsettling enough, but now a jolt of pure emotion shot through Della, nearly causing her to gasp, and making her cling suddenly to Kent for balance.

That he felt something similar was obvious from the way his arms encircled her, supporting her, while his mouth covered hers far more completely than she had expected. His lips, his arms, his body, all felt wonderful. Without conscious thought, she parted her own lips slightly, allowing him to deepen the kiss.

The cheers of their audience brought her abruptly back to herself. She stiffened and Kent released her, though with obvious reluctance. As they slowly parted, his eyes asked an urgent question, one she silently answered in the affirmative. He looked nearly as dazed as she felt, but he smiled—a smile that held incredible promise.

She knew her face must be brilliant scarlet—and Kent's was only a shade less bright—as they turned to face their teammates. Kent bowed and Della curtsied, signaling the completion of the first act.

It took the Eastons only a moment to correctly guess "kiss" as the answer to their charade, which had been no charade at all.

Della went through the acting out of the second syllable as though in a dream, approaching Kent from the opposite end of the saloon, silently exclaiming in greeting, then clasping hands as they "met." For a moment she thought he would sweep her back into his arms, but, with apparent effort, he only shook her hand—much to her relief, as she could not have resisted.

Now the Eastons held a protracted debate between themselves as to the second syllable, but Addie finally pronounced it *-met,* as that fit best with their first half. The other team applauded and acknowledged that the word had indeed been *kismet.*

The Pattersons went next, acting out the word *maritime* for the Birches to guess. Della paid little attention to their pantomime, first of a wedding and then the reading of a pocket watch. Since that shattering kiss and the silent exchange that had followed it, she could think of nothing but the coming night. Though no words had been spoken between them, she knew what they had both agreed to.

Had she been in any doubt, Kent's behavior during the remainder of the evening would have dispelled it. He now sat close against her on the bench, one arm draped around her in a seemingly casual gesture—but something he had never done before. She was acutely aware of the warmth of his hand at her waist, searing through the fabric of her dress and shift. Soon, if she had read him correctly, she would know the feel of that hand against her flesh. Further ahead than that, she would not think.

When the Eastons performed their piece, a bit

more attention was necessary, but she and Kent had a far more difficult time than they should have. They had to demand the whole before they were able to guess the word *millrace*. Then it was the Birches' turn, with Billy drawing laughs, as usual, as he acted out the first part of *horseshoe*.

No one seemed inclined to play another round, as the evening was by now well advanced. When Kent accompanied her to the cabin rather than lingering behind as was his custom, it did not occur to Della to object. She now faced the night ahead with a sense of inevitability—a path already chosen. Kismet?

As Kent pulled the cabin door softly closed, his eyes met hers across the tiny room. Again she silently communicated her willingness to proceed—to commit herself to him for however long she could have him. Even if that proved to be only this one night.

He took a step toward her, and she moved to meet him halfway. As naturally as breathing, she placed her hands on his shoulders and lifted her face for his kiss. His arms enfolded her, and their lips met in a mutual vow of passion. She would not assume it was more than that. For now, it was enough.

She thought she was braced for the emotions that would surge through her at the touch of his lips, but she was wrong. Now that they were alone, with no spectators, the impact was even more profound than before. It was as though they became one when they kissed, two parts of a whole finally fused and healed.

And she wanted more.

Parting her lips, she invited him inside, and he accepted the invitation eagerly, probing the recesses of her mouth with his tongue. The sweet violation set her vitals to burning. She wanted to draw more and more of him into herself until she engulfed him completely.

With a tiny moan, she clutched at him, pulling his head more firmly down to her, deepening the kiss until it could be no deeper. Still she wanted more, but didn't know what to do next.

He showed her. One hand still pressing into the small of her back, holding her tightly against him, Kent slid the other up her side, then around, cupping her breast through layers of fabric for an instant—too brief an instant—before beginning to unbutton his shirt.

Eagerly she helped him, then drew back slightly to begin on her own long row of buttons. Kent broke the kiss then, to speak at last. "Are you sure—"

Della laid a finger on his lips to silence him. Words were more than superfluous right now. They were a threat. Without them, she was certain of what she wished to do, but if he asked her outright, she would have to consider the possible consequences—something she very much preferred not to do right now.

He accepted her muting of his question, to her

relief, and now turned his attention to helping her with her buttons as she had helped with his. So many buttons! But at last they were undone—only to reveal her corset and shift. Cursing the layers convention bade her wear, Della began working on her laces.

Again Kent helped, if a bit awkwardly, and she found his very awkwardness endearing. It told her what she had already suspected, that he was no practiced seducer of women—that, while this might not be so novel an experience for him as it was for her, at least it was not routine.

Between them, delayed by frequent kisses, they freed her from her corset and hoops. Now they clung again, she clad only in her shift and he only in his trousers and boots. By mutual consent, they sank down upon her bunk to make removal of these final encumbrances easier.

She began unbuttoning his trousers, hesitating for a moment at the plain evidence of his desire. So much was new here, so much she was eager to experience. He lifted her shift and pulled it over her head, and when she could see again, he had freed himself entirely from the trousers. He was as magnificent under his clothing as she'd imagined during all those nights when she'd been able only to hear him undressing.

Now nothing separated them. The sensation of warm skin against warm skin was an entirely new one for Della. She'd dreamed of this moment, but her imaginings fell far short of the reality. The feel of Kent's hard, masculine body against hers, the clean sandalwood scent of him, and the sounds of his sighs against her lips, all overpowered her senses. She felt she could die right now and be happy.

But he had more pleasure in store for her.

Sliding both of them into a reclining position, Kent again cupped her breast, now bare, with one hand. Della gasped, unprepared for the difference. He smiled, then shifted further onto his side so that he had both hands free. Teasing her nipple with his thumb until she thought she could stand no more pleasure, he slipped the other hand lower, until he found the cleft between her legs.

With one finger, he stroked her most sensitive spot. Della arched her back, her body demanding more of the incredible sensation he was producing. And he obliged her. While she clung almost helplessly to his shoulders, dizzy with pleasure, he probed more deeply, showing her levels of ecstasy she'd never dreamed existed. And still her body cried out for more.

Just as she was certain she must reach a pinnacle or explode, he moved his hips against hers and slid his rigid shaft into the place that had become the very center of her being. Instinctively she wrapped her legs around him, drawing him into her, inviting him to thrust more deeply.

And thrust he did. Once, twice, and then Della did explode, or so it seemed. Wave upon wave of pure sensation crashed over her, becoming her, completing her. A moment later, with the deepest thrust yet, Kent clasped her even more tightly and held himself deep within her, pumping his life into hers.

Together they sighed. In a warm haze of happiness, Della knew that whatever was to come, this moment, here, now, was worth it all.

Kent felt his heartbeat gradually slowing. Never had a woman affected him as Della did, her essence demanding a response from every fiber of his being. This was no mere physical joining. Their very souls had been entwined.

He'd decided two days ago that he was willing to risk any consequences in order to make her his. He'd rehearsed speech after speech to communicate his feelings, but when the time had come, words had not even been necessary.

Kissing her once more, he slid a hand up her back to run his fingers through her fiery curls—something he'd wanted to do almost since first seeing her. They were just as soft and silken as he'd imagined. Finally she opened her eyes and regarded him with something akin to wonder in their green depths.

"Now I know I made the right decision," she said on a sigh.

Though startled by her phrasing, he smiled. "What decision was that, exactly?"

"To seize the moment while I could. And oh, what a moment!"

Kent was happy to know her pleasure had apparently matched his own, but he needed to let her know the depth of his commitment. "More than just a moment, I hope. Della, I want you to stay with me, even after we reach New York. I want this to be for a lifetime."

Instead of the delight he'd expected, she frowned, pulling away from him until only their hands touched. "Kent, I went into this with my eyes open. You don't have to—"

"Don't you understand what I'm saying?" he interrupted her. "I want you to marry me, Della. To become my wife in truth, and forever."

But still she did not smile. "Yes, I understand. And I won't deny that I've dreamed you might ask. But you've only known me for two weeks, so—"

"The best two weeks of my life," he interjected.

"So while I'm grateful," she continued, "I won't hold you to any promises just yet. This is enough for me for now. I'm content to let the future take care of itself."

Frustrated at her unwillingness to understand, he tried again. "But I *want* to plan for the future. I need you to know this isn't just a passing fancy for me. You mean far too much to me for that. I want to take care of you, to protect you with my name, my position."

She did smile now, finally, but he thought something was missing. "Very well. I will consider myself engaged to Kenton Bradford, of the New York Bradfords—at least for the remainder of the voyage. As long as we can continue as husband and wife in all the ways that matter."

Though still not satisfied, he reluctantly nodded. Della had had a hard life, he reminded himself. It was no wonder she found it difficult to trust. He would simply have to convince her. As long as she allowed him the time to do so, he had no doubt he could accomplish it.

"You may consider it temporary if you wish. Just as long as you know that I do not."

He kissed her firmly, hoping to show her with his lips what he had apparently failed to do with his words. She responded enthusiastically, and soon they were joined again. It was more than an hour later before they both finally fell into an exhausted, sated sleep.

ELEVEN

Sometimes a-dropping from the sky
I heard the sky-lark sing;
Sometimes all little birds that are,
How they seemed to fill the sea and air
With their sweet jargoning!

—SAMUEL TAYLOR COLERIDGE,
The Rime of the Ancient Mariner

THE MORNING BELL AWAKENED DELLA. Even before the fog of sleep cleared from her mind, she knew something momentous had happened. At a slight movement in the berth beside her, full memory came flooding back.

She rolled onto her side to face Kent just as he started to sit up, and she accidentally knocked him off the narrow berth entirely, onto the cabin floor. Despite the carpet, he made a surprisingly loud thump.

"Oh, my goodness! I'm so sorry—are you all right?" she exclaimed, sitting up in her turn.

He sat on the floor, rubbing his elbow ruefully and looking rather dazed. "Why do they make these bunks so damned narrow?" he grumbled.

Her concern relieved, Della began to giggle at the sight of him sprawled on the floor, stark naked and complaining. He shot her a glare, then chuckled himself. "You must admit, these beds weren't exactly designed for honeymooning couples," he said.

That sobered her abruptly. "No, I should say not." She successfully kept her sudden nervousness from her voice. Had that been a reference to his proposal of marriage last night, or had it been a mere jest?

Before she could decide which would be better—or safer—he scrambled to his feet. "We should reach port shortly after breakfast, I believe. Let's go take a look, shall we?" He was already pulling on his underclothes.

Though she knew it was silly, Della felt belatedly modest. "You go on ahead and I'll catch up. I fear I'll need the cabin to myself to get into my hoops properly." Even as she spoke, though, she realized the other married women aboard must manage that operation—and other, more embarrassing ones—every morning with their husbands present.

Kent did not argue with her, though he shot her a rather knowing glance. "Very well—if you're certain you don't need any help."

Still embarrassed, she shook her head. At the very least, she needed a few minutes alone to sort through her thoughts about the changes last night had wrought in their relationship. A moment later, Kent left the cabin, and she jumped out of bed to attend to her own toilette. Though she tried to think rationally while she dressed, all she could seem to focus on was how Kent had made her feel last night. Never had she even imagined . . .

Della finished dressing, brushed her hair back and tied it with a ribbon, then left the cabin, no closer than before to a settled way of looking at things. All she had managed was a determination not to raise her hopes too high too soon.

Most of the passengers had breakfasted quickly and were already watching the rapidly approaching shoreline from the promenade deck or through the windows of the dining saloon. Kent handed Della a plate as she reached him, and she needed no encouragement to hurry. After two weeks at sea, she found she was as eager as any of them to feel solid ground beneath her feet again, however briefly.

"We are scheduled to dock at around eleven o'clock," he informed her as she took a big bite of pastry. "I recall that the train across the isthmus takes no more than four hours or so, which means we should be boarding the steamer on the other side by late afternoon."

As he spoke, he draped an arm across her

shoulders. With the memory of last night fresh in her senses, she found it both distracting and intensely pleasurable. She turned to him with a smile.

"I've just had my first ocean voyage, and now I can look forward to my first ride on a train. What an adventure I'm having!" Though she didn't mention the other, more significant "first" she had experienced, he clearly read the unspoken addition in her expression, for he tightened his hold on her.

"One you'll recall with fondness for the rest of your life, I hope," he said, infusing his words with a meaning that made her drop her gaze.

Clearly he still thought they could make this work as a lasting alliance—a real marriage. Della still had serious doubts, but after a moment she lifted her head and smiled at him again. Whatever the future held, she was determined to enjoy the time she still had with him. She would let the future take care of itself. *Carpe diem*.

"I'm certain I will," she declared, adding silently, *No matter what*. Whatever else might be taken from her when they reached New York, the memory of her time with Kent would be hers forever.

Gulping down the last of her coffee, she declared herself finished. "Come, let's go topside for a while, before we need to come back down to our cabin to pack."

* * *

Kent felt warmed by the confiding, natural way Della slipped her hand into the crook of his arm as they went up to join the crowd at the railing. The approaching coastline was lush and green, and Della exclaimed over it, as it was unlike anything she had seen before.

He reminded her that they were near the equator, where tropical conditions reigned year-round.

"Will we be passing through real jungle in Panama?" she then asked him eagerly.

Kent smiled down at her. What lust for new experiences she had! What zest for living! "Unless things have changed since my trip west, yes—for most of the train ride, in fact."

"Might we even see wild animals?"

He hid his amusement, not wanting to dampen her excitement even slightly. "Some have reported seeing monkeys, crocodiles, and even jaguars," he replied, "though I don't recall seeing any wildlife beyond parrots on my own trip."

"Oh, my," she breathed.

He considered her enthusiasm a hopeful sign. At any rate, if she was anxious to see the jungles, she'd be unlikely to desert him when they reached Panama—not that he really believed she would, after last night. Still, he had an uneasy feeling that she was holding a part of herself back from him.

Not her body—she had been gratifyingly, eagerly generous last night, so much so that he'd hoped her last objections to marriage had been swept away. But now he still sensed an emotional distance that he suspected only time and trust could bridge. Again he vowed to take the time and build that trust.

He placed a hand at her waist, and she did not object, continuing to stare ahead with great interest. In half an hour they had entered the gulf surrounding the Pacific side of the isthmus. Regretfully Kent suggested they return to their cabin to pack up their belongings.

"I'm just as glad now that I have so few," Della commented. "Packing should take me no time at all. I very much want to see the docking."

True to her word, she had her valise filled and fastened in only a few minutes. Alone with her in the cabin again, Kent nearly suggested lingering for another taste of new physical delights, but restrained himself. He didn't want to spoil the wonder with hurry. Besides, though Della would likely agree, she would miss the docking.

Sternly suppressing his desire, he held open the cabin door for her so that they could return to the promenade deck for the steamer's final approach to the docks at Panama.

"All packed?" Robert Patterson greeted them as they reemerged into the late morning sunshine. "I had Mary do hers last night, for fear we'd miss debarking if she left it till today. What a lot of clothing women feel compelled to unpack for such a brief trip!"

Mary gave a self-deprecating smile of agreement before turning to talk to Della. Kent found himself thinking how glad he was that Della wasn't afraid to speak her mind to him—and that she had such a quick mind, with opinions worth voicing. He'd never noticed that in a woman before, and wondered how uncommon it truly was.

". . . and actually saw an ocelot!" Mary was saying, relating her previous trip across the isthmus a year ago. "At least, that's what Papa thought it was. Spotted, and more than twice the size of an ordinary cat—and with such a long tail! I still remember it quite vividly."

Della was listening with rapt attention, though her gaze strayed to the city just ahead and its surrounding jungle. "Kent recalled seeing parrots as well. I can scarcely wait! It's like a different world."

The steamer slowed and turned, its engines churning noisily as it eased up to the dock so that the gangplank could be extended. Excitement aboard was at a fever pitch, with nearly everyone eager to be among the first ashore.

"Should we have brought up our luggage?" Della asked Kent softly when Mary's attention was claimed by the activity on deck. "A few others seem to have done so."

He shook his head. "Those are steerage passengers. Stewards will handle ours. They're most efficient, as I recall. We should find our bags waiting in our new cabin on the other side."

"Oh . . . of course."

He realized again that luxuries he took for

granted were still novelties to Della. Somehow that knowledge only served to endear her to him all the more. He very much looked forward to showering her with *real* luxury when they reached New York. Stubbornly, he refused to think about the various obstacles to their happiness they might face there.

"Tell me what I can see," she said to him now. "Are those ruins over there, beyond the clustered buildings?"

He nodded. "Panama is a very old city by American standards. The Spanish settled it early in the sixteenth century, though little from that era survives. The pirate Henry Morgan razed it some two hundred years ago, and the rest was rebuilt afterward by the Colombian government and businesses."

"How fascinating! Did you learn its history when you passed this way before?"

"Before that, actually. Knowing I was to travel through this part of the world, I made it a point to research it in advance."

She looked up at him speculatively. "Do you always plan everything out to the last detail?"

Though she spoke playfully, he thought for a moment before answering. "I've always prided myself on doing so, but I'm beginning to discover certain rewards to acting on impulse."

Her green eyes twinkled. "I'll make an adventurer of you yet, Mr. Bradford," she declared.

Before he could respond in kind, the gangplank was opened, and they had all they could do to avoid being separated by the sudden surge of bodies in that direction. Knowing how eager Della was to see the city, Kent guided them to where the other first-class passengers had gathered, to be among the earliest to disembark. The steerage and second-class passengers were restrained by the stewards while the wealthier folk crossed the gangplank first. Kent barely noticed Della's small frown as they passed Mrs. Benbow among the waiting crowd.

Almost the moment they set foot ashore, the travelers were accosted by dozens of local tradesmen, chattering in Spanish as they thrust their wares forward. To Kent's surprise, Della answered one or two of the nearest in the same language.

"You speak Spanish?" he asked in amazement.

She glanced back at him and nodded. "A bit, anyway. There are quite a lot of Mexicans in California, you know. I found it useful to be able to communicate with them."

Good for business, he presumed she meant, but still he could not help but admire her resourcefulness. Every time he thought he knew her, she found new ways to surprise him.

"Is there anything here you'd like?" he asked, indicating the various wares the natives proffered, from cheap beads to pieces of fruit. She hesitated, and he remembered she had little money with her. "My treat, of course," he added quietly.

Della gave him a long, enigmatic look, then nodded. "That green scarf is lovely," she said, pointing. "And perhaps a bunch of bananas to take along on the train?"

The natives knew enough English to transact business, so Kent was easily able to purchase the sheer green scarf, bordered in deep blue, and a large cluster of golden bananas, all for well under a dollar. With a flourish, he presented them to Della, who accepted them with a smile and an exaggerated curtsy. They had a few minutes to look around them at the mellow stone buildings and the picturesque ruins beyond.

"It's a shame we can't stay here for a day or two," Della commented. "This place is so unique, I'd love to have time to explore it."

On his trip west, Kent had thought the city of Panama a dirty, impoverished place, though its long history compensated to a degree for what it lacked in elegance. Seeing it through Della's eyes, he realized there was far more to it than he'd perceived—or been willing to perceive—before. Now, however, they were obliged to hurry on to the train station, where they were to board momentarily.

They found themselves seated with the Eastons when the train pulled away half an hour later.

"I'm so pleased to see that you two have worked out whatever problems you were having," Addie confided to Della as the train gathered speed.

Both Kent and Della looked at her in surprise. "Problems?" Della asked.

Her husband frowned warningly, and Addie looked rather abashed. "Well, perhaps not problems, precisely, but I could not help but notice a restraint between the two of you that seemed most unusual for a newly married couple. Today, however, I could see it was gone. You both look so much happier. I couldn't help but think you had resolved something between you."

Della put a hand on her arm. "I thank you for your concern, Addie, and you are quite right. There *were* a few issues causing occasional friction between us, but we have learned to deal with them. You'll excuse me, I'm sure, for not going into more detail."

"Oh, certainly! I did not intend to pry, you know. I merely wished to congratulate you on your newfound happiness." She squeezed Della's hand, and Kent saw Della return the pressure.

A moment later, she glanced at him, a hint of alarm in her eyes. He felt precisely what she must be thinking. Had they been so obvious, both before and now? Apparently so. No wonder Nelson Sharpe had been suspicious! It would seem neither of them was so proficient at acting as they had believed.

Now, however, all was resolved, he told himself, resting an arm along the back of the seat, across Della's shoulders. They would marry as soon as they could, he was determined, making their fiction truth. He would have a bit of unpleasantness to deal with when he reached home, but it would be nothing to signify. He and Caroline had never been in love, nor was his mother in a position to dictate whom he should marry.

Della leaned her head on his shoulder most satisfactorily as she watched the exotic scenery flit by. Yes, this felt right—as though she belonged here, next to him. He breathed a sigh of contentment.

A moment later, however, Della sat up and leaned forward. "Parrots! There are some of the parrots you mentioned. Oh! And something large just moved in the underbrush there, but—no, it's gone now. I could not see what it was."

For the rest of the four-hour trip, Della paid more attention to their surroundings than to him, but Kent didn't mind. He enjoyed her excitement, vicariously sharing it. Under her influence, he could almost feel himself loosening up, shaking off the staid conservatism on which he'd prided himself for the past ten years and more. It was a freeing feeling.

By the time they reached the terminus at Aspinwall, Della had identified two different species of wild cats, a wild boar that Ansel Easton claimed was a peccary, and dozens of parrots. Her eyes shone with the experience. Tonight, Kent vowed, he would introduce her to further delights.

The *Central America*, the steamship that was to take them the rest of the way to New York, was already waiting at the docks in Aspinwall—a city the natives called Colón. It was very similar to the *Sonora* in size, shape, and even coloring, with a gay red stripe running the nearly three-hundred-foot length of its black hull. As they approached it, Della let out a small sigh, but whether of resignation or admiration, Kent was not certain.

"Are you tired, darling?" he asked her.

Her eyes widened, and he realized belatedly that the endearment had slipped out involuntarily.

"No, not really. I was merely wishing we could have a lengthier stay on land before steaming off into the sea again. Not . . . not that I'm reluctant to reach New York, of course."

So that was it. Not that he blamed her. Though he would do everything he could to shield her from the inevitable unpleasantness there, he knew she wouldn't be able to escape every barb directed her way by his mother and Caroline's friends—and perhaps Caroline herself. Clearly she knew it, too. "We still have at least ten days," he reminded her gently.

She nodded vigorously, then smiled up at him with an expression that made his heart beat faster. "Yes, we do. And I intend to make the most of every minute!" If there was a hint of desperation in her tone, Kent dismissed it as the product of nerves—very natural, given their situation.

They stepped off the train and waited with the others while the baggage was loaded onto carts. "It's a lovely ship," Virginia Birch commented, "but I can't say I'm anxious to be afloat again so soon." It was apparent from various murmurings that most agreed with her.

"Still, it means we're but ten days out from New York now," said Addie Easton. "I'm very much looking forward to arriving there."

"Oh, so am I!" agreed Mary Patterson. "I haven't seen my sisters for more than a year, and Gwendolyn had her first child while I was away. I can scarcely wait to see my little nephew!"

That brought forth a clamor of recollections from those who called New York home or who had frequently visited there and had acquaintances in the city. Della, not surprisingly, remained silent—and so did Kent, observing her. She looked more somber than he had ever seen her, frowning abstractedly in the direction of one of their fellow passengers, a retired judge who stood swinging his walking stick as they waited to board.

"Regrets?" he asked gently, for no one's ear but hers.

Immediately she shook off her seriousness and smiled. "Regrets? Never!" she declared. "New York sounds like just my sort of city—big and bursting with new sights and sounds."

He continued to watch her for a long moment, but her smile never wavered. Finally he nodded. "Yes, I think you'll fit in there quite well. I find I'm very much looking forward to showing you around my hometown."

The group started toward the ship then, urged on by one of the stewards, who seemed most anxious that they not deviate from the schedule by so much as a minute. The *Central America* was to sail at four o'clock, and not a moment later.

As they stepped on board, Kent was struck by the ship's familiarity. "I could swear this is the same steamer I took from New York back in February, but it can't be," he commented aloud. "How many ships are on this route? Does anyone know?"

"Just two, I believe," said Nelson Sharpe from behind him. "Why?"

Kent shook his head. "I was simply marveling at the similarity between them. This ship is much like the *Sonora*, of course, but it appears virtually identical to the *George Law*, on which I sailed from New York to Panama six months ago."

Sharpe burst out laughing. "I would imagine that it does! It's the same ship, my boy. They rechristened it two months since, when Mr. Law left the United States Mail Company. Politics, you know."

Feeling rather foolish, Kent grinned back. Had Sharpe noticed the difference in his relationship with Della, as Addie Easton had? And if he had, would that subdue his suspicions or raise new ones? He realized he'd been unconsciously avoiding the man ever since his remark about the Irish a week or more ago.

"Will our cabin be in the same area on this

ship that it was on the *Sonora*?" Della asked him then, interrupting that disturbing train of thought.

"Let's ask one of the stewards," he suggested, seizing on such a plausible reason to again put distance between himself and Nelson Sharpe. He preferred not to think about what the man's reaction might be once they reached New York if he should discover Kent had not previously broken off his engagement.

If anything, their cabin aboard the *Central America* was even more luxurious than their previous one had been. Della exclaimed with pleasure over the larger trunk, in particular. The first moment they had alone, she demonstrated in no uncertain terms that this cabin would be just as enjoyable as well.

Before he could follow up on her overtures with more than a heated kiss, however, the dinner bell rang. They'd have to leave their unpacking—and more pleasurable pursuits—for later.

As they left the cabin, the Eastons joined them again. While the women chatted animatedly, Ansel said to Kent in an undertone, "I'd have insisted on waiting for the next steamer had I known before we boarded that this one had been rechristened."

Kent recalled the old superstition that it was unlucky to change the name of a ship or boat. For a brief moment he felt a finger of premonition touch his spine, but impatiently shrugged it off. He was not, after all, a superstitious man.

"You surprise me, Easton," he said teasingly. "I had thought you firmly grounded in reality. At any rate, try not to alarm the ladies with talk of ill luck."

"Of course not," Easton agreed, but he frowned as they proceeded to the table.

TWELVE

The Sun now rose upon the right:
Out of the sea came he,
Still hid in mist, and on the left
Went down into the sea.

—SAMUEL TAYLOR COLERIDGE,
The Rime of the Ancient Mariner

DELLA SIGHED. SHE WOULD MUCH RATHER have stayed in the cabin alone with Kent. Ten days was such a brief time to have together, and despite his assurances, she could not convince herself that she could depend on having more than that. Which meant she grudged every moment not spent enjoying each other.

The dining salon was nearly full already. The tables were laid out much as they'd been on the *Sonora*, and Della took her accustomed place beside Kent, surrounded by their honeymooning friends. As there'd been no opportunity for a proper lunch on the train beyond the fruit some of them had bought in Panama, everyone was hungry. After just a few eager bites, however, forks began to slow.

"It would appear there's one area in which this half of the voyage may not measure up to the first," Robert Patterson commented, voicing the general opinion. Indeed, the food—on this first evening, at least—was noticeably inferior to what they'd enjoyed aboard the *Sonora*.

Della nearly said that she'd had far worse, but she caught herself. The others didn't know about her years in the mining camps or the periods of poverty she'd experienced. Particularly if Kent hoped to extend their charade beyond the voyage, she'd best keep those details to herself.

One or two nouveau riche first-class passengers who had made their fortunes in gold voiced her opinion, however. While there was nothing fancy about it, at least the bread was fairly fresh and the vegetables edible, if mushy. Recalling the iron-hard sourdough loaves in the camps, and months on end with no greens at all, Della joined them in silently offering up thanks for the food, as well as her current situation.

Turning, she found Kent watching her, a smile she couldn't decipher playing about his mouth. "No complaints?" he asked softly while most of their tablemates continued to abuse the fare before them.

She shrugged slightly. "I've had better—and worse. The company more than makes up for any shortcomings."

Billy Birch, on her other side, overheard her. "That's the spirit, Mrs. Bradford! What is a bit of wilted lettuce when we all have each other, and this fine ship to travel upon?"

As usual, the minstrel had a cheering effect on everyone, and conversation turned to more pleasant channels as they finished the meal with few additional complaints. One of the stewardesses, a middle-aged black woman, clapped Billy on the back.

"There you go, sir!" she exclaimed. "And our service will make up for any other problems, you'll see. Any of you lack anything, just ask old Lucy Dawson and I'll see you get it."

Della was just as glad that the attention quickly shifted away from her. All day she'd felt as though some outward evidence of her amazing experience of the night before must be visible. How could it not, when it had changed her entire outlook on life? The idea made her uncomfortable before the scrutiny of others, to the point where she had to stop herself from offering some sort of explanation to those around her.

Kent leaned close just then, his warm breath tickling her ear and causing the most delicious sensations to race up and down her back. "I believe I'll excuse myself from the nightly card games and retire early, if you're amenable."

Those delicious sensations multiplied. "Most amenable," she whispered with a grin.

He pulled her closer with one arm, and they sat touching from shoulder to knee as they waited impatiently for an opportunity to make their excuses. Giddy with anticipation, Della wasn't sure she'd ever been happier in her life.

Then, across the saloon, she saw Nelson Sharpe watching them from where he sat, now at this captain's table. Beside him, to her dismay, sat the man with the walking stick—the one she'd seen speaking to the police just before the *Sonora* sailed from San Francisco.

That Sharpe still had his suspicions was obvious—and when they reached New York, he would likely discover that they had been justified. And there was no knowing what the other man might have told him. What damage might Sharpe be able to wreak on Kent's business because of her?

She was called from such sober reflections when she heard Kent making their excuses to the others at the table. "It's been a long day, after all, with a lot of excitement. Della has expressed an interest in writing down her impressions, and I've offered to add my observations to hers."

"How famous!" exclaimed Addie Easton. "I am keeping a journal of the voyage as well. We must compare notes before it ends."

Della agreed, though it meant she would now have to produce the diary Kent had just invented.

Rising to accompany him from the saloon, she decided that would be no bad thing. If her memories were to be all she could keep of this trip, it might be nice to have them in tangible form.

Not now, though. Now she wanted to focus on Kent and nothing else. The moment they were shut into their cabin, he made it clear he shared the same goal, sweeping her into his arms for a long, passionate kiss.

"I've been wanting to do this for hours," he murmured when he finally lifted his head, his arms still enfolding her against his chest. "Do you think anyone would notice if we never left our room again before reaching New York?"

Della sighed. "That sounds heavenly. I'd much prefer to spend all my time with you alone, and pretend that the real world doesn't exist. Perhaps we could ask Lucy Dawson to have our food sent in to us."

She was joking, but he regarded her seriously. "Do you find it a trial to face the others, then? Are you still worried about reaching New York?"

Not quite meeting his eyes, she shrugged. "Perhaps a bit, but I'm sure I'll get over it." She didn't want him to perceive her very real doubts. She just wanted to snatch whatever time they might have remaining. If that meant pretending she believed all would be well once they reached the end of the voyage, she was willing to do just that.

But Kent was not so easily fooled. "You're still

not sure, are you? You still think I'll change my mind once we leave the ship and I'm back among my family. I won't, you know." His voice was gentle rather than accusing, but still she tried to defend herself.

"I do trust you. It's just that we've known each other such a very brief—"

He cut off her words with another kiss. "I've thought of a way to relieve your doubts," he said after a moment. "Tomorrow I'll speak to Captain Herndon and ask him to marry us in a private ceremony in his quarters. Then I wouldn't be able to change my mind even if I wanted to—which I won't."

Della stared. "You're not serious? What if anyone were to find out? Your credibility—our credibility—would be ruined." In particular, she thought of Mr. Sharpe, who appeared to be on as friendly terms with this captain as he'd been with their last one. What might he do with such information?

"No more so than when the truth comes out in New York," he said reasonably. "But think! Once we're well and truly married, we can plan for the future. My home is on the outskirts of New York City, right on the Hudson River. We can live there, or build another house nearby, if you prefer. It's a lovely area, within an easy drive of my business offices. You'll make friends with the other women in the neighborhood, have them over for tea. We can raise our children there."

Though the picture he evoked was everything Della had ever longed for, she felt a surge of panic. This was too much too soon. And it seemed so terribly unlikely. "Do you really think those society ladies—or your family—will so easily clasp me to their bosoms? Me, the daughter of an Irish prospector? And what of your fiancée and her family?"

Kent's jaw hardened stubbornly. "Any initial resistance will not last long. I won't allow any of them to insult you, I swear."

With a derisive little laugh, she pushed out of his arms. "How can you possibly swear any such thing? It's obvious you know little of women's society. They won't insult me in your presence. They'll simply exclude me from their circle and tell each other how I seduced you away from your intended bride with my lowborn charms. They'll teach their husbands to think the same, possibly to the detriment of your business."

He shook his head. "No! I—"

But she plowed on, unable to stop now that she had begun to put her fears into words. "You may well find that all of your friends and associates, even your own family, will turn their backs on you because of me. Your business, your prospects, could be ruined. If we do not marry, you may be able to explain me away as a passing fancy, a final fling before taking your proper place in society. People will frown, but they'll soon forgive you. Marry me, and they will not."

"You don't know that. Not everyone is so narrow-minded, even in the East."

"But many are."

Reluctantly he nodded. "Some, yes. But I refuse to shape my life to their expectations. That would make me no better than they are. I hope I've learned better by now—thanks to you, Della."

She took a deep breath. "You give me more credit than I deserve, I fear. There is still one matter in which I've been less than honest with you."

"Oh?" He regarded her intently, only the smallest flicker of uncertainty in his eyes. "An important matter?"

"You may judge. It's . . . my name. I told you it was Gilley, when in truth it is Gilliland." There. It was said. And now . . .

To her amazement, he chuckled. "Is that all? For a moment I was almost worried. Now I think of it, it's just as well, as I incautiously let the name Gilley slip at the start of our voyage. So you see, your instincts were sound. Can you not trust them now, when they tell you I can make you happy?"

In her relief at having unburdened herself of her last secret and her happiness at Kent's reaction, she felt herself softening. She wanted so much to believe it could work! But her entrenched realism wouldn't quite let her. "I believe you mean everything you say, Kent, but I can't be the cause of your downfall, any more than you would wish to be the cause of mine. Can't you see that?"

He gazed deeply into her eyes, clearly willing her to read what was written in his own. It made her catch her breath. "Losing you would be my downfall, Della. Nothing else counts for anything compared to that."

With a tiny cry, she came to him, lifting her face for his kiss. He eagerly obliged her, and then they were frantically caressing each other, unbuttoning, unfastening, untying in a heated frenzy until a few moments later all of their clothing lay in a heap on the cabin floor.

Still kissing her, Kent swept her up into his arms and carried her the two short steps to her bunk. Tenderly he laid her upon it, then stretched his length beside her on the narrow bed. She explored his body with her hands, learning his every curve and angle, committing it to memory, even as he did the same.

Now that she had voiced her fears, they had lost much of their power over her. She was willing to believe that it was just possible things might work out, with a large slice of luck. And she'd always had more than her share of luck.

Then, as Kent's hands narrowed their focus, she ceased thinking of anything but him and this precise moment in time. If anything, the sensations he produced in her were more intense than before, now that some of her fears were allayed. She shifted, opening herself to his probing fingers, his searching lips.

Her own explorations became more goal-oriented as well. Sliding her hands down his firm stomach, she found his shaft and researched its length, its hardness, the drop of moisture at its tip. Kent gave a throaty growl and pulled her against him so that her most sensitive spot and his tantalized each other.

Pushing with her legs against the wall of the berth, she scooted higher to grant him access, her breasts massaging the curly-haired roughness of his chest. Capturing her mouth, he kissed her deeply, plunging with his tongue to make her even more eager for a parallel plunging below. Lifting one knee, she parted her legs and invited him inside.

He accepted her invitation, but slowly, tantalizingly. One of his hands was still trapped between them, and now he made use of it, stimulating her sensitive nubbin with his thumb. She gasped, fireworks exploding in her head at the incredible wash of pure sensation he evoked.

Now he plunged, driving her to ever more amazing heights until she crested, only to spiral slowly down in waves of gradually ebbing pleasure. She had not yet reached the ground when he thrust again, driving her back upward, higher and higher, until she crested again, even as he reached his own climax.

Together they began their descent, heartbeats mingling as they gradually slowed. As the capacity for thought returned, Della realized this had been a bonding that went beyond last night's experience. She knew now that in all the ways that mattered they were truly one. Whatever might separate them in the future, she felt certain some measure of that bond would endure—forever.

With a sigh as much of relief as of satisfaction, Della burrowed her head against the beloved man at her side and slept.

Kent gazed down at the fiery head pillowed on his chest, a wave of tenderness sweeping over him. How had she become so dear to him in such a short time? He had no idea, but the fact was undeniable. Della meant more to him than life itself.

Until she'd unburdened herself to him, he hadn't realized how deeply her fears of the future had run. Nor had he considered the various ways she might be hurt, despite everything he could do to protect her. The fury he'd felt at the very idea of New York society rejecting her had startled him—and made his feelings for her even clearer.

He'd meant it when he said that losing her would destroy him. He now realized that made him vulnerable in a way he'd never been before. By threatening Della, an enemy could have Kent at his mercy—and Della herself had the ability to wound him beyond healing. Not that he believed she would. Not now.

They had forged a lasting bond tonight. He felt it, and he knew she felt it, too. Where that bond would lead them, they had yet to decide, but it would not break. Of that he was certain—and determined. He drifted off to sleep, to dream of a future in which Della played the central role, and in which he was able to make her every dream come true.

The morning dawned clear, and as soon as he rose, Kent sought out the captain to make his request. Though Captain Herndon was startled to learn that he and Della were not already wed, he expressed his willingness to rectify the matter at their earliest convenience. To Kent's relief, he accepted without question Kent's rather vague explanation of a delay in California that had prevented them from having time to marry before boarding the *Sonora*, as they had intended.

After breakfast, Kent and Della walked along the deck arm in arm while he related his conversation with the captain. He half expected a renewal of last night's protest, but it did not come. Della now seemed content to leave the planning of their future to him—for the moment, at least. After agreeing to meet with the captain just after luncheon, they continued along in companionable silence. All too soon, however, they were interrupted.

"Della! Kent! Have you heard?" Mary Patterson, accompanied by two or three other women, hurried toward them. "This ship has had its name changed! My Robert says that is the unluckiest thing in the world, and now we are all worried."

Addie Easton and Virginia Birch nodded anxiously. "Is there cause for concern, do you think?"

asked Virginia. "Billy trusts your judgment, I know."

Gratified by the compliment, Kent did his best to allay their fears. "That belief is a mere superstition. Certainly many ships have had names changed along with ownership over the years, and the vast majority of them never foundered."

"And I've enough luck to make up for any lack," declared Della, her eyes twinkling with special meaning. "Besides, look at this sea. If we have such weather the whole way, as we did on the Pacific, we shall certainly have nothing to fear."

The other women seemed comforted by their calm replies. A few of the gentlemen came up then, and as they clearly wished to discuss business concerns, Della excused herself and went with the other ladies to talk and walk along the deck.

Kent watched her for a wistful moment before turning to join in the masculine conversation. He found Nelson Sharpe regarding him shrewdly. For the next hour the discussion turned upon shipping concerns, but when the other gentlemen drifted away, Sharpe remained.

"I've frequently noticed that a man's passion for his wife subsides quickly once the first days of marriage are past," he said without preamble. "It's quite unusual, however, to see the opposite occur. You are to be congratulated yet again, my friend."

Something in Sharpe's expression told Kent

that the other man's suspicions, never entirely allayed, had been aroused again. "I certainly think so," he agreed easily. "Della and I had such a brief courtship that we had little opportunity to get to know each other well before marriage. Now we find we are even better suited than we realized."

"Indeed?" Sharpe still appeared skeptical. "On the surface you appear very different indeed. You, after all, come from one of the oldest and finest families in New York."

Kent had to fight down a surge of anger at the implied insult to Della. "I have no doubt my wife will do both me and my family credit," he said with icy politeness, though he'd have preferred to remove Sharpe's smile forcibly, with his fist. The violent impulse startled him.

"Oh, no doubt, no doubt," Sharpe continued, oblivious. "I was simply observing the uniqueness of your situation and your behavior over the past few days. If I didn't know better, I'd almost think your marriage hadn't been consummated until just a day or two ago."

Forcing a smile to his lips, Kent replied, "Not that it's any of your business, of course, but my wife and I did have a few difficulties to work out—some simple differences of opinion. She had some of the same concerns you've voiced about our dissimilar backgrounds, but all is settled now to our mutual satisfaction."

Something of his anger must have come

through in his tone, for Sharpe blinked and took a step backward. "No, none of my business at all. Apologies, Bradford, of course. Glad to see everything is working out so well." With a quick tip of his hat, he decamped, much to Kent's relief. He wasn't sure how much longer he'd have been able to restrain himself.

"You're looking thunderous." Della's voice came from behind him, making him wheel around to face her. "I take it you don't care much more for Mr. Sharpe than I do. Does he still suspect something, do you think?"

With an effort, Kent brought his face and voice under better control. "He did, but I believe I've finally convinced him that we've just had newlywed jitters, now over."

She breathed a sigh of relief. "I hope so. That man has set my teeth on edge from the moment I met him. He seems the sort who would cause trouble for sheer enjoyment—unless it would interfere with his profit."

Again he was amazed by her perceptiveness. "Precisely my own assessment of his character. But enough about Sharpe. In a few hours his suspicions will be groundless. The day is fine, the water is smooth, and the deck spacious. Let's enjoy our wedding day, shall we?"

Captain Herndon welcomed them into his private cabin shortly after luncheon. Della regarded him with interest—a smallish man with thinning hair that must once have been as red as her own but now was shot with gray.

"So," he greeted them in a voice that seemed too large for his frame, "in your haste to leave California, you somehow neglected to wed, I hear. Let's rectify that oversight at once."

Della glanced at Kent in some confusion. Had he told the captain about her flight? But he met her eyes and gave a tiny shake of his head. It was merely the captain's figure of speech.

The ceremony was quiet and brief. Della surprised herself by answering the captain's few questions so calmly, considering the monumental change in her circumstances that was taking place. But when Kent repeated his own vows and put her mother's wedding ring back on her finger with new significance, she felt a calm certainty that she was doing the right thing.

That night, when Kent finally slumbered after the ecstatic consummation of their union, doubt reared its ugly head again, but Della sternly ordered it away. Now that they were wed, she and Kent could handle anything life threw at them—neither censure nor poverty could be a match for their united love. Still marveling that she was actually Mrs. Kenton Bradford, Della drifted off to sleep, secure in the knowledge that the *Central America* had become her ship of dreams.

The next three days, as they steamed through calm seas toward Havana, were idyllic. Kent and

Della spent nearly all of their time together, walking, sitting, standing at the railings, alternating between conversation and companionable silence. Kent had never been happier in his life.

Now that they were well and truly married, no longer did Della allude to the difficulties she feared lay ahead. Kent, too, was content to let tomorrow take care of itself. He knew as well as she did that all would not be smooth sailing ahead. For one thing, there would be the scene, possibly ugly, with Caroline and her family to get through. But he saw no point in spoiling his present happiness worrying about it.

On the afternoon of September seventh, they steamed through the narrow entrance of Havana's harbor. "What is that?" Della asked him, pointing to a structure high upon the land to their left. "It looks like a castle!"

Kent smiled down at her, remembering her excitement in Panama over the new sights. "Yes, that's Morro Castle. It dates from the late sixteenth century, as does that." He pointed to a smaller castle on the right-hand side of the harbor entrance. "The Castillo de la Punta."

"Why, Kent! I thought you didn't know any Spanish," Della chided him with a grin.

"I don't. I only know the name—not what it means."

"Castle of the Point," she translated. They were now passing the towering El Morro, which shielded the harbor, and on which the Castle

Morro perched. Kent pointed out other items of interest upon the shore as they passed them—those he knew about, anyway.

The buildings became denser as they progressed, nearing the heart of Havana. It fanned out along both arms of the harbor, a far more populous city than Panama or Aspinwall. Half an hour later they dropped anchor, joining several other ships already in the harbor. Immediately a bevy of small boats, some no bigger than canoes, surrounded them, their occupants shouting up to the *Central America*'s passengers.

"What do they want?" Della asked, joining the others at the crowded rail.

"I imagine they wish to sell us things, just as the natives in Panama did," Kent guessed. "We're all rich Americans to them, after all."

"Oh, my! Look at the size of those oranges." She listened a moment. "Only ten cents? An orange like that would cost five times that in San Francisco!"

Smiling indulgently, Kent dropped a few dimes down to a boat below them, then leaned out to catch the oranges tossed up in exchange. "The food aboard is such that I don't mind supplementing it a bit," he admitted.

"Will we be able to go ashore?" Della asked after wrapping her two oranges in her shawl. "I'd love to see the city!"

"I'm not sure. On my previous voyage, as I said, we had a day in Havana, but our schedule may not allow it this time. I'll ask the captain."

Captain Herndon, when Kent found him in the wheelhouse, nodded, his eyes twinkling behind his gold-rimmed spectacles. "I'll allow you and your bride an hour or two ashore if you'd like, Mr. Bradford. We'll be transferring a few passengers this evening, then continue on in the morning. I'll ask everyone to be back aboard by full dark, however. I don't want to risk a paid-through passenger getting so involved in the nighttime pleasures of Havana that he misses the sailing."

Kent returned to Della with the news, and she quickly prepared to go ashore for a brief tour. "I've been pinning my hopes on Havana for the chance of a new dress," she admitted. "Let's hurry!"

With the Eastons, they spent the next hour in the quaint Havana shops. Together the ladies agreed on a gaily striped ready-made dress of blue and green as Della's best choice. Kent paid for the gown, glad of the chance to finally buy her something of substance, though it was but a token compared to what he planned to do in New York. His whole fortune could scarcely repay Della for the riches she had given him.

All too soon it was time to return to the ship. "I'll model my new gown for you tonight," Della promised him with a wink as they regained the deck of the *Central America*. "Then you can help me to take it off again."

"A good plan. I heartily approve." He pulled her close against him, and they moved to the railing to watch the transfer of cargo and passengers. A dozen or so well-dressed people accompanied the stevedores, and a corresponding number of current passengers had gathered near the waist of the ship with their baggage—those bound for destinations other than New York.

One or two of these were people Kent and Della had befriended, so they went over to say their goodbyes. They were still trading pleasantries when the new arrivals came aboard.

"Bradford! Kenton Bradford!" A once-familiar voice boomed across the crowd, making him turn with a stifled oath. No, his ears had not deceived him. Striding toward him, a broad smile on his fleshy face, came the bulky form of Francis Cadbury.

Caroline's brother.

Though a hard knot formed in his stomach, Kent managed to summon a smile. A hundred recollections assailed him as the other man advanced: of being bullied by Francis, who had surpassed him by two years and twenty pounds when they were boys; of his possessiveness toward Caroline and his comments that Kent was not good enough for her; and, more recently, of his obsequiousness when Kent was in a position to benefit Francis financially.

All of this passed in a flash, and then Francis stood directly before him. "Good to see you again, Francis," Kent lied. Then, after only the slightest hesitation, "Let me introduce you to Della—my wife."

THIRTEEN

The harbour-bay was clear as glass,
So smoothly it was strewn!
And on the bay the moonlight lay,
And the shadow of the Moon.

—SAMUEL TAYLOR COLERIDGE,
The Rime of the Ancient Mariner

DELLA NOTICED KENT'S SLIGHT HESITATION and quickly guessed the cause. This was someone he knew from New York—someone who knew of his engagement to Caroline and would be startled to hear of their marriage. She extended her hand with a smile, prepared to explain again the whirlwind nature of their "courtship," but froze at the incredulous outrage in the other man's face.

"Wife? Did you say wife?" His beady gaze swung from Della to Kent and back. "What the hell is this, Bradford?"

Startled, Della realized, fell far short of describing his reaction. "We met in Sacramento," she offered, wondering what his connection was to Kent—who seemed momentarily tongue-tied. "We were married only two days before taking ship."

Pure fury blazed from the man's small eyes, making her recoil in alarm. "And what of Caroline?" he demanded of Kent, his fleshy cheeks quivering with his anger. "Is she to discover this only when you arrive? If you make her an object of ridicule, I'll—"

Della suddenly understood that this must be a relative of Caroline's—a brother or cousin, perhaps. "Kent wrote to her," she improvised quickly. "She should have received the letter by now." Anything to keep this man from attacking Kent, as he seemed on the verge of doing.

Kent now found his voice. "I'll make my explanations to Caroline, not to you," he said calmly. "Della, Francis Cadbury, Caroline's brother."

"And protector," Francis added ominously. "To think I changed my travel plans just so that I could join you aboard this ship. I always said that you weren't worthy of her, Bradford."

Rocking back on his heels, Kent looked down his nose at the man. Though half Francis' girth, Kent topped him by several inches in height. "I seem to recall that you changed your tune when you thought I could benefit you. I return now with a substantial infusion of gold for Bradford Shipping and its related enterprises. Are you certain you don't wish to remain on good terms with me?"

Kent must have known the workings of this man's mind well, for immediately his shrewd little eyes became speculative. "How substantial?" he asked.

"I'll discuss the details with you later. First, however, you will apologize to my wife." Never, not even when he had given her his original ultimatum on they day they met, had Della heard Kent sound so implacable.

Francis Cadbury frowned, clearly waging an internal struggle between loyalty to his sister and greed. Greed won out. "Sorry, Mrs. Bradford. Took me by surprise, that's all."

Again Della extended her hand, this time with her most gracious smile. "Quite understandable, Mr. Cadbury. It does you credit that you care so for your sister, and I hope I won't be an instrument of pain to her."

He seemed uncertain what response was called for, but he took her hand briefly and sketched a faint bow over it. Then, turning immediately back to Kent, he said, "Details?"

"Of course. If you'll excuse us, my dear?"

More than willing to put some distance between herself and Francis Cadbury, Della nodded and moved away. Glancing around, she was relieved to discover that none of their closer friends on board had witnessed this exchange—only those slight acquaintances who were leaving momentarily anyway. Still, it gave her a foretaste of what she and Kent were likely to face when they reached New York.

Caroline herself might very well be waiting at the dock, she realized. She'd have received no letter, of course, and would doubtless see Della as a scheming fortune hunter who had stolen Kent from her.

And would she be so very wrong?

Certainly that had not been Della's intent at the outset. She'd wanted only a plausible excuse for being aboard the Sonora so that she could escape being arrested for murder. But as she'd come to know Kent, she *had* wanted to engage his interest, and though she hadn't known about his fiancée at the time, she'd made no inquiries, either. Once she'd known, the knowledge had not been enough to overcome her desire for Kent. And now . . .

Now she was in truth what she had claimed to be the moment she met him. She was also hopelessly in love with him. And he, she knew now, loved her in return. But would his love withstand the ruining of his business and social interests? Would it have been more noble for her to have refused him despite their love?

"Della, why the long face?" Addie Easton broke into her disturbing thoughts. "Are you disappointed that we were able to spend such a short time ashore? I'd have liked to stay longer, too. Havana seems a fascinating city."

Eagerly Della seized on this excuse for her pensiveness. "Yes, I had hoped we might be able to stay ashore overnight." She sighed, willing away her worries over what the future held.

"We'll just have to come up with something special to do tonight to make up for it, don't you think? And Ansel and I have been invited to join Captain Herndon at his table for dinner tomorrow night. I'm sure he'd be delighted if you and Mr. Bradford were to accompany us. I'll go suggest it."

She hurried off, leaving Della to smile at her kindness. How pleasant it was to have friends! Della had cultivated few over the years and, beyond her sister, none who were close. First there had been the embarrassment of Papa's drinking and their rapid return to near-poverty. Then she had moved about so much that friendships had been impossible to maintain.

For a moment she allowed herself to imagine a rosy future in New York, married to Kent and with dozens of friends, couples they could socialize with, ladies she could gossip with . . . But then the pleasant vision faded. It was far more likely she'd be a social pariah, accused of snaring Kent and injuring Caroline.

She'd heard stories of the eastern monied elite. They wouldn't easily admit an outsider like her to their ranks, she knew, however Kent pretended otherwise. But he'd promised to protect her from them, so she would simply have to trust him. She had passed the point of no return when she married him.

Addie returned then, to tell her that she and Kent were more than welcome to join them at the captain's table the next evening. "And tonight we'll have a grand time on deck, watching the lights of Havana. There may even be dancing, as a group of musicians has agreed to play for us."

Della agreed that it would be fun, and then Mary Patterson and Virginia Birch joined them with the same news. For a while, Della was able to forget her worries, chattering happily with her newfound group of friends.

The sun was sinking by the time the last of the passengers and cargo had been transferred. The gangplank was drawn up, and the *Central America* rocked gently at anchor as evening fell with a glorious scarlet sunset. One by one, the lights of Havana gleamed out across the placid waters of the harbor.

Kent made his way back to Della, where she stood near the railing, talking with some of the other women. He had made an uneasy truce with Francis Cadbury, based largely on the quantity of gold Kent carried and was promised by his investors. Some untruths had been necessary to mollify the man, however. He knew they would be exposed in a few days, when they reached New

York, but he was willing to risk future embarrassment to prevent further unpleasantness toward Della for the remainder of the voyage.

"Are you all resigned to staying on board tonight?" he asked the group when he reached them. "Mr. Patterson did try to convince Captain Herndon to allow a few of us to spend the night ashore, but without success. It appears he had a bad experience once before with a passenger who found the Havana rum so much to his liking that he was unwilling to leave with the ship. He had to be carried aboard forcibly."

The ladies laughed at the image this conjured, but Kent was aware of Della's questioning glance. When the conversation turned again to the possibility of a dance that evening, she moved to take his arm.

"Come, let us go enjoy the sunset before it is gone," she suggested—for the benefit of the others, he was sure. Though not particularly eager to make explanations, he acquiesced.

"Well?" she prompted once they were out of earshot.

"Well what? I thought you wanted to watch the sunset," he teased.

She was not amused. "Don't evade me, Kent. What did you and Mr. Cadbury discuss? Will he try to pitch me overboard before we reach New York?"

Kent started before he saw that she was smiling. Still, her latter question shook him. As a boy,

Francis had been quite capable of violence. "Of course not!" he said emphatically, to convince himself as much as her. "He's far too eager to use my wealth and influence for his own ends to risk such a thing."

Della must have caught the uncertainty he tried to conceal. "You don't like him, that's clear, and he most certainly doesn't like the fact that I exist. Have you known him a long time?"

"Since we were boys. And I'll admit he was a bit of a bully when we were young." What an understatement that was! "But he's an adult now, and no fool when it comes to his own business interests."

"I'm relieved to hear it." But she still looked unconvinced. "What, exactly, did you tell him? I wouldn't want to inadvertently contradict you should he catch me alone."

Kent was determined not to allow that to happen. Still, "I told him Caroline and I had been corresponding," he said. "That her recent letters hinted that she found our betrothal a burden. Since he had mercenary reasons to want to believe me, he wasn't hard to convince."

But Della sighed. "I blurted out that bit about the letter without thinking, for fear he was about to do you an injury. Not until afterward did I realize how easy it would be to disprove. Suppose he encounters Mrs. Benbow?"

"Damn! I hadn't thought of that. And if she lived so near his mother, he may well know the woman by sight." He thought for a moment, then shook his head. "We'll simply have to deal with that problem when—if—it arises. Perhaps it won't."

"And then there's the fact that we said on our first day aboard the *Sonora* that there'd been no time for any letters at all," she reminded him.

Kent groaned. "I'm such a pitiful liar. I wish I'd never attempted it." Then, realizing what he'd said, he turned quickly to Della. "That is to say—I didn't mean—"

"No, I understand." She smiled, but he could see the hurt in her eyes. "I've complicated your life terribly, haven't I? I'm so sorry, Kent."

He snatched her to him in a hard embrace. "You've brought me more happiness than I've ever known," he said fervently. "You have nothing to apologize for, Della. Ever."

She sighed, leaning her head against his chest. "I hope you still think so when we reach New York. You may discover that fleeting happiness can't compensate for the long-term consequences of deceiving others to attain it."

"Fleeting? Perhaps not. But ours will be a lifelong happiness, Della—well worth any momentary embarrassments or slights. You'll see."

Again she sighed, but this time he dared hope it was in relief. At any rate, she advanced no more arguments. Arms around each other, they watched the last crimson sliver of the sun sink behind the western arm of Havana's harbor. Then, as they continued to watch, lights appeared in the city, one by one. Before it was fully dark, Havana glittered more brightly than the stars above.

"It's beautiful," Della breathed.

"It is. San Francisco looked much the same the first time I saw it from the sea, just after sunset. I should have known such beauty presaged a change for the better in my life." He squeezed her waist.

"This is the first time I've seen a city at night from the water—but I thank you for the compliment." She tightened her own clasp in return, just as the dinner bell rang. For a moment they clung together, as though fearing this brief idyll might be among their last. Then they turned to go down to supper, hands still clasped.

The talk at the table was all of the dancing planned for later, the ladies having apparently convinced the captain and their husbands to allow the entertainment. So eager were they to begin that the meal was concluded swiftly. The ladies then excused themselves to their quarters to freshen up before returning to the men on deck.

Kent joined the other men in clearing a wide space on the promenade deck, moving coiled ropes and other paraphernalia out of the way and then repositioning some of the ship's lanterns to supplement the moonlight and starlight illuminating their makeshift dance floor. They were just congratulating themselves on the result when the ladies began to reappear, exclaiming with delight.

"Why, it's just like a garden party, only better," cried Mary Patterson. "Instead of a pool to reflect the lights, we have the entire harbor around us!"

The others laughingly agreed. The musicians, a group of steerage passengers whose talents had been belatedly discovered by those in first class, began to tune up their instruments. Della appeared just then, and moved at once to Kent's side. She had donned her new dress and woven the green-and-blue scarf from Panama through her red curls for a bewitching effect.

"You look lovelier than ever tonight," he murmured when she reached him.

"It's the new dress," she replied with a grin. "Thank you for buying it for me."

"Husband's prerogative. This dress becomes you—but I think you'd make a burlap sack look good." And he meant it. Della was more beautiful every time he saw her.

"I hope we won't have to put that to the test!" she exclaimed with a laugh. Just then the musicians struck up the first tune.

Kent extended his arm. "Shall we dance?"

But Della hung back. "I'm afraid I've had almost no chance to learn—just a few lessons during our one year of prosperity. I may embarrass you."

"Impossible," he said firmly, and led her out to join the other couples assembling in the middle of the deck.

Nor did she embarrass him. Though she hesitated occasionally, Della was light on her feet and quick to improvise if she didn't know a step. The musicians mainly knew lively folk tunes, so after just a few dances, everyone was breathless, flushed, and happy. The stewards and stewardesses entered into the spirit of the evening, producing bowls of fruit punch to refresh them all for another hour of dancing.

All in all, it was a magical evening. By the time people started drifting toward the stairs, to descend to their cabins, all agreed it was the most pleasant evening of the voyage yet. Kent was smiling, imagining future dances in New York, as he linked arms with Della to return to their quarters. Passing through the saloon, however, he saw Francis Cadbury near the far windows, deep in conversation with Nelson Sharpe.

He hurried Della into their cabin, hoping she had not noticed the two men. To his relief, she made no mention of them, and when he began helping her out of her new dress, she responded with gratifying eagerness. Kent's fleeting worries faded as together they recaptured the magic of the evening, exploring new ways to pleasure each other. If there was an urgency to their passion, he attributed it to desire—and love.

Later, however, as Della slumbered by his side, Kent stared up into the darkness at the berth above them. With the engines silent, he could hear every creak of the ship, every lap of water against the hull outside their cabin. But that was not what kept him awake. The memory of Sharpe and Cadbury in private conference haunted him. Whatever tomorrow might bring for him, he was determined it would involve no unpleasantness for Della.

Again he reflected on the change she had wrought in his outlook. For the first time in his life, he cared more for another person than he did for himself or for his family name. And for the first time, he realized that this was how life—and love—were supposed to be.

Another beautiful day dawned, and at nine o'clock the *Central America* steamed out of the Havana harbor to resume its journey to New York. Della watched the colorful city recede with some regret, wondering if she'd ever again be as happy as she'd been last night.

In less than a week they would reach New York—perhaps in as few as five days, if the weather continued as fine as it had been. Once there, everything would change—and not, she feared, for the better.

"Penny for your thoughts," said Kent, coming up just then to stand by her side at the rail.

"Oh, I was just thinking over the past few weeks and realizing what a lucky woman I am." She turned to give him a smile and a kiss. "If you had been any other sort of man, I might have spent most of that time in irons, and now be on my way back to San Francisco to stand trial."

Kent glanced around in alarm but relaxed when he saw that no one was within earshot. "I doubt they even have irons on these luxury ships," he said with a grin. "But if you want to cast me as heroic rescuer, I won't quibble."

"Good. Because I do." The light breeze ruffled their hair, and Della thought Kent looked handsomer than ever. For an instant, however, she had another flash of foreboding—that their days together were numbered. On impulse, she kissed him again, even though they stood in full view of the others on the deck.

Though he looked a bit startled, he was quick to respond. "After the big breakfast we just had, I'm in the mood for a nap," he said, his golden eyes twinkling. "How about you?"

"Absolutely," she agreed, and they returned to their cabin for some more precious time alone.

In spite of the lovely weather, they spent most of the day closeted away from the others. Della had no illusions about why their lovemaking had taken on such urgency. Though he didn't say so, clearly Kent felt as uncertain of their future as she did. For now, however, that only heightened their passion and made for a pleasurable, if tiring, day.

They agreed to a turn on the deck before dinner, which they were to take at the captain's table, along with the Eastons and a few other passengers. The moment they stepped out of the stairway, Della noticed the breeze.

"Oh, that feels lovely! I can't say I regret how

we've spent the day"—she gave Kent's arm a squeeze—"but it certainly is cool and comfortable out here."

"Almost makes me wish we could open the window in our room to freshen the air," he agreed.

She laughed. "Almost. But we'd want to close it in a hurry if salt water accompanied the breeze, I think."

Most of the other passengers were also on deck, enjoying the unaccustomed breeze after so many days in the tropical heat. The sunset was spectacular, turning both sky and sea crimson. Della vaguely recalled that this was supposed to be a weather omen of some sort, and asked Kent about it.

"Red sky at night, sailor's delight," he quoted with a smile. "Though that may only apply to more northern climes, for all I know."

"And what is that?" she asked then, pointing to what appeared to be a plume of smoke far behind them. "Another ship? Surely we're too far from Havana to see anything ashore."

One of the stewards, overhearing, answered her. "That'd be the *Empire City*, madam. She was to leave port an hour after we did."

Della recalled seeing the other steamer anchored near them in the Havana harbor, nearly as large and fine as the *Central America*. It seemed companionable, somehow, to see the smoke from its stacks. All too soon, the dinner bell rang, summoning them below.

Addie Easton beckoned, reminding them that they were invited to Captain Herndon's table. He rose as they and the Eastons approached. Privately Della thought, as she had yesterday, that he looked more like a merchant than a sailor, but then he greeted them in his booming voice, developed, no doubt, from years of shouting commands at sea.

"Welcome, welcome! I hope you're enjoying your stay aboard my ship thus far?" He gave Della a ghost of a wink.

"Very much so," she replied with an answering twinkle, and the others agreed. She and Addie were introduced by their husbands, and the captain showed that he possessed social as well as nautical skills by pretending he had never met Della before while paying the ladies outrageous compliments as they were all being seated.

He then turned to two other men just joining them at the table. "Mr. Sharpe, I believe you said you were acquainted with both the Eastons and the Bradfords, but I'd like to make you all known to Judge Alonzo Monson, an acquaintance who has taken ship with me on more than one previous occasion."

Judge Alonzo Monson. The man with the walking stick.

Della felt that her smile must be frozen on her face. She'd actually heard of Judge Monson, of the Sacramento courts, but hadn't realized this was he. He was known as both a notorious gambler and a rigid legalist—and he'd been speaking with the police, the police seeking *her*, just before the *Sonora* sailed! Did he know? Would he denounce her now, in front of everyone?

Her fears were partially allayed by his first words. "Aye, I've made this voyage a few times now, but this is likely to be my last for some time. I've finally resigned my post in Sacramento and plan to put down roots where I began, in New York."

His glance when he acknowledged her held no special portent—nothing that distinguished it from his bow to Addie, in fact. Della began to breathe again, only now realizing that she'd stopped.

"*If* we reach New York," Ansel Easton said then, distracting her from her own worries. "What think you, Captain Herndon, of commanding a ship with a changed name? Many ships have sunk after being rechristened, or so I've heard."

"Doesn't worry me in the least," replied the captain. "More ships have gone down with their original names than without, after all."

Conversation then turned to famous shipwrecks, with Mr. Sharpe relating the story of a recent one in which the captain and crew had saved themselves at the expense of their passengers. Captain Herndon roundly abused such cowardice as unworthy of a seaman.

"I'll never survive my ship," he declared. "If

she goes down, I go under her keel." Then, noticing the ladies' concerned expressions, he added, "But let us talk of something more cheerful."

Both Judge Monson and Captain Herndon had a knack for storytelling, and throughout the meal they regaled the others with tales of their colorful careers. The captain's tales of the Amazon jungle, where he had led an exploratory expedition some years earlier, were particularly fascinating—and amusing. Della, almost giddy with relief from the nagging worry that had plagued her for three weeks, enjoyed herself immensely.

As the group lingered over claret after dinner, the wind became audible at times. Addie expressed some concern, no doubt recalling the earlier conversation about shipwrecks, but Judge Monson and Mr. Sharpe both laughed at her fears.

"I've run into one storm or another every time I've come back East," Monson advised her. "September is rife with them here in the West Indies. But even should this develop into yet another, we'll be in no danger. The *Central America* is a stout ship—one of the best afloat."

The other men agreed. Della hadn't been as worried as Addie, but hearing Monson, Herndon, and Sharpe speak so casually of hurricanes and cyclones both reassured and excited her. She didn't actually hope to run into one, however sound their vessel, but rather envied them their experiences.

An hour or so later, Captain Herndon excused himself to make his rounds, promising to return for a few hands of whist with Monson, Sharpe, and whomever they could find for a fourth. The two couples took this as their cue and bade their tablemates good night. Heading toward their cabins, they were all in good spirits.

"What an interesting life Captain Herndon has led," Addie commented. "I thought I should die laughing at his story about the monkey!"

The others chuckled in agreement. "Thank you for arranging our invitation," Della said to Addie with perfect sincerity, for now she could enjoy the rest of the voyage that much more, all fear for her safety removed. "I had a wonderful time."

"As did I," Kent added. "A good omen for the remaining days of the voyage, I should think."

"Let's hope so," said Ansel. "With luck, the wind will abate by morning and we can pass these last few days as pleasantly as the ones preceding. Good night!"

But once inside their cabin, the wind sounded louder than ever to Della. "Do you think this might really be one of those West Indian storms brewing?"

Kent gave her a quick hug before beginning to strip off his jacket. "I doubt it. But even if it is, you heard what the others said. This ship has weathered them before, and certainly can do so again. The most we need worry about is a day or two of seasickness—and I'm confident we can avoid even that."

Though a hurricane might be exciting, the prospect of seasickness held no charm for Della whatsoever. Once they were in bed, however, she could not quite ignore the moaning of the wind, nor the slight rocking of the ship as the sea rose. Not, at least, until Kent pulled her to him, distracting her most effectively for the next half hour.

FOURTEEN

But in a minute she 'gan stir,
With a short uneasy motion—
Backwards and forwards half her length
With a short uneasy motion.

—Samuel Taylor Coleridge,
The Rime of the Ancient Mariner

KENT WAS AWAKENED BY AN UNACCUSTOMED vertical motion of the ship the next morning. A glance at the porthole, combined with the evidence of his ears, showed that the wind had increased rather than decreased overnight. Della still slept, so he tried to rise without waking her—unsuccessfully.

"Mmm. What . . . ? Goodness!" She sat up, looking adorably tousled and confused. "This *is* turning into a storm, isn't it?" Shaking her head to clear the last vestiges of sleep, she jumped up to press her face to the porthole.

"I'm certain it will blow itself out in a few more hours." Kent tried to speak reassuringly, though he knew no more about storms at sea than she did. "There's no real cause for concern."

She turned back to him, and he saw that her expression was more eager than worried. "No, I'm sure there's not, but how exciting! Think of the stories we'll have to tell later. I'd begun to fear that the entire voyage would be uneventful."

He felt a smile tugging at the corners of his mouth. He should have known Della would require no soothing. "Uneventful? I'm wounded."

"Oh, you know what I mean. Our days—and nights—together have been the most momentous of my life, but those are scarcely stories with which we'll regale our grandchildren. A hurricane at sea, however—"

"I hope it won't come to that," he said quickly. Despite the brave front she put on, he thought she must be worried underneath. "Come, let's see what the more experienced voyagers have to say about the situation."

Though slightly hampered by the motion of the ship, which once or twice lurched unexpectedly, they dressed quickly, and Kent even managed to shave before they ventured out into the saloon. It was only sparsely populated, most of their fellow passengers having apparently elected to remain in their cabins.

Nevertheless, breakfast was served right on time by the indefatigable "Aunt" Lucy, and Kent was relieved to find he still had an appetite. His journey west had involved a few brief rain showers, but no pitching to compare with what they were experiencing now, so he hadn't been sure how his stomach might respond.

"We'd better eat while we can," Della commented, echoing his own thoughts. "If this storm lasts much longer, or worsens, the cook may decide against preparing another meal for a while." It appeared that she, too, was not particularly prone to seasickness.

As they finished eating, a few more passengers ventured out of their cabins, though several looked rather peaked. "Ansel assures me that I'll feel much more the thing if I get some fresh air," Addie Easton said doubtfully as she joined them. "I confess I don't dare eat much beyond a biscuit and some coffee, however."

Della spoke soothingly to her, and while the two women were thus engaged, Kent took the opportunity to draw Ansel Easton and Billy Birch aside. "Do you think there's any danger?"

Though Easton's eyes reflected some concern, the other man shook his head. "Not yet, I shouldn't think." He spoke as quietly as Kent had ever heard him. "Once we've eaten, we can go up and take a look at the sea, but I've heard stories of far worse storms that did not the least bit of damage to a ship."

"As have I." Kent remembered some of Captain Herndon's tales from last night. He sat back down next to Della, who was keeping Addie and Virginia company with a second cup of coffee and chatting about the antics of one of the steerage children. She appeared to be taking the weather in stride.

In fact, when the men expressed their intention of going up onto the deck, she insisted on joining them. "Why don't you come, too?" she suggested to the other ladies. "I'm sure the wind will revive you as nothing else could."

The others reluctantly agreed, and the ladies all linked arms to follow the men up the curved stairs to the promenade deck. A light, flying rain was falling, but more daunting were the waves that occasionally broke across the bow of the ship, sending a heavy spray of salt water over them all.

Kent concluded, upon watching the waves for a few moments, that they had nothing to fear, and said so clearly for the ladies' benefit. Seeing the ship's second officer nearby, Kent called out to him, hoping to verify his analysis of the situation.

"This storm is nothing out of the ordinary, is it, Mr. Frazer?"

The seaman actually laughed. "Storm? I'd not call this a storm yet—it's naught but a bit of a blow. You might want to keep your ladies below, though, if they don't like salt water in their skirts." Even as he spoke, another wave broke across the bow, showering them all. The ladies' hoops danced wildly in the wind.

Addie was already tugging at her husband's

sleeve, urging him back toward the stairs, and he went willingly enough. The Birches followed. Della hesitated, however.

"Can't we stay out here a bit longer? The sea and sky are so different, so fascinating. It's almost like riding a fast horse into the wind."

Now that the crewman had allayed his lingering worry, Kent was willing enough. "Don't forget that you have only two changes of clothing, however," he reminded her.

She made a face at him. "Spoilsport. This old lilac will just have to be my topside dress, then, until this blows over. I'll save the two green ones for drier pursuits."

They stood side by side, clinging to the rail and steadying Della's hoops, laughing as the spray drenched them repeatedly. Though windy, the air was still fairly warm. Even so, after an hour Kent noticed Della shivering.

"Come, let's go below for a bit. We'll both want to dry off before lunchtime, I think." He suspected that she'd deny being cold, but given a reasonable excuse to go in, she did not protest.

"Very well—for now. I'll want to come back out later, though," she warned him with a grin.

He leaned forward and kissed a drop of seawater from the tip of her nose. "Whatever you say—unless it really does become dangerous."

"You heard what Mr. Frazer said. 'Naught but a bit of a blow.' I'd like to experience it while it lasts."

Kent wondered whether her thirst for new experiences would ever be sated, but he had to admit it was contagious. On his trip west, he'd been careful not to allow the rain they encountered to dampen or disarrange his conservative attire. Now he found himself actually looking forward to another drenching on deck, with Della by his side.

She was good for him. As they reached the saloon again, he turned to tell her so, but the sight of Nelson Sharpe striding toward him, accusation blazing from his eyes, brought them both up short.

"I knew there was something havey-cavey going on," Sharpe said without preamble. "I gave you more than one opportunity to come clean about it, too. Suppose you tell me the truth about your new bride—and your fiancée in New York?"

•

Della tightened her grip on Kent's arm, trying to communicate silently that she'd support him whatever he said—or did. What could this odious man have discovered now?

"I have no idea what you're talking about," Kent responded with as much disdain as one might expect if he were truly ignorant of any deception.

Sharpe looked nonplussed for a moment but did not back down. "I've been talking to your would-be brother-in-law, Cadbury. He left New York less than a month ago, and at that time, he says, his sister still considered herself engaged to you. Jilting the daughter of one of Philadelphia's wealthiest families is not an action likely to endear you to your investors, Bradford. It might make them wonder whether you'll be as faithless with their money as you've been to that poor girl."

"Caroline is no 'poor girl' by anyone's measure," Kent retorted with a coldness that made Della shiver—or perhaps that was just the seawater soaking through to her skin. "Your money is perfectly safe, Sharpe."

"You can be sure it is—safe in my cabin." He gestured across the saloon. "And it will remain in my possession, every bit of it, until I get to the bottom of this matter."

Della's fingers twitched, but Kent covered her hand with his own. "I don't see how my private life is your concern, Sharpe. I had a falling-out with Caroline Cadbury, and her brother has understandably taken her part. What more needs to be said?"

Sharpe's shrewd eyes narrowed, as though he would bore holes in Kent with them, but Kent remained impassive. After a moment, Sharpe snorted. "I'll be very interested to hear which story prevails when we reach New York. Till then, I'll reserve judgment."

"Always a wise course." Della marveled that Kent could sound so calm even knowing, as he must, that their deception would be exposed shortly after the ship docked.

"You won't find Cadbury so patient, however," Sharpe warned him. "He spent last evening in conversation with a Mrs. Benbow. It appears you told her rather a different story from the one you told him. I imagine he'll wish to discuss it with you."

With a mocking smile, he tipped his hat and headed for the far end of the saloon to join one of the card games just forming.

"What do you think Mr. Cadbury will do?" Della asked anxiously. She remembered how the big man had behaved at first. Just last night she'd rejoiced that her physical safety, at least, was assured. But now she was fearful for Kent's.

"Nothing to you, I promise," said Kent soothingly.

But that was not the reassurance she sought. "To you, I mean. He doesn't seem the type who would easily forgive being lied to."

"No—unless he sees a profit in doing so. Which he will."

"Do you really think he'll be that rational? I saw how close he came to attacking you when he came aboard, even though you were surrounded by people."

She thought Kent hesitated for a moment before replying. "I can handle him, Della. I've done so before."

For his sake—and hers—she hoped he was right.

By lunchtime, a few more people had tired of

their cabins, though not many seemed inclined to eat. The weather remained the primary topic of conversation, as the wind had not yet abated at all—if anything, Della thought, it had increased. Even so, as soon as she finished eating, she went to change back into her damp lilac gown—sans hoops—for another foray onto the deck.

Kent did not try to dissuade her, though he looked as though he wanted to. She couldn't explain the need she had to face the wind, to experience the raw elements. Somehow, she found it cleansing to brave physical rather than social dangers. Eagerly she mounted the steps again.

At the top, however, they were nearly driven back by the wind, which had increased more than she'd realized over the past two or three hours. The waves crashing across the bow seemed to have doubled in size, and now sent ankle-deep swirls of seawater along the deck at regular intervals.

"I don't think—" Kent began.

"No, please, just for a few minutes," she interrupted him. After that encounter with Mr. Sharpe, and in all likelihood an even more unpleasant one with Mr. Cadbury to come, she needed the perspective of the storm. "Look—the sailors seem not the least bit concerned, so surely there can be no real danger even now."

Kent gave her a long look, then slowly nodded. "I don't pretend to understand, but I can see you really want to do this. Come on, then." Supporting her against the wind with one arm about her waist, he accompanied her to the windward rail.

She saw that they weren't the only passengers on deck, after all—though the others appeared to be here from necessity rather than desire, lined up as they were to lean over the leeward rail. She felt a surge of sympathy for the poor, wretched souls. What a mercy that she was unaffected by seasickness—so far, anyway. She was glad she had left her hoops below, however.

Della turned her face to the wind and rain, reveling in the way it whipped her hair to a frenzy and scoured her skin. This, surely, was life at its most intense! Petty concerns about her reception in New York fell away as the power of nature, far greater than any human machinations, bore down upon her.

All too soon, Kent recalled her. "Darling, you are drenched again, and shivering, however you try to hide it. Let's go below."

In truth, she hadn't even noticed her own trembling, but at his words she discovered he was right—she was chilled to the bone. "How long have we been here?"

"Nearly an hour. Were you seeing visions or simply communing with the elements?" he asked teasingly as he guided her away from the rail and back toward the stairs.

"Both, I think," she responded in the same vein. "I was trying to draw on the power of the wind and sea to shore up my own weakness."

He squeezed her shoulders as they began their descent. "Weakness? Della, you are the strongest woman I've ever known."

She looked at him curiously. "Really? I've never thought of myself in that way. Certainly I haven't been one to resort to tears or fainting spells in the face of trouble, but I always regarded that as practicality rather than strength."

"I suspect the two are rather closely related." His eyes were twinkling again, and she only belatedly realized he'd been worried about her.

She knew now that there were certain things she needed to make clear to Kent—to be sure he understood. And things she needed to know herself. "Let's go back to our cabin, where I can dry off," she suggested. "And there's something I'd like to talk to you about."

He had already been leading her in that direction before she spoke. "Of course. And then I mean to fetch you a cup of something hot, which you can sip while wrapped in at least two blankets."

She wrinkled her nose at him. "Don't start treating me like a brainless child. I'm fine. Just wet, but that can be easily mended."

"I won't have you neglecting yourself or falling ill," he said firmly, and the concern was back in his eyes. "Go on in and dry off, and I'll be back in a moment with some tea."

Abruptly Della understood that she herself had become a point of vulnerability for the man she loved, that his feelings for her had the power to injure him—that *she* had that power. The idea frightened her.

She'd become accustomed to being on her own, knowing that should she disappear or die, no one but herself would be affected. That was no longer the case. For the first time since her sister reached adulthood, she had a responsibility to take care of herself for someone else's sake. The thought left her both shaken and warmed.

"Thank you, Kent." She hoped her eyes expressed the gratitude for which her words were inadequate.

He bent to kiss her lingeringly on the lips, then left her. Della had her sea legs—or storm legs—now, and was not hampered by the motion of the floor as she quickly stripped off her sodden lilac gown. She pressed as much water out of it as she could with a towel before draping it over the top bunk to dry somewhat. Then she removed her wet bloomers and shift and put on her night rail, her driest undergarment.

She started to pick up her newest gown, but then recalled what Kent had said and put it back down, instead pulling on her wrapper and then draping a blanket over her shoulders. Sitting on the edge of her berth, she tucked her feet under her for warmth just as Kent returned with two steaming cups.

"This should take away the chill," he said, handing her one. She took a long swallow, then sputtered.

"This isn't just tea!"

"No, I added a drop of brandy, courtesy of the Eastons. It'll warm you more quickly. Drink up!"

She sent him a speaking glance at such coddling, but obeyed. The heat of the spirit-laced tea coursed through her veins, warming her to her toes in minutes. Contentment swept through her as well, almost making her forget what she'd wanted to talk to Kent about—but not quite.

"I know a way to finish the warming process," he said suggestively when she set down her cup. But she put up a hand when he began to rise from his seat on the trunk, his eyes alight with desire.

"Before you distract me—which I well know you can—I want to discuss something."

He settled back on the trunk, a slight frown between his dark brows. "There's something we haven't already discussed?"

"Actually, I want to finish a discussion we began some days ago. Kent, you've spoken confidently of how we'll sweep away all barriers once we reach New York, but . . . what if we can't?"

He shook his head, as she'd known he would. "I told you, we'll manage. I'll manage. I won't allow—"

"No, Kent, I want to discuss realities now. I tried once before, but you swept away my objections without truly addressing them. After seeing Mr. Cadbury's reaction to our marriage, however, and Mr. Sharpe's this morning, I believe we must consider all possibilities, even the most unpleasant ones."

His chin jutted out stubbornly, but at least he didn't interrupt this time. She continued.

"Suppose, just suppose, that the majority of your acquaintances and family respond as Mr. Cadbury has. That they reject me—reject us as a couple—utterly. That your own mother refuses to receive me." He made a convulsive movement, but she plowed on, not allowing him to interrupt. "No, Kent, it could happen. The society columns in the newspapers may vilify me—us. Your business could suffer, to the detriment of your mother and sisters as well as you personally."

"It would still be worth it," he declared.

She smiled at his naïveté, for all that he was ten years her senior. "You say so now, in the first days of infatuation—and yes, it *has* been only days. But what of a month, a year from now, when we perhaps have a child to provide for and no friends or family to turn to? Kent, think—you could be giving up your entire way of life for me. I can't help but believe, should that happen, that eventually you would resent me for it."

"No!" He spoke emphatically, but she thought she saw a glimmer of doubt in his eyes. He really hadn't thought it through before.

"Just think about it, that's all I ask." She now allowed softness and sympathy to color her voice. "I've long believed that if one prepares for the worst, it is less likely to occur. I love you, Kent.

You know that. And I believe you when you say you love me, and that losing me would cause you pain. But there are other ways I might cause you pain, and I wish to avoid that if it is in my power."

Kent regarded her pensively now. "I've tended to think of myself as the realist between us, and you as the impulsive dreamer, but I see I've been mistaken. Had you not been so practical, you wouldn't have survived and prospered as you have.

"Very well." He sighed. "I will give the matter some thought—but it will not change how I feel. Should things fall out as you imagine, you would be the one to suffer most, despite what you say. For that reason alone, I'll consider ways we might counter such a scenario. Will that suffice?"

As an answer, she held out her arms to him, and he came to her most willingly.

By suppertime, even the seasoned crew members were willing to admit they were in the grip of a storm. The motion of the ship made serving the meal—to those passengers still willing to eat—difficult, but the stewards and stewardesses valiantly performed their duties.

Virginia Birch, who had spent most of the day in her cabin, emerged to lie upon one of the sofas in the salon, but when Aunt Lucy fussed over her, she declined to be served anything but a little wine. Addie Easton was feeling slightly better, but Della noticed that her appetite was still far from hearty. Of the Pattersons there was no sign.

In fact, of the nearly six hundred passengers aboard the ship, it appeared that more than half were by now afflicted with seasickness. Della feared it might get worse before it got better, though the gentlemen assured the ladies that the storm was sure to abate by morning.

"These late summer squalls blow up suddenly but are soon over," Judge Monson claimed, and the others who had previously sailed these seas agreed with him. Captain Herndon again played at whist, with Monson and Sharpe making up his party along with Mr. Brown, a friend of the Eastons' who was traveling to New York for his own wedding.

The game had already begun when Mr. Cadbury entered the saloon, having either skipped supper or taken it in his cabin. Visibly irritated by his inability to join the captain's foursome, he looked about the room, his eye finally lighting upon Della, who sat commiserating with Virginia on a sofa.

With some misgiving, Della watched him cross the room. Kent had briefly excused himself to fetch something from their cabin to aid in a discussion he was having with Ansel Easton, so she was on her own for the moment.

Mr. Cadbury wove his way across the floor, whether from drink or the motion of the ship, she wasn't sure—though she hoped it was the latter. Finally he heaved his bulk to a halt before her, his little eyes glittering with malice.

"So, my fine lady. Think you're better than my sister, do you?"

Della had seen enough men in their cups to know reason was more likely to anger than appease him. Still, she had to say something. "I'm sure your sister is the most admirable of women," she offered.

"Damned right she is! The best woman living, and partly to my credit. I made sure she never suffered an insult in her life, even when she was a schoolgirl. Sent more than one spoony to the rightabout, too, when they presumed to pay her court. Not good enough for her, any of 'em."

"No doubt the perfect man is still out there, searching for her," Della suggested.

He snorted. "Perfect or not, she set her sights on Bradford. I tried to talk her out of it, but she made it clear that's what she wanted—a place in New York's society as well as Philadelphia's. But now you've taken that away from her. Not sure I can allow that."

Virginia struggled to sit up despite her queasiness. "Sir, are you threatening Mrs. Bradford?"

Cadbury's mouth worked for a moment. "Take it as you will. I've said nothing incriminating. But I'll be damned if I let my sister suffer because of some upstart Irish wench."

Billy Birch came up just then, before Della could decide how best to respond. "Here, now, we can't have you swearing in front of the ladies. Come, there's a poker game just starting over here. Why don't you join in? I'll have the steward bring you another glass of claret."

Cadbury glowered at the smaller man but allowed himself to be led away. Billy turned to wink at the ladies over his shoulder, and Della sent him a grateful smile. The incident had reinforced her doubts, but when Kent rejoined the party a moment later, she was able to enter the discussion that resumed as though nothing was amiss.

After all, she thought lightly, perhaps the ship would go down in the storm and she'd never have to deal with any of the worries that plagued her.

FIFTEEN

And the coming wind did roar more loud,
And the sails did sigh like sedge;
And the rain poured down from one black cloud;
The Moon was at its edge.

—Samuel Taylor Coleridge,
The Rime of the Ancient Mariner

KENT THOUGHT HE NOTICED A SHADOW IN Della's eyes when he rejoined her, but he wasn't certain until just before the party broke up for the evening. Under cover of making plans for the next day, Billy Birch pulled him aside and told him about Francis Cadbury's hectoring, though he hadn't heard much of the conversation.

"Three sheets to the wind, the man was, and in an ill temper to boot. I was able to distract him, but he bears watching."

Kent nodded slowly. "I know he does. I'll be more vigilant in the future. Thank you, Billy."

Rejoining Della, he waited until they were back in their stateroom before speaking. "I understand you had an unpleasant encounter with Francis Cadbury earlier. I'm sorry I wasn't there to defend you."

He was more than sorry—he was frustrated and ashamed. If he couldn't protect her from insult even in the restricted environment of the ship, how would he do so in New York? So much for all his fine promises.

"It's just as well," she said, to his surprise. "He was drunk and spoiling for a fight. Had you been there, he might have found one, and that would have done none of us any good." The shadow did not leave her eyes, however.

"Della, you must know that most easterners are nothing like Francis," he said urgently. "Even as a boy, he was a cowardly bully, harassing those who were younger or weaker than he, or who could not retaliate. I've never considered him a friend, despite our mothers' closeness. He's not in the least representative of the people I'd have you associate with in New York."

She smiled, the shadow lightening. "It wouldn't say much for my judgment if I believed you enjoyed the society of a man like that. I'm glad, though, to hear he was never a friend of yours. I feared I was perceiving him as worse than he is, because of my own selfish—and, yes, jealous—leanings."

Kent enfolded her in his arms. "You have

nothing to be jealous of, Della. Not ever. My betrothal to Caroline was one of convenience and family alliance for the sake of wealth and connections, never one of love. Not even she ever pretended it was anything else."

Della pulled back to look up at him doubtfully. "Truly, Kent? It has tormented me to think I must cause her pain. If she cares for you even half as much as I do, our news will be a terrible blow to her."

"The only blow will be to her pride and ambitions, I assure you." He gathered her close again, resting his chin on top of her head.

"We were friends as children, seeing each other frequently when our mothers visited, but as we grew older, her interests turned to fashion and gossip, and mine to business. My mother persuaded me we would be a good match, and as I assumed I'd marry eventually anyway, I made her an offer. She accepted as coolly as I offered. No protestations of passion or dreams of happiness, just mutual satisfaction at the prospect of a profitable alliance."

Della's arms crept around him almost shyly. "I have trouble imagining you as such a mercenary."

He sighed, ruffling her hair with his breath. "But I was. Until I met you, I don't believe I knew what true happiness was. Thank heaven I found out in time, before binding myself in a union that would have precluded it for the rest of my life."

Now she pressed her cheek against his chest.

"I'll do my best to make you happy, Kent—as I know you'll do for me."

"I will." He made it a vow.

Della was rudely awakened the next morning by being nearly thrown from her berth. Clutching at Kent with one hand and the edge of the bunk with the other, she looked around wildly as the last shreds of a pleasant dream fled. The wind had by no means abated—she could hear it wailing and screaming just outside the hull.

"Another day of this?" Kent was awake now, too. "You were the one who wished for excitement, were you not?"

"I take it back," she said wryly, sitting up. Yes, the floor was rocking more steeply than it had yesterday. Remembering her errant thought last night about the ship sinking, she swallowed. Really, in the future she would have to be more careful about what she wished for!

Her lilac dress was still damp, but she pulled it on anyway, again dispensing with the hoops. She had realized yesterday that in this wind they were more than an inconvenience—they were a positive danger.

"Does your wardrobe selection mean you intend going on deck again?" Kent asked as he completed his careful shave, despite the pitching. She heard the hint of worry in his voice.

"Just for a peek. I won't stay up there if it seems too dangerous, I promise."

A few minutes later, Kent had no need to remind her of that promise. They made their way up the curving stairs to the deck with some difficulty, hampered by the pitching of the ship and by the occasional gushes of seawater that came under the door at the head of the stairs. On opening the door, a fearsome sight met them.

Della stood aghast, watching as a huge wave, many times the height of the ship, rushed toward them. Certain that this was likely to be the last sight she'd ever see, she clutched at Kent, unable to tear her gaze away from the terrifying tower of water. It leaned over them from on high, and then, just as she was sure they would be engulfed forever, the ship lurched and rose as though hoisted by an invisible, giant hand.

Water crashed across the deck, dousing them both thoroughly and filling her eyes. Blinking to clear her vision, she saw that they were now on a mountain with valleys all about them—and then they were rushing downward again.

With her heart in her throat, Della watched the process repeat itself, and then again. It seemed a miracle that the ship was still afloat, and the pitching they'd felt below was more than explained.

"Seen enough?" Kent murmured in her ear—or, rather, shouted, for the shriek of the wind and crashing of the waves made anything less inaudible.

She nodded mutely.

They backed through the door and pulled it closed before descending again to the saloon. Not surprisingly, it was nearly deserted. Aunt Lucy was individually serving the few hardy souls who could stomach breakfast, but she made no pretense of laying out a full meal. Della wondered how on earth the cook had managed to prepare anything at all with the ship rocking so violently.

Of those they knew, only Judge Monson and Billy Birch were in evidence, speaking to a small cluster of obviously terrified passengers. Approaching, Della heard Monson declaring yet again that there was no cause for alarm.

"These ships weather worse than this several times a year," he was saying. "Hurricanes are common in these latitudes, and ships are built to withstand them."

"But . . . ships *do* go down sometimes," one woman pointed out shakily. "Mightn't this be one of those times?"

Billy spoke up. "If it is, we'll go down singing! Worrying won't change things, so let's put it aside until the captain himself tells us to worry, eh? I spoke with him an hour ago, and he was perfectly cheerful. As he's promised to go down if the ship does, he'd hardly be so if he thought we were likely to sink!"

His breezy manner seemed to soothe the others as Monson's sober assurances had not. The fear fading from their eyes, the passengers dispersed.

"Is the captain really so confident as you say?" Kent asked the two men in an undertone once every woman but Della was out of earshot. She took it as a compliment that he did not attempt to shield her from the truth.

"He certainly seems so," said Monson. "And while I've not personally experienced a storm at sea quite so severe, certainly many ships have weathered them intact."

Della wondered that she could ever have been afraid of this man. Right now she wanted to hug him for the confidence he exuded.

As they stood speaking, Captain Herndon himself entered the saloon. At once he was bombarded with questions, but he responded just as Billy had reported. "I've a good crew and a good ship. Keep up your spirits, and we'll come through for you."

He hurried away then, but everyone seemed much cheered. Della, however, noticed how tired the captain looked. Had he slept since the storm first blew up? She rather doubted it.

Ansel Easton had emerged from his stateroom while the captain was speaking, and now he looked after him darkly. "Have I not been saying all along that a ship with a changed name will be dogged by ill luck?"

But Billy clapped him on the back. "Come now, Easton, we haven't gone down yet!"

"We haven't reached New York yet," he replied. Then, noticing Della in the group, he shook off his unaccustomed grimness and smiled. "But no doubt the captain is right. Certainly he has had far more experience at this sort of thing than I have."

Della refrained from telling him that he need not dissemble for her sake, instead asking, "How is Addie this morning?"

"Horribly seasick," he replied, worry once more coloring his voice. "I've only ventured out to fetch her some tea in hopes of settling her stomach somewhat."

"Poor thing! Would she appreciate a visit, do you think?"

He hesitated, then shook his head. "She'd have my head if I allowed anyone to see her as she is just now. But perhaps later. I'll let you know—and thank you." He hurried after the stewardess to procure the required beverage.

Kent smiled down at Della. "That was kind of you."

She looked up in surprise. "Why, it's nothing to the kindness Addie has shown me since leaving San Francisco—even though she knew nothing of me at all when we sailed. I only hope she'll allow me to be of some service to her if she continues ill."

Kent merely shook his head, leaving Della to wonder how he could love her as he said if such a minor show of sympathy surprised him. Perhaps it was simply that most women of his acquaintance would not have responded so, but still she wondered.

Della had thought that the weather could not get worse without sinking the ship, but as Thursday progressed, so did the hurricane—as even the crew was now calling it. The storm was all anyone spoke of, and it was clear that despite the brave front the captain, crew, and other gentlemen aboard put on, everyone realized that the ship was in very real danger.

Steerage passengers now outnumbered first- and second-class passengers in the dining saloon, as many had come there to escape the stench of seasickness below. With all but a handful of the wealthier passengers holed up in their staterooms, no one protested their presence there.

Though even she now felt the occasional twinge of nausea, Della tried to occupy her thoughts by befriending some of these poor, frightened souls—especially the children. Just as the men tried to keep up the spirits of the women, so she and the other women tried to distract the children from the danger. They told stories and played games, and when the meager evening meal was brought out, they made sport of trying to eat while the tables tilted back and forth.

As darkness fell, the creaking of the hull seemed to grow louder still. Several first- and second-class passengers ventured out to learn what news there might be, and to escape the close quarters of their staterooms. A few had no choice—seawater from the main deck had spilled into their staterooms, making them uninhabitable. These stretched themselves on the sofas in the saloon, complaining bitterly.

The gentlemen made no pretense of playing cards this evening. All anyone could talk of was the storm and their chances of surviving it.

"I fear, as bad as it is now, we have not yet seen the worst," Della overheard Thomas Badger, a former ship's captain himself, saying to one of the engineers. To her dismay, the other man agreed.

"If we can keep the boilers lit, we may ride it out yet," the engineer said, "but if we develop a leak, I fear we may be lost."

"Is there any sign of one?" asked Captain Badger in a voice Della had to strain to hear.

The engineer's only response was a tightening of his lips, then finally a quick shake of his head.

Della debated whether to tell Kent of the exchange but decided against it. If this was to be their last night together—their last night alive—she didn't want either of them to spend it in fear.

"What I can't affect, I won't worry about," she murmured to herself. "But my own outlook is under my control." Taking a deep breath of the humid, fetid air of the saloon, she went to find her husband.

She found him in concerned conversation with Judge Monson. They were just saying something about signal rockets when Kent caught sight of her and turned. "Ah, there you are, my dear. Are most of the children gone to their beds?" The warmth in his eyes buoyed her spirits.

"I believe so. One poor woman from Lima is traveling with three little ones, and speaks almost no English. Thankfully, I was able to calm them all—for the moment, at least."

Judge Monson bowed to her respectfully, murmuring something about her charity, then left them alone.

"So your Spanish has paid off once again," said Kent when the judge had gone. "It appears to be far more useful than the Latin and Greek I learned in school."

Though she suspected he spoke of such things merely to distract her—and perhaps himself as well—she answered in kind. "That's me, practical rather than classical. Though my mother did teach both my sister and me a smattering of Latin, and threw our way every book she could get her hands on."

Kent's eyebrows rose. "No wonder you appear unusually educated for your circumstances."

"So you think I can convince the society crowd that I'm not just an ignorant Irish prospector's brat after all?" She tried to speak lightly, but knew some of her irritation showed in her voice.

He realized his error at once. "I never said—I didn't mean—"

"No, I know you didn't. I'm just overly sensitive—my nerves are frayed by this endless storm." She linked her arm through his. "Come, it's late. We may as well attempt to sleep, as there's no knowing what tomorrow may bring."

Or whether we'll see tomorrow at all, she added silently.

Though Della spoke cheerfully, Kent could see the worry in her eyes. He felt it, too, but saw no more point than she did in speaking of it. What would come would come. For now, they still had each other. Bidding the others good night, he accompanied her to their stateroom.

The air there was close, but still fresher than that of the saloon, now that so many people had gathered there. Closing the door quickly behind them, he breathed deeply to clear the stink from his nostrils. Then he smiled across at Della, who had braced herself between wall and bunk to remove her shoes.

Today had shown him another side of her, a compassionate, giving side that he found he admired greatly. Though he himself had always given generously to charities, he had done so because it was expected of a man in his position, not out of tender feelings for his less fortunate brethren. Della really cared. It was yet another example of how she embraced life, whereas he had only gone through the motions of living.

"What?" she asked, and he realized he had been staring.

He shook his head. "I was only marveling that you can still look so beautiful after a day like today."

She laughed. "Beautiful? With my new dress a

crumpled mess and my hair all undone? I probably have dirt on my face as well." She made a movement toward the mirror to check.

"Only a smudge on your nose. I find it rather charming," he said with a grin. "Come here, Della."

The mirror forgotten, she turned toward him, her green eyes alight with an emotion that both humbled and aroused him. What had he ever done to deserve such a woman? He closed the gap between them with one long stride and lowered his lips to hers.

She seemed as eager as he, willingly parting her lips for him as she slid her arms up his back. With an urgency born of the danger facing them, the knowledge that this might be their last night together, he deepened his kiss, skimming his hands along her body. Frustrated by the layers of clothing, he began unbuttoning her gown, while at the same time she worked on his shirt.

In a moment they were both bare to the waist, savoring each other with hands and lips. Della ducked her head to touch one of his flat, hard nipples with her tongue, and he shuddered with pleasure before returning the favor. Lingeringly he kissed first one firm breast, then the other, drawing the nipple into his mouth and gently suckling. Clutching his shoulders, Della threw back her head and inhaled deeply.

Suddenly his trousers seemed far too tight. Still suckling, he unfastened them. Just as he had worked them to his knees, however, the ship pitched. Hampered as he was, Kent lost his balance and fell to the carpet in an ungainly heap. Della tried to catch herself by grabbing the middle berth, but after a swaying scramble, she lost her purchase and landed right on top of him.

For a moment, they lay in startled silence, but then Della began to chuckle. Kent joined in, and in a moment they were both gasping with laughter that held an edge of hysteria, with the sudden release of the tension they'd been under all day.

"Why don't we just stay here?" Kent suggested when he could speak again. "I'd hate to be pitched out of the bunk right in the, er, thick of things."

"My thoughts exactly." Rising to her knees, Della pulled his trousers the rest of the way off, then proceeded to unfasten her skirt. "I don't know why we didn't think of this before. The carpet is far more spacious than the bed." With a wicked twinkle in her eye, she kicked her skirt and pantalettes to one side and climbed astride him.

Startled, but pleasantly so, Kent grinned up at her. "Do you mean to have your way with me, young lady?"

She nodded. "What do you intend to do about it?" As she spoke, she leaned down to brush her breasts tantalizingly along his chest.

Kent put his arms behind his head. "I throw myself on your mercy."

"No mercy," she replied with a grin before fastening her mouth on his. She moved above him, sliding her body along his, stimulating every nerve he possessed to a fever pitch. Finally, just when he thought he could bear no more, she settled her hips against his, allowing his eager shaft access to her waiting depths, moist and ready to receive him.

With a groan, he lifted his own hips to drive himself deeper, at the same time grasping her by the waist. Again the ship rocked violently, but this time the motion only served to intensify their pleasure, plunging him yet further inside her. He pulled her face down to his for another kiss.

Now Della began to move again, easing him out and back into her in a rhythm as old as humanity itself. Kent ran his hands up and down her back and then around to her belly, her breasts, the sensitive nubbin at the place of their joining. As he plied his thumb, she began to moan, rocking faster, pulling his tongue into her mouth to massage it with her own.

Then she broke the kiss and straightened, arching her back and lifting her face to the ceiling, her hair streaming down behind her, as she climaxed. Her tightening drove him over the edge. Thrusting upward once, twice, three times, he shattered within her with an impassioned cry.

She collapsed atop him, pressing her cheek to his, relaxing by degrees as her heartbeat slowed along with his. "It's just as well the hurricane is so noisy," she said after a moment. "We might have embarrassed our neighbors otherwise."

He rolled to one side so that she lay beside him on the carpet. "Trust you to find a silver lining even for these dark clouds." He loved her more than ever—more than he'd imagined it was possible for anyone to love another. "But you are my silver lining, Della. Because of you, I'm happier than I've ever been, even knowing . . ."

"Even knowing we may have only hours to live," she finished for him. Her eyes reflected no fear, however—only love.

Reluctantly he nodded. "I can think of no other way I would choose to spend my last moments."

"Nor I. Thank you for marrying me, Kent."

He pulled her to him for another kiss. "We go on too fast. It is still possible the storm will blow itself out by morning, and that we'll reach New York only a day or two behind schedule."

A faint frown furrowed her brow, and for a moment he thought she was about to say something, but then she smiled. "You're right, of course. As long as the ship is intact, we have every chance of weathering the storm. We need only keep our courage up."

What a remarkable woman his Della was! But even she must be tired after the day she'd spent among the children. "Come, let us see if we can remain in our bunks long enough to catch a few hours of sleep," he suggested.

She nodded and sat up. "Perhaps if we tuck the blankets tightly around us, they will act as a sort of restraint against the pitching of the ship."

Kent agreed, and they took a blanket and turned it sideways so that they could tuck it in at both sides across them. Even so, and as tired and sated as they were, they slept very little.

In the darkness, with nothing to distract him, all Kent could think about was his helplessness to protect Della should the ship founder. What use was social position, wealth, even physical strength in such circumstances? Still, he vowed over and over to do whatever he could, even if it killed him.

Della lay silently beside him, snuggled within his arms, but he could tell by the tension in her body that she was as wakeful as he. Once or twice he nearly asked her what she was thinking about, but decided against it. If he could honestly reassure her, he wouldn't hesitate to speak, but he knew he couldn't—and he wouldn't lie to her. Not again.

It was nearly dawn when they both fell into a heavy slumber, finally oblivious to the crashing and shrieking outside the ship and the creaking and moaning within. It must have been close to noon when they were both abruptly awakened. Their restraining blanket gave way, and they were violently tossed out onto the carpet to roll against the cabin door.

Dazed, they looked at each other confusedly for a moment, and then Kent grabbed Della and braced himself for a corresponding pitch to the other side, one that might hurl them against the ladder trunk under the porthole. But it didn't come. The floor remained pitched at an unnatural angle, with the door beneath them and the porthole above, on the opposite wall.

Della was the first to speak. "What on earth? Give me a boost and I'll look outside to see if I can figure out what has happened."

He helped her to reach the bunks, and, using them as a sort of ladder, she made her way to the porthole. For a long moment she was silent, and then she spoke the words he'd been dreading. "Dear God," she breathed. "I do believe the ship is sinking."

SIXTEEN

See! See! (I cried) she tacks no more!
Hither to work us weal;
Without a breeze, without a tide,
She steadies with upright keel!

—SAMUEL TAYLOR COLERIDGE,
The Rime of the Ancient Mariner

HOLDING TIGHTLY TO THE MIDDLE BUNK, Della stared down at the sea far, far below them. The wind still lashed the waves in fury, and the ship still rocked, but now it lay nearly on its side. Surely this was a very, very bad sign.

Kent made his way up the steeply pitched floor to join her at the porthole, clutching the trunk fixed in place below it. "I fear you may be right." His voice was remarkably calm. "I'd best go out and see if there is anything I can do."

"I'm coming with you." To her relief, he didn't argue.

Quickly they pulled on their clothing, dispensing with all but the necessary items. As soon as they unlatched the door, it swung out and down to show the dining saloon in a state of chaos. Passengers were scrambling up the slope toward them, using the tables and benches, which were bolted to the floor, to help themselves along. Most were clearly afraid that the other side would soon be under water, though at the moment it appeared dry enough.

Della saw the Eastons nearby, having made their way up from their stateroom opposite. "Our porthole is completely underwater," Addie informed her when she joined them. "I fear—"

But just then Captain Herndon's voice cut through the commotion in the saloon. "All men prepare for bailing the ship! The engines have stopped, but we hope to reduce the water and start them again. She's a sturdy vessel, and if we can keep up steam, we shall weather the gale."

Kent and Ansel Easton started forward at once, pausing only to take leave of the women. "We'll do everything we can," Kent assured Della. He looked almost relieved at the prospect of action.

Beside her, Addie was saying to her husband, "Oh, Ansel, if you hadn't married me, you wouldn't have been in all this trouble!"

He kissed her. "If I knew it all beforehand, I should do the same again."

And then he and Kent were gone. Della was

glad to see that Ansel's assurances had left Addie with a smile on her face. For a moment the two women clung to each other, watching their men join the others to form a bailing crew at the captain's direction. Could they really make a difference? Della had no idea.

"Come," she said rallyingly to Addie. "Let's see if there is anything we can do to improve the spirits of the other women and the children."

"Yes, let's," Addie agreed, clearly as eager as Della was to keep her thoughts and hands occupied. "You were wonderful with the little ones yesterday. I wish my Spanish were as good as yours. I know only a very little."

"Only a few of the passengers do not speak English, so that should be of little importance," Della assured her. "There, I see Mrs. Ellis, poor thing. I'm sure she would like some assistance with her brood. Dr. Ellis has gone to join the bailing party."

Lynthia Ellis had the care of four children—her own three as well as another traveling with them. She and her husband hailed from Ohio, and yesterday she and Della had spent some time talking of her home state while helping to amuse the children. Now Mrs. Ellis, one of those who had suffered most from seasickness, was even more grateful for Della's assistance, as the children were all sobbing with fear.

In contrast, young Harriet Lockwood and Augustine Pahud, both about ten years old, found the pitching of the ship and the resultant breaking of plates and glassware amusement enough. Laughing each time another dish broke, they continued to eat the meals that had been served them just before the ship heeled over, bracing themselves sideways against a table. Della rather envied them their ignorance of the danger.

More and more passengers crowded up from the lower decks, the men joining the bailing lines and the women grouping together in small, serious knots. Della and Addie gathered together as many of the children as they could—more than a dozen—and organized a game to keep them distracted and out of the way of the men. Soon most of them were interested and took turns naming things beginning with successive letters of the alphabet. Even the few who spoke only Spanish were able to play, with some assistance.

"How long can we keep this up?" Addie whispered to Della at one point, glancing anxiously in the direction the men had gone.

"As long as we have to," Della whispered back determinedly, trying to keep the grimness she felt from her voice. She didn't see how any of them would survive unless the ship could be righted and the leak stopped. At the moment, with the *Central America* still buffeted by high seas, both seemed unlikely prospects.

Addie nodded. "Whatever happens, we'll try to keep these little ones from being frightened until . . . until the very end."

Della smiled encouragingly at her, and Addie

resolutely stopped her lips from trembling and smiled back. "Now, where were we?" she asked the child nearest her, and the game resumed.

"I'm not a man to say I told you so," Ansel Easton murmured to Kent as they took their places in one of four bailing teams. The lines of men wound up the stairways from the hold and across the decks, passing along buckets, pitchers, and ewers of water to be emptied back into the sea where it belonged. "But—"

"But you did tell us so," Kent finished for him. "It appears your superstition may have been well founded." Mechanically, over and over, he took one after another water-filled vessel and passed it to Ansel, who passed it to the next man, who tossed out the contents and handed it back.

"What of the pumps? Why aren't they doing this job?" panted a man a few places closer to the stairs, a Mr. Jones, from Kentucky. He had earlier reminded Kent of his brother, Charles—a handsome fellow with an eye for the ladies and a high-stakes card game.

"The donkey engines, what run 'em, won't go," offered another man, a steerage passenger Kent hadn't met. "All mucked up, they are. Engineers ought to be horsewhipped."

A general murmur of indignation arose, though the buckets never slowed. They all realized that their very lives, not to mention those of their wives and children, depended on their labor.

"There's nothing to be gained right now by placing blame." Kent lifted his voice above the others. "If we survive this, no doubt there'll be an inquest. Until then, I recommend we conserve our strength for the task at hand."

No one could disagree with this, and a few minutes later Billy Birch, from his place on a lower deck, began singing—a song that was taken up by the rest, helping them to keep up their rhythm and their spirits. As the day wore on, however, everyone grew silent again as hope and energy alike waned, and still the ship listed over.

What little daylight the storm allowed was beginning to fail when Captain Herndon again came along the sloping deck. "We're going to cut away the foremast," he shouted into the gale, "and hope that will help to right the ship. The water has been lowered somewhat, so we'll try to restart the engines."

He, the first officer, the boatswain, and Captain Badger all set to work cutting through the rigging and unstepping the mast until it fell over the side. Kent heard it give a sickening thud against the hull as it went, and offered up a silent prayer that it had not punched another hole in the ship, undoing all their efforts.

His arms felt leaden, and with each bucket he passed he wondered if he'd be able to lift the next. Several men had already fallen out of the line, to be replaced by others. Now, with the mast away, Captain Herndon gave a general order that the bailing crews work in shifts. Ashby, the chief engineer, had gathered up another group of men to take their places for a while, so that they could rest.

Passing one last bucket along, Kent gladly gave his spot to a Mr. Frederick, a German steerage passenger. Staggering with weariness, he and Ansel went below to find their wives.

Della and Addie were still in the saloon, singing with raspy voices to fifteen or twenty children, some pillowed on their mothers' laps, others clinging to each other, and some sleeping on piled blankets between the tables. Their eyes lit up at the sight of their husbands, and after finishing their song, they left the next to two of the mothers.

"Come sit down, both of you," said Della, hurrying to greet them. "You look ready to drop."

Addie threw herself into her husband's arms, which, tired as they were, still had enough strength to clasp her to him. "We've been so worried about you! Virginia went to offer our assistance in the bailing to the captain, but he wouldn't allow it."

"You're doing more good here, I think," Kent told her, and Ansel nodded in agreement. "There are still quite a few men who haven't had a turn at the bailing, though I believe the women's offer motivated many more to join in. We'll be working in shifts now, until the water is out."

Della took his hand and forced him to look at her. "Is there really any hope of that?" she asked quietly.

He pressed his lips together for a moment, debating, then decided he owed her the truth. She had as much right as anyone to decide how to spend her last hours. "Very little," he finally confessed. "Cutting loose the mast didn't—"

"Look! Look!" Addie interrupted him, pointing to the ornate chandeliers suspended from the ceiling of the saloon. "The ship is righting itself."

They all turned to look. Sure enough, the lamps were slowly, slowly returning to their proper position until, after almost half an hour of breathless watching, they hung nearly perpendicular to the ceiling once again. A moment later, a dull throbbing sound signaled the restarting of the engines, and everyone in the saloon cheered.

Kent allowed himself to breathe more easily, but his relief was short-lived. Not five minutes later, the engines stopped again, to universal groans of despair.

"But still, we are level," Addie said to all who would listen. "That puts us in better condition than we were before."

Della pulled Kent aside again. "What is it? Why could they not keep the engines running, do you think?"

He shook his head. "I imagine the water has reached the boilers, though I don't know. But it stands to reason that once the ship took on enough water, she would right herself—before beginning to sink. I'm afraid this may not be the good sign Mrs. Easton thinks it is."

She glanced over to where Addie and Ansel sat together, hands clasped and heads bowed in prayer, and nodded. "I feared as much. But let's say nothing to the others—not yet. Allow them to hope while they may."

He gave her a hug, though his arms were still heavy with fatigue. "Have I told you today that I love you?"

Della grinned at him, but before she could reply, a shout came from the stairway. "More men! We need every man available to bail out the engine room!"

With a sigh, Kent rose. It appeared his conjecture was all too accurate.

Even as he ascended the stairs again to resume his place on deck, he saw bright trails of fire in the sky. The captain must have ordered the distress rockets launched, in hopes that another ship might see them and come to the aid of the *Central America*. Kent knew that the women below had likely seen the rockets through the skylights or windows of the saloon, and momentarily wished he could be down there to offer Della additional comfort.

But she was strong—stronger than he, in many ways. She would be one of those offering comfort right now, not receiving it. The thought bolstered his courage and his strength as he stepped forward to take the next bucket—actually a fancy porcelain pitcher—coming along the line.

* * *

Through the window at the end of the saloon, Della watched the fiery trail sputter out against the waves. "A distress rocket, of course," she said calmly, in response to the questions going up on all sides. Over the past several hours, she had become a leader of sorts—one the others looked to for answers and encouragement.

"Now that it is dark," she continued, "there's a very good chance another ship will see it and come to our aid. Then, even if the men can't ultimately keep us from sinking, we should all be rescued to continue aboard another vessel."

Nods and general murmurs of agreement greeted this piece of reasoning, to her relief. Privately she rather doubted anything could be seen for more than a mile or two in the raging storm. Nor did she have great confidence that another ship would be able to reach them under these conditions of wind and wave, even if they were spotted. Still, it was something to hope for, and hope was all they had right now.

As the night wore on, the children fell asleep, exhausted by fear and the storm—and by lack of food, as the kitchens had sent nothing up since noon except some dry bread and water. Rumor held that the storerooms had been swamped. Occasionally the men would return, singly or in pairs, for a few minutes of rest before resuming their labors.

Each time she saw Kent, he looked more exhausted, more hopeless—as did the other men.

Though the women had insisted on giving the men the lion's share of their scanty bread and water, it was by no means enough to sustain the energy they were expending. At about nine o'clock, watching Kent and Ansel heading wearily back to their places after only the briefest break, Della came to a decision.

"The children don't need us now, as they're nearly all asleep. I'm going to help bail."

Addie stood up beside her. "So will I. You're perfectly right, Della. Virginia?"

"Of course," Virginia replied, rising a bit shakily.

Together the three women made their way to the nearest bailing line—away from the one their own husbands occupied. Comparative strangers, they hoped, might be more willing to let them help.

"Come, take a rest. I'll take over for a few moments," said Della, laying her hand on the sleeve of a man in his sixties who looked ready to drop. Addie similarly accosted a boy in his late teens, while Virginia tried to take a pail from another man.

All three men paused for a moment, apparently in confusion, but then, almost in unison, shook their heads. "Thank ye for offerin', missie, but we can't have that," said the older man gruffly. The others, all up and down the line, agreed.

"But it's our own lives we'd work to save as

well," Della argued. "If we can make a difference, surely you would let us?"

The men, however, were adamant. With renewed vigor, they passed their sloshing vessels along, resolutely ignoring the women's pleas. Sighing in frustration, Della motioned the others to follow her to one of the other bailing teams, out of sight of the first. But they met with the same resistance there, and again at yet a third bailing line.

"Chivalry indeed," Della muttered as the three women resumed their places in the saloon. "Stupidity, more like. If sheer stubbornness can save this ship, we shall all be fine."

That forced a chuckle from the others. "They really are behaving most heroically," Addie commented, "though I do wish they would let us help. Most of those men don't even have wives or children aboard, yet they work just as hard as the others."

"They may well work themselves to death, whether we sink or not," Della replied sourly. "No one can keep on like that indefinitely, particularly with no food and little water."

Addie blinked at her. "Oh! Oh, my goodness!"

"What?"

"I've only just remembered! Our hampers—wedding gifts—in our cabin. Most are filled with crackers, cheese, wine, and other edibles. I'd completely forgotten about them!"

Della looked across the saloon toward the Eastons' cabin. "Do you think they're still dry?"

"Let's go see." The three women rose again and hurried between the tables to the door of the stateroom. Addie opened the door, and they were relieved to discover the cabin tumbled but dry, the hampers she'd mentioned lying along one wall.

Gleefully Addie plunged into one after another, unearthing more than a dozen bottles of wine, numerous tins of biscuits and crackers, wax-wrapped cheeses, and other delicacies. Della took the corkscrew Addie produced from one hamper and opened three of the wine bottles, while Virginia cut up one of the cheeses with a knife.

"Let's each take a bottle," Della suggested, "along with some crackers and cheese, and go down the bailing lines, handing it out. Once it's gone, we'll come back here for more."

This sort of help the men were more than happy to receive from the women, they discovered a few moments later. The wine bottles were passed along the line between the bailing buckets, each man taking a swig to wash down his mouthful of cheese and cracker. With a heartiness surprising in such tired men, they thanked the women, dubbing them blessed angels of mercy.

"Somehow I knew you'd find yet another way to help," said Kent when Della brought him his portion.

"I still think you should let us bail, but at least this will give you all a bit more strength," she said, leaning in to give him a quick kiss on his stubbly cheek. Despite the gravity of the situation, she could not help thinking that the day's growth of beard gave him a dashing, heroic look.

"More than you know," he agreed, turning to seize the next ewer of seawater from the man behind him.

"Addie really gets the credit for this." Della spoke loudly enough for Ansel, just ahead of Kent, to hear her. "She remembered the hampers and had no hesitation in offering every bit of the contents to the men."

Ansel grinned at this praise of his young wife. "A courageous, generous spirit Addie has," he declared.

"She does indeed," Della agreed, turning back to replenish her supply of victuals.

Kent stopped her with an urgent hand on her arm. She looked up at him with a surprised frown, but before she could ask what he wanted, he kissed her, firmly and fiercely, on the lips. "And so do you," he murmured. He had to release her then, to pass back an empty bucket, but his words and look bolstered her with a warm glow as she headed back down to the saloon for more wine and cheese.

Over the next few hours, hope alternately grew and then waned in the faces of the passengers, male and female. Though the distribution of wine and cheese had given the men heart for a while, it was consumed all too quickly. Full as those hampers had been, it was still scanty rations for nearly five hundred men. Della suspected they were as heartened by the gesture as by the wine itself.

Even so, there were several men who refused to work at all. Francis Cadbury had joined a bailing crew at first, but Della had seen him retire to his cabin even before the first break, many hours earlier, and he had not reappeared. She rather suspected he had his own stash of spirits and by now had drowned his fears in them. Nor was he the only one. Despair, in some cases assisted by drink, had induced several men to slink away and work no more.

More than ever, Della wished the women might be allowed to help bail. But barring that, she was determined to assist the men by keeping their spirits up. Once the food from the hampers was exhausted, she gathered all available women—those without sleeping children in their arms—around her.

"We can't just sit here and do nothing," she said, to general agreement. "If we can't bail, we must do what we can to encourage the men. You saw how affected they were by Mrs. Easton's generous gift. Let's all go up and down the lines, offering our support, as well as what water is left."

At least a dozen women rose at once, clearly eager for a chance to do something—anything—to distract themselves from the ghastly waiting. As night crept toward dawn, Captain Herndon added his encouragements to theirs.

"Just a few more hours of work, and we may all be saved," he shouted. "I feel in my bones this storm will drop with daylight, making rescue likely if we can but keep her afloat."

Taking their cue from the captain, the women kept the men apprised of the time and weather. "Only an hour till dawn!" they cried. "The wind is lessening—can you hear it?"

And indeed, as gray daylight penetrated the clouds, the storm really did seem to be lessening, the sea and wind less fierce. The men drew on unsuspected reserves to bail with renewed vigor.

"The captain was right!" Della exclaimed to Kent, pausing in her endless trips up and down the bailing lines. "The storm is blowing itself out. He says that if we can only bail till noon, the ship may yet be saved."

Kent gave her a weary smile. His sweat-soaked shirt flew about him in the wind, occasionally revealing knotted muscles hardened by his night's work. Della thought he'd never looked more handsome.

But then he shook his head. "The people, perhaps, but not the ship." At her questioning look, he continued. "Think—there are tons and tons of iron in her belly, and the engines covered in water. The *Central America* is doomed."

"But—"

"But we do have a fighting chance," he continued, passing along yet another bucket. "With daylight, there's a good possibility of rescue.

These are busy shipping lanes. If the storm abates enough for visibility, another ship may well come to our aid."

"Then every bucketful extends our hope," said Della, wishing for the hundredth time that she could help bail. "Is there no way to get the water up more quickly? Perhaps some sort of pulley system, such as I've seen used in the mines?"

Kent shook his head, but then frowned. "Actually, something like that just might work. You there! Murray! Take my place for a moment while I go speak with the captain."

Della followed, wondering exactly what he would suggest. They found the captain on the weather deck, directing a crewman to hoist the Stars and Stripes—upside-down.

"A distress signal," he explained, turning to face them as the flag flew aloft. "With daylight, a ship keeping a sharp watch with a glass may well see it and come to our aid."

The fact that both Kent and the captain said the same thing encouraged Della mightily—as did the lessening wind. Remembering their errand, she nudged Kent.

"Captain Herndon, I've an idea to put to you," he said quickly, at her reminder. "Might we be able to bail out the hold more efficiently by rigging barrels on some sort of pulley? Perhaps we could adapt the winches I saw used for bringing trunks and crates aboard in Aspinwall and Havana."

The captain was already nodding. "One of the

engineers suggested something similar. I'll put the crew on it at once. You're right, Bradford, we must find a way to bring the water up faster." At once he turned to shout new orders to the nearest crewmen.

Kent did not wait to see the results of Della's idea, but returned to the bailing line. Della, however, watched with interest as a wheel and ropes from the mizzen stay were fixed in place above first one aft hatch, then another. The men not already working in a bailing line were organized, some to fill the barrels at the bottom and others to heave them over the rail topside.

In an hour, half a dozen such pulleys were working over both the fore and aft hatches. Water by the barrelful was emptied back into the sea, then the barrels lowered again to the ship's bowels for another load. By nine o'clock, a report came up from below that they were gaining on the water.

Not only Della's but nearly every heart aboard was heartened by the news. Yet again she and several other women petitioned to be allowed to help bail, and again they were repulsed, but the men seemed to have gained a second wind now, cheered by the news of the receding water and by the patches of blue beginning to peek between the clouds above.

Going back to refill her pitcher with fresh water to distribute to the men, Della had paused near the wheelhouse when she heard the chief engineer speaking urgently to the captain.

". . . rising again," he was saying. "Fourteen feet deep now in the engine room, up nearly to the second deck."

"Aye," Captain Herndon replied heavily. "I feared as much. If only—" He looked up and saw Della loitering within earshot. "But we won't give up hope, right, Mrs. Bradford?"

Della forced a brilliant smile. "Not for a moment, sir! I was born with more than my fair share of luck, I've often been told. I'll trust it to see me through this as well."

Herndon nodded. "That's the spirit, madam! Go along, then, and give those men another drink. They'll need it."

Honored that the captain trusted her with the truth, Della kept the grim news to herself as she dipped out water up and down the bailing lines. Men without hope wouldn't work as hard, she knew—and right now, their work was buying precious time.

Soon, however, the again-rising water became evident to all as it began lapping at the stairwells, plain to see. And then, around noon, the clouds thickened again and the wind picked up. The waves, only just starting to subside, began once more to toss the ship and break across her decks.

Still, Della was amazed by the grim determination she saw on almost every face. As hope died, the men kept working and the women stoically encouraged them or comforted the children. Still, every now and then a man would fall out of the line, shaking his head in despair. Despite urging and even bullying by the crew and the other men, some refused to return.

Della watched Kent, his face drawn with fatigue and sorrow, mechanically passing bucket after bucket. Descending again to the once-elegant saloon, she listened to the mothers desperately trying to soothe their frightened children, not believing their own words. She wondered when the end would come. All too soon, she feared.

A shout came from above, but with the renewed wailing of the wind, she could not decipher the words. She heard the shout again, and then a loud *boom* that could only be the firing of the ship's signal guns. Incredulous, afraid to hope, Della ran back up the stairway. Could it be possible?

"Sail ho!" came the cry again as she reached the deck. Staring hard in the direction everyone was pointing, she finally saw it—a tattered pair of sails, still more than a mile away, but moving perceptibly closer.

Another ship had spotted them.

SEVENTEEN

A speck, a mist, a shape, I wist!
And still it neared and neared:
As if it dodged a water-sprite,
It plunged and tacked and veered.

—SAMUEL TAYLOR COLERIDGE,
The Rime of the Ancient Mariner

DELLA RAN TO KENT, AND HE MET HER WITH arms outstretched. Grabbing her, he swung her around, laughing. "What did I tell you?" he shouted. "It paid off! We kept her afloat long enough for help to arrive."

Similar celebrations were taking place all over the deck, but after a few minutes of laughing and crying, the captain exhorted the men to keep bailing. "I don't know how many boats the other ship will have, but we have only a handful. It will take some time to get everyone off, and we must stay above water until then."

Reluctantly Della left Kent to his work, but then remembered that the women still below might not have heard the news yet. Hurrying back down the stairs, she shouted it out to all who would listen. "A ship! A ship is coming, to take us all aboard!"

A similar scene of rejoicing occurred below, and women who had resolutely refused to shed a tear while hope waned now wept copiously with relief. "I knew it," Addie Easton declared over and over. "I knew our prayers would be answered!"

After making certain she wasn't urgently needed in the saloon, Della went back up on deck to watch the approach of the other ship, which soon proved to be a two-masted brig. With dismay, Della realized it was less than half the size of the *Central America*. Would it be able to hold everyone? And how, in this still-raging sea, were they possibly to get to it?

The bailing had all but stopped again as the men crowded to the rails to watch the other ship's approach. At first Della could not find Kent, but then she saw him in close conference with Captain Herndon, Judge Monson, and Captain Badger. They broke apart when she approached, but not before she saw the concern on all their faces.

Kent donned a smile when he saw Della coming toward him, but not quickly enough. He doubted he'd ever be able to fool her anyway, so it was useless to try.

"It won't be an easy task, transferring the passengers to that brig," he replied to her urgent query. "With so few boats, the captain wants to be certain there's not a panic, with everyone rushing them at once. He's enlisted my help, among others, to try to prevent that."

She bit her lip, and he thought her adorable even with her hair in tangled tendrils about her face and her once-lovely green dress soaked and stained. "I hadn't thought of that," she confessed. "Will the other ship hold us all? It looks so small."

"We don't know yet. The captain has been watching through his glass and says that her sails are in tatters, making it difficult for her to tack against this wind. I only hope she can get close enough to launch her own boats to supplement the few we have."

"Few indeed!" she exclaimed indignantly. "What can the Vanderbilt Line have been thinking to supply only six, with six hundred passengers aboard? Nothing like a hundred people can fit on any of those boats."

"Forty, under ideal conditions, Captain Herndon said." Kent tried to keep his tone matter-of-fact. "But if the brig can maneuver close enough, we should be able to make several trips with each. Unfortunately, we're now down to five boats. The storm smashed one against the wheelhouse last night."

"Surely, though, the other ship will have at

least that many? Not every shipping company can be so shortsighted."

"Let's hope so." Kent recalled, however, that his own company's ships carried but two lifeboats apiece, as they shipped cargo rather than passengers. This brig might very well be the same. "Look, she's nearly here."

Unfortunately, the brig now looked even smaller—and more crippled—than she had from a distance. Still, Kent thought, she seemed in no immediate danger of sinking, and thus offered far more hope than they'd had an hour ago.

The moment she was close enough to hail, Captain Herndon strode to the rail. "We are in a sinking condition," he shouted, his deep voice cutting through the wail of the wind. "You must lay by us as long as possible."

The captain of the brig, which they could now see was named *Marine*, agreed, and rounded the stern of the *Central America* to get to her leeward side, the starboard. At once, Captain Herndon ordered all women and children below, to be fitted with life preservers.

"Only the women and children?" asked Della in dismay. "When you men have worked so hard for more than twenty-four hours?"

Kent guided her to the stairs. "It's always been customary to take the women and children off first. The men will follow, of course."

He had noted how poorly the brig maneuvered in the wind, and hoped she would be able to hold her position that long—but he was doubtful. Still, his words seemed to reassure Della, and she accompanied the other women who had ventured on deck back below to the saloon.

"Launch the boats!" came the next order. Of the five remaining, four were of wood and one of metal. Two of the wooden ones were cleared first, to be lowered over the starboard side. Kent helped to operate the winch, so he was able to see what a tricky operation this was.

The first boat was nearly swamped when it hit the water, and only heroic efforts by the oarsmen kept it from smashing into the hull of the *Central America*. The second went down a bit more easily, but the third launching was disastrous. A huge wave swept between the steamer and the brig, now lying about a hundred yards away, just as the third boat touched the water. Before they could release the lines, the sea flung it high, then hurled it against the side of the ship to shatter into pieces. The oarsmen escaped alive, but had to be hauled into one of the other boats.

"So now we're down to just four boats," Kent heard Ansel Easton mutter grimly from where he worked beside him.

"At least no passengers were in them, so no lives are yet lost," he replied. He had wondered at first at the launching of empty boats, but now he understood completely.

The next boat was successfully lowered, and then only the metal lifeboat remained. Ashby, the chief engineer, rode that one down, but it hit the water at a bad angle and was immediately swamped. It sank like a stone and Ashby disappeared beneath the waves, but only for a moment. Grabbing on to the now-useless lines that had lowered the boat, he was hauled back aboard.

The women began appearing back on deck now, clad in only their outer dresses and life preservers, the officers having instructed them to remove all petticoats to lessen the danger of drowning. Kent eagerly sought Della's face, so that he could read her expression.

While serious and concerned, she did not appear frightened, he was proud to note. Still, she had to know the truth. "We have lost two more boats," he told her. "But the three remaining appear to be sound."

She paled but still did not panic, simply asking, "What can I do to help?"

The crewmen were herding the women, many of whom were unwilling to leave their husbands, toward the starboard rail. "See if you can keep them calm, and make sure none—especially the children—are left behind," he murmured.

She nodded and went to speak with Mrs. Ellis, who was pleading for Dr. Ellis to be allowed to accompany her.

"I'm so weak," she was explaining plaintively, "and I have four little ones to care for. I need my husband to help me."

The crewmen, however, were adamant that no men should be allowed in the first boats. Kent understood their position, unfair as it must have seemed to Mrs. Ellis. If they let even one man board, a rush might ensue that could be the death of them all.

"It will be all right, Lynthia," Della assured her. "Here is Mary Patterson, and she will help you with the children—won't you, Mary?"

Mary had been nearly as prostrated by seasickness as Mrs. Ellis, but she quickly agreed. "Of course I will. Here, I'll take little Betsy." She lifted a girl of about four into her arms, then allowed herself to be fitted with a rope harness so that she could be lowered to the waiting boat.

Other women stepped forward to help, and Mrs. Ellis was persuaded to go. Lowering the women to the boats turned out to be no easy feat, however. For all the efforts of the oarsmen, the boats could not be held in position, tossed about by the choppy sea as they were.

The men held Mary, clutching little Betsy in her arms, suspended by ropes over the boat until an opportunity came to lower her. She missed the boat, however, and ended up in the water. They hauled her back up, sputtering but still clutching the child, to try again. The second attempt was successful, though it appeared that she landed hard enough in the bottom of the boat to have the wind knocked out of her. The moment she and the little girl were safe in the boat, the oarsmen unhitched the harness so that it could be pulled aloft for the next woman.

This process was repeated, with most women getting at least one dunking before landing safely in a lifeboat. Aunt Lucy, the black stewardess, was crushed between a lifeboat and the hull, however. When they hauled her into the boat, it was clear even from the deck that she had been badly injured.

Glancing up, Kent saw that the *Marine* had already drifted well away from them and seemed incapable of tacking closer. Even getting all of the women and children to the brig would be a challenge, should the boats need to make more than one trip.

By the time the first boat was filled, it had a mile of open sea to cross, but the oarsmen pushed off at once and began rowing. The second boat began to fill, one woman at a time. Della and Addie Easton, both wearing their cork-and-tin life preservers, moved among the other women, comforting and encouraging and making certain all of the children had a hand to hold. As the third boat filled, Kent and Ansel left the rail to urge their wives to board.

Della shook her head firmly. "We're staying. We've decided it between ourselves. Once all the other women are off and they begin allowing men to leave the ship, we'll accompany you. We can do more good here."

Kent admired their fortitude, but Ansel grasped

Addie by the shoulders. "You *must* go," he told her. "We will join you on the *Marine* before the day is out, but we'll be able to work here with much better heart if we know you are safe."

"Yes, you really must," Kent echoed, holding Della's worried green eyes with his own. "There goes the last of the children, and only a handful of women are left. By now, you'll be needed on the other ship to do the same outstanding job you've been doing here. Please, Della."

Slowly, reluctantly, she nodded. "I'll make certain all three boats come back, as well as every boat the *Marine* carries," she promised. "Oh, Kent!" She flung herself into his arms and fastened her mouth on his with the passion of parting for perhaps the last time.

He returned the kiss with equal fervor. "Goodbye, my darling wife. I'll see you soon."

And then he was fitting her into a harness, as Ansel had already done for Addie. Kent knew that, for all his brave words, it was extremely unlikely that he would ever see Della again.

Kent had just finished buckling her harness when Della was shoved roughly from the other side. "Oh, no you don't!" shouted Francis Cadbury, getting between her and the rail. "If anyone's going down on this ship, it'll be you, you slut!"

The man was clearly drunk, but that made him no less dangerous. He swung at her again but lost his balance, and Della was able to duck.

Before he could make another attempt, Kent put a fist into his face, sending him to the deck in a heap. Immediately he signaled the men to hoist Della over the side.

She felt the fearful lurch, then looked back. Mr. Cadbury lay sobbing on the deck, crying out broken apologies to his sister Caroline. Kent stood beside him, somberly watching her. He raised one hand in farewell as she was lowered out of sight of him.

Dangling above the pitching boat, so tiny from this height, Della felt her strongest surge of fear since the storm had begun. Not fear for her own safety, though that seemed precarious enough at the moment, but fear that by leaving she had just doomed Kent to founder with the ship. What might Mr. Cadbury try to do to him when he recovered?

But then she had no more time for regrets, as the rope holding her went suddenly slack, dropping her more than ten feet—into the sea. As the water closed over her head, she shut her eyes against the sting of salt and clawed for the surface. Before she could reach it under her own power, however, the line yanked her aloft, to again dangle above the lifeboat.

She sputtered and coughed, squinting to see where the boat lay below. Just as she found it, she was dropped again, and again missed the boat to land in the water beside it. This time she saved her effort and merely held her breath until the men winched her out of the sea again for another try.

Only a few feet away, she saw Addie swinging in her own harness for a moment before the crew successfully landed her in the boat. Moments later, Della dropped again, this time smack into the center of the boat, much to her relief, though the landing twisted her left ankle painfully.

"At last!" she cried, and turned to embrace Addie as their harnesses were unhooked. Just then, a barrelful of water, thrown by the bailers above, drenched them both and half filled the boat.

"As if we weren't wet enough already!" Della exclaimed, drawing a smile or two from the other women. Picking up a tin pot from the bottom of the boat, she began to bail it back out. A few others joined her efforts, their doleful expressions momentarily lightened.

Mrs. Badger was one of the last to land in the boat, muttering about all the gold she'd had to leave behind. Della was just about to remark sharply on the woman's misplaced priorities when the great bulk of Mrs. Benbow landed squarely on top of Mrs. Badger, effectively silencing her.

All of the women had apparently been evacuated now, for the next two slings held men—an elderly gentleman and Judge Monson. "I merely wished to send a message," Monson was protesting, looking confusedly up at the *Central America* towering above them.

"They're signaling that this lady behind you is the last to come, Judge, so it's no matter," said one of the oarsmen. "But we'd best head out before any others get it into their heads to try to jump down. We're nearly full as it is."

The moment the last woman reached the boat, the men plied their oars and began the long haul to the *Marine*, which had now drifted so far that it was out of sight. "Wait! My baby!" the woman cried, pointing back at the steamer. Looking up, Della saw that indeed a crewman held a little girl of about two—but the oarsmen were paying no attention.

She grabbed the sleeve of the man nearest her. "We have to go back!" she cried.

"Too late," he grunted. "Someone'll bring the tyke on the next trip."

The woman, a Mrs. Small, sobbed quietly, but there was nothing else to be done, with the wind pushing them away from the steamer even more rapidly than the oars could do. The lifeboat began to leak, though not badly, and Della was almost glad for the excuse to do something.

As the men were occupied with rowing and steering, she organized as many women as there were tins to bail as they went along. She made certain that Mrs. Small had one of the tins, as she desperately needed the distraction.

"Captain Herndon will make sure your daughter is safe," she assured the woman, praying that the boats would indeed be able to make at least one or two more trips before the *Marine* drifted out of reach.

In fact, it took more than two hours to reach the *Marine*, and Della was sure the distance had widened to at least three miles by that time. One by one, they jumped or were hauled aboard as the surges of the sea brought the boat nearly level with the deck of the small ship. Della was dismayed to discover that the *Marine*'s deck was awash with nearly a foot of water, with more waves breaking across it all the time.

Captain Burt greeted them, welcoming them aboard his ship. "I can't promise you haven't left one sinking ship for another, but we'll do our level best to get you all safely away."

"But the others?" gasped Addie, at Della's side. "There are hundreds of men still aboard the *Central America*."

"The first two boats have already gone back," the captain assured them. "As this one will, as soon as all are aboard."

"What of your own boats, sir?" asked Della. "Have you sent them as well?"

He shook his head sadly. "I've only the one, and it's stove in—and too small, anyway, to survive in a sea like this."

Della swallowed hard. Peering through the rain and mist, she could just barely make out the huge hulk of the steamer, a mere dot on the horizon. At most the boats would manage one more trip before dark—maybe two. And Kent, she knew, would go down with the ship before he would take part in an undignified scramble for safety—which was sure to occur now that the women were off.

Just then Virginia Birch, who had been on the first lifeboat, accosted them. "Oh, I can't tell you how happy I am to see you both! Was Billy well when you left him? When I saw a few men on this boat, I hoped . . . But the others will be returning soon, I'm certain."

Della and Addie embraced her in turn. "He was working hard alongside the others when we saw him last," Della assured her. "I have no doubt— What on earth?" A muffled chirp had sounded from the bodice of Virginia's dress.

"Oh! I'd nearly forgotten him." She reached into her bosom and pulled out her little canary, bedraggled and wet, but still with a bright eye. "I wonder if there might be a cage aboard?"

"You brought your bird?" Addie and Della asked in unison.

Virginia giggled. "Billy said the same, that I was being unforgivably foolish when so much was at stake, but I couldn't bear to leave him in his cage to drown."

A few queries yielded a small cage among the cargo of the ship, and Virginia placed the bird inside. Immediately he began to sing, cheering all hearts around them.

"Billy may think you were foolish, Virginia, but I thank you," Della said with a smile.

Worry returned soon enough as they waited for the first lifeboat to return, every woman hoping to see her own husband aboard it. Another hour passed before they were able to descry a small vessel coming toward them. To their surprise, it contained three or four women, as well as a dozen men.

"We weren't the last after all," Della commented. Then, "Look, Mrs. Small! One of the women has your little girl. I knew she wouldn't be left behind." Mrs. Small hurried to the rail, and her two-year-old daughter was the first passenger of the boat to be handed aboard the *Marine*.

Della stood silent, arms linked with Addie and Virginia. None of their husbands was aboard the boat. "But there are two more yet to come," said Della encouragingly, and the others nodded bravely.

Mr. Ashby, the chief engineer, was among the passengers on the first returning boat, and the moment he was aboard the *Marine* he began exhorting Captain Burt to work the brig closer to the sinking steamer.

"I've been trying these hours past," the captain replied, "but with only one intact sail, she won't tack against the wind."

Ashby argued with him, offering him five hundred dollars if he would comply, but it was clear to everyone that the captain was telling the truth, however they might wish otherwise. Just then, another lifeboat was seen returning through the flying spray, and the women again crowded the rail, their hope renewed. This boat held only men, but barely more than a dozen.

One steerage woman spotted her own husband and cried out with relief, but Della swallowed hard. Kent was not aboard, nor was Billy Birch, Ansel Easton, or Robert Patterson. Their vigil continued.

By now, most of the women, even those whose husbands had not yet arrived, had retired below, out of the wind and spray. Mary Patterson, after seeing her husband was not in the second boat, joined the others below, weeping. Della, Addie, and Virginia, however, remained at the rail, their eyes straining into the darkening mist.

The first boat, manned by the boatswain John Black, headed back for a third trip, though Della overheard him say to an oarsman that they would now have five miles to row. The *Central America* had disappeared from view nearly an hour before. Mr. Ashby was shouting for volunteers to take another boat back, but no one stepped forward.

Della touched his arm. "I'll row."

He stared at her in disbelief for a moment, then turned back to the other men as though she hadn't spoken. "I need three more men!" When still no one responded, he cried, "For God's sake, please help me to save more lives!"

The oarsmen, utterly exhausted, refused. When Ashby appealed to the steerage men who had been rescued, there was some grumbling, and one said, "Damned if I will. I'm as good as the first-class passengers, and I'll not risk my neck to save them."

"I will," Della said again, more loudly, hoping at least to shame a few men into going. Still no one paid any attention, though Virginia and Addie regarded her admiringly.

"Look! Another boat!" someone shouted, and they all turned.

The daylight was failing, but Della strained her eyes to pick out the faces of the men aboard. For a moment, her heart leaped at the sight of a tall, dark-haired man, but when he turned his head she felt a sharp stab of disappointment. It wasn't Kent. Like the last, this boat held only a handful of men, none of whom she knew.

The last two boats, with no one to man them, were now tied to the brig. "There will be one more boat," Della said, trying to sound encouraging, but with so little hope in her own heart, she doubted she was successful.

Just then, one of the men from the third boat approached them. "Mrs. Easton?" he asked.

Addie looked up fearfully. "Yes?"

"Your husband gave me this note for you." He extended a folded scrap of blue paper.

Thanking him, Addie quickly scanned its contents. "Oh! Oh, Captain Burt!" She hurried over to where he stood, Della and Virginia following close behind. "Captain, please, please do send one more boat back—just one boat."

"My dear Mrs. Easton," he replied, "I wish I could, but in such a sea as this and in the darkness, even a sound boat could not make the trip."

"But they may all die before morning," she implored. "Anything—ten thousand dollars, my husband offers, if you will send another boat." She pulled a few bills out of her husband's coat, which he had put on her just before she left the steamer.

Captain Burt regarded her sadly. "My dear, dear lady, if I could send it, one should go without a cent of money. But a boat such as we have would not live a moment. I've given orders to tack around in a circle as best we can, and we will try to take the brig nearer the steamer. She will probably float until the morning."

Addie turned away in despair, and Della put her arm around her to lead her away. "Would you like to go below until the last boat returns?" she asked, but Addie shook her head.

Virginia, swaying from exhaustion and days of seasickness, did make her way down the stairs, leaving Della and Addie as the only women on deck. Shoulder to shoulder, they sat staring into the gathering darkness.

EIGHTEEN

Under the water it rumbled on,
Still louder and more dread:
It reached the ship, it split the bay;
The ship went down like lead.

—SAMUEL TAYLOR COLERIDGE,
The Rime of the Ancient Mariner

KENT WATCHED AS THE BOAT CARRYING HIS wife to what he devoutly hoped was safety moved away. He could see a few women bailing, apparently led by Della. Even in this extremity, knowing he might never see her again, he had to smile at her mettle. After a moment, the waves and mist obscured the little boat from view, and then the captain was calling everyone to resume bailing.

A general murmur of rebellion arose. "What's the use, now the boats are gone?" one man asked loudly.

"The boats will come back for us, but it may take two or three hours," the captain said sternly. "Our job is to stay afloat in the meantime."

"What shall I do with this?" asked a crewman, coming up just then with Mrs. Small's toddler.

The captain seemed at a loss, clearly unaware until that moment that the child had been left behind. Then a feminine voice came from the stairwell. "I'll take her."

Turning, the men saw an elderly woman, a steerage passenger, standing there. "Madam, I had believed all of the women to be gone in the lifeboats," Captain Herndon exclaimed. "Are you the only one left?"

"No, there are two others. We'll take charge of the child until the boats return."

The captain nodded, and the crewman handed her the little girl. She disappeared back down the stairs with her burden, but the men had all been reenergized by her appearance. Knowing now that there were yet women aboard, they returned to their bailing without further complaint.

Wearily Kent picked up the ewer he had set down while helping Della into the last boat. A glance showed Francis Cadbury beginning to stir, but Kent did his best to ignore the man, not wanting to waste energy on anger that could be spent bailing—and perhaps increasing his chance of a reunion with Della.

A look around the decks, however, showed that more than five hundred men, passengers and crew, remained aboard. Reason told him that no more than a tithe of them were likely to survive the sinking.

Clearly Captain Herndon had also come to that conclusion. Once the bailing lines were reestablished, he gave new orders to every man not actively working. "Take all doors off their hinges," he told them, "and pull off the hatches. Gather up those barrels over there and lash them together."

Watching these operations as he bailed, Kent realized that the captain was liberating everything from the ship that was likely to float, presumably to serve as rafts after the sinking. When the others caught on, many abandoned their places in the bailing lines. As many others had given up hours ago, there were soon only enough men to operate the pulleys. Kent redirected his energies toward helping to haul the barrels of water over the sides.

Every now and then Billy Birch attempted to rally the men in song, but by now no one had the spirit for it, and all lapsed into silence after only a bar or two. Billy, as exhausted as the others and as weakened by seasickness as his wife had been, eventually gave up the effort.

On his way back from yet another trip to the rail, Kent saw Sharpe, who had been absent for the past two hours or more, dragging a large trunk up the stairs from the saloon onto the deck. "What are you doing?" he asked. "If you have energy to spare, we can use some help with this next barrel."

Sharpe just looked at him with something between a smile and a sneer. "What's the point? I mean to be on the next boat, and she'll float that long with or without my help. And if no boats return, this is all wasted effort anyway."

Kent frowned. "If all take that attitude, we can be assured of losing nearly everyone remaining aboard."

"They're as good as dead anyway. Look around you, Bradford! The ship won't last till morning. The water's already swamping the second deck—I looked while I was on the first just now. It'll be every man for himself in short order, and I mean to be prepared."

"With that?" Kent nodded at the trunk.

Sharpe nodded. "Fifty thousand dollars' worth of gold bullion. Enough to reestablish me, wherever I end up. And in here, notes for all monies due me." He patted his vest pocket.

Kent stared at him in disbelief. "Are you mad? What good is money if none of us survive?" He broke off to help with the next full barrel, and by the time he returned, Sharpe had moved to a spot near the stern rail, still dragging his trunk behind him.

The hurricane deck was being taken apart now, he saw, under the captain's direction. A sense of doom, which he'd been fighting since Della left, settled heavily upon him. Still, he did his part in the bailing, determined to save at least the remaining women, and as many men as he could.

Finally, after what seemed like endless hours, a shout greeted the return of the first lifeboat. Bailing was suspended as men rushed to the rail to watch the small boat approach. As it rounded the stern of the steamer, the captain shouted for the remaining women to be brought up on deck.

Francis Cadbury, who had been sitting in a corner near the wheelhouse nursing his head for the past two hours, struggled to his feet. "Women be damned," Kent heard him mumble. "This boat's for me." While crewmen were still helping the three women into their harnesses so that they could be lowered to the waiting boat, Francis sidled over to the railing.

Kent stepped up next to him. "What do you think you're doing?"

Francis glared at him, reminding him forcefully of the bully he'd been as a child. "Don't try to stop me, Bradford. I'm getting off this deathtrap, and I'll make sure your bogus bride gets the reception she deserves—if she reaches New York at all."

The rage Kent had ruthlessly held in check since Francis' attack on Della abruptly boiled over. He lunged at the man and was gratified to see Francis' eyes widen with fear—the same fear he used to inspire in Kent when he was a boy of seven. Francis tried to jump backward but missed his footing. Before Kent could grab him, he hit the railing sideways and went right over.

"Damn!" Angry as he'd been, Kent didn't

want Francis' death on his hands. He looked down, only to see him surface not five feet from the lifeboat. With an exclamation of disgust, he watched as two of the oarsmen hauled him into the boat to lie wet, fat, and panting in the bottom. All Kent had managed to do was grant Francis' wish of being first on the boat.

"Away from the rail!" Ashby, the engineer, roared then. Other men, seeing what had happened, were already preparing to jump. "We'll do this in an orderly fashion or not at all!"

Kent, Ansel Easton, and one or two of the other prominent men aboard helped to restore order before a free-for-all could ensue. Though some grumbled, the men moved back while the last three women, one holding the child, were harnessed and lowered into the waiting boat.

After a quick, quiet consultation with Captain Herndon, Mr. Ashby went next, swinging down a rope into the boat. "I promise you, Captain, I'll return with as many boats as the brig has on her!" he shouted up as he reached the boat.

At this point, however, discipline among the men remaining on board disintegrated rapidly, despite anything Kent could do. A final sweep of the lower decks had ascertained that no other women or children remained aboard. With that, all chivalry seemed at an end. One man jumped overboard to land near the boat, and more were lining up to follow when Ashby, in the boat below, pulled out a long knife.

"I'll slice any man who tries to get on in that way!" he cried, waving the dirk. Captain Herndon, however, shouted for Ashby to put away the knife and shove off. At this, one or two others vaulted over the side and were pulled aboard the lifeboat as it began to row away.

"The other boats will return soon," Kent shouted, trying to stave off a mass exodus that might swamp the boat. In a moment, though, it was far enough away that no others were willing to risk the swim, even though it held only a dozen people besides the oarsmen.

Kent, Ansel, and the first officer tried to organize bailing parties again, but most were too busy watching for the next boat. Nelson Sharpe was busily bargaining with a crew member for a spot in the next boat for himself and his chest, offering him several hundred dollars in gold for his help. The crewman eagerly agreed.

A few minutes later, though it seemed like another hour or more, another boat appeared out of the mist and rain. As it rounded the stern of the steamer, no pretense was made of rigging harnesses or lowering ropes. Men threw themselves overboard willy-nilly, scrambling for a chance at safety.

Kent heard Sharpe remonstrating with the crewman he had paid. "Come on, man, help me lower my trunk! I'll pay you double."

But one of the oarsmen below shouted up that the boat was taking on water, and Captain Herndon ordered it away before more men could swamp it. The boat headed off, this one with no more than ten men aboard.

A short time later, the third boat appeared, and chaos erupted again. This boat appeared sound, and more men were able to get aboard. Sharpe, sobbing and cursing, frantically tied ropes around his precious chest of gold as the boat filled.

"Shall we make the attempt?" Ansel Easton asked Kent as he watched Sharpe in bemusement. "It's likely to be the last chance we'll get to join our wives."

Kent glanced over to where Captain Herndon stood, grim and resolute, showing not the slightest trace of fear or regret as he prepared to go down with his ship. "You go, Easton. I'll do what I can here."

Ansel took a few steps toward the rail but then stopped. "No, you're right. Besides, I believe the boat is already pulling away."

It was. No others were likely to return, for the daylight was starting to go. All told, perhaps twenty male passengers and as many oarsmen and crewmen had escaped, along with the sixty women and children who had been aboard. Fully five hundred men remained aboard the *Central America* as the stormy skies ushered in an early dusk.

"They're gone, Nelson," Kent said to his one-time associate.

Sharpe looked up in disbelief from the knots he was tying. "Gone? They can't be. I've paid good money for a seat in that boat." He returned to his efforts.

"You'd do better to find something that will float, instead of that gold-filled anchor," Kent advised him.

"No! You just want it for yourself," Sharpe cried. "Get away!"

Kent shook his head and walked away. "Here! You men! Let's get to bailing again," he called to a dejected-looking group near the rail. "If we can stay afloat till morning, they'll send the boats back, or another ship may come by."

He knew both were unlikely, but felt physical activity would be preferable—for both him and the others—to merely waiting for fate to overtake them. Apparently many others agreed, for with a few more words of encouragement, two bailing parties soon formed.

With each barrel of water he helped to heave over the side, Kent thought of Della. He could almost feel her thoughts wending toward him over the miles of open sea. The return of the third boat told him she must have reached the *Marine*. He imagined her staring into the gloom, watching for the returning boats, and pictured her disappointment when she discovered that he was not in any of them.

"I'm sorry, darling," he whispered into the whirling wind.

But no. Della was strong. She would survive, with or without him. She would mourn him—he had to believe she loved him enough for that—but she would recover and go on. Still, it pained him to think he would not be there to ease her way.

"Sail ho!" came an excited cry, breaking into his thoughts. Indeed, a small schooner was approaching. Already the captain was hailing her, telling her to send whatever boats she had and lay by them till morning.

A wave of excitement swept through the men on deck, and their bailing efforts were redoubled as new hope arose. They waited and worked, but no boats came, and after fifteen minutes it was obvious that the schooner, like the *Marine* before her, was drifting away from them.

"Why don't they help?" cried a man beside Kent. "Why are they going away?"

He only shook his head. "Perhaps they have no boats and can't hold their position. All we can do is bail and hope."

Even as he spoke, a tearing, wrenching sound reverberated from below, making the whole steamer shudder violently. "The second deck has burst its fastenings," shouted one of the crewmen. "The water is nearly to the first cabin."

Bailing was clearly pointless now, even as a distraction. Kent reluctantly threw down his pitcher along with the others and went to help distribute tin life preservers to everyone aboard who wasn't already wearing one. Some men, including Sharpe, were now so dejected that they couldn't even be bothered to put one on, but sat helpless while others fastened their preservers onto them.

A distress rocket was launched, and then another. Fights began to break out over the best rafts and other objects likely to float. "Come on, Bradford," Ansel Easton called, hauling a large piece of wood behind him. "It's my cabin door. It will easily hold both of us. Help me tie a few ropes onto it, so we'll have something to grip when we're in the water."

Nodding, with one glance back over his shoulder to where Sharpe sat slumped against his chest of gold, Kent joined him. "When she goes down, she may go fast," he warned. "She'll pull everything and everyone with her unless we can get well away. It may be wise to swim some distance before that happens."

"But when is that likely to be, do you think?" asked Easton. "The captain seems confident she'll float till morning, but I admit I'm skeptical."

"I'll be surprised if she lasts till midnight," Kent agreed. "We'd best be prepared." He helped Easton lash two more ropes around the door, then they hauled it to the leeward rail. A faint shout upon the waves drew their attention.

One more lifeboat had returned, and John Black, the boatswain, stood up in its stern and hailed the steamer. When they deciphered his words, however, their brief spurt of hope died.

"She's stove and leaking," the bo'sun shouted. "I'm sorry, Captain!"

"Keep off, then," Herndon shouted back from the top of the wheelhouse, where he and Mr. Frazer were struggling with another rocket. "Stay back at least a hundred yards."

Kent and Easton exchanged a glance, then in unspoken agreement went to join the captain and first officer. "Can we be of assistance?" Kent asked as they climbed up beside them.

Captain Herndon turned, and Kent was struck by the quiet resignation in his face. He'd meant it when he'd promised to go down with his ship, that first night out of Havana. But all he said was, "Give me your cigar, Easton, for this last rocket."

Ansel handed the captain his cigar, but just as he touched it to the rocket fuse, a massive wave hit the ship, making it shudder from bow to stern. To Kent's surprise, the captain directed the rocket downward at an angle toward the sea, rather than upward. Then, with a sickening start, he remembered that a rocket fired downward was a maritime signal for imminent sinking. Intercepting his look, Captain Herndon nodded sadly.

"This is it, gentlemen. It has been my honor to know you, and I apologize that I was unable to bring you safely to New York."

Another great wave hit the ship, and the bow began to rise as the stern was slowly sucked beneath the water. Screams and shouts arose as men began to abandon the ship on all sides.

"This is our cue," Kent told Easton. With difficulty, they clambered down the tilting ladder to the main deck, only to find that their raft was already gone—either washed overboard or seized by other desperate passengers.

"Over the side, then," said Kent urgently. "We've life preservers. It's our only hope."

Even as they leaped—and the ship rode so low in the water now that they had only to jump a few yards—the bow rose higher and began to turn, almost idly, in a circle.

"A whirlpool," Easton gasped as they attempted to paddle away from the ship. "She's caught in a whirlpool!"

Their progress was painfully slow. It was obvious to Kent that they could not get nearly far enough from the ship to avoid being sucked down with her. Indeed, even as he thought it, the *Central America* sank in a rush with a great creaking groan, her lights disappearing beneath the waves to engulf them all in terrifying darkness.

Kent took a deep breath a split second before he was pulled under—far under—along with everything else within fifty feet of the steamer. He felt the straps of his life preserver giving way, and clutched at them desperately, knowing it was his only hope. Just as he thought his lungs would burst, he felt himself moving upward again. Kicking hard against the water, he fought for the surface.

After what seemed an eternity but could have been only seconds, his head broke through to blessed air. He sucked it into his lungs once, twice, three times, and then he heard an ominous rumbling below him. Jettisoned from far beneath the surface by their own buoyancy, boards, doors, spars, barrels—and bodies—shot upward. A large piece of decking erupted less than two yards from him and was propelled ten feet into the air, arcing directly above him. It reached its peak, then fell. All Kent could do was brace himself for the impact before everything went black.

Della and Addie huddled together under a blanket the captain of the *Marine* had thoughtfully given them. More than two hours had passed since the last lifeboat had left for the steamer. During that time, Captain Burt had managed to tack in a wide circle, and now, at last, approached the *Central America* again from the windward side. Her lights shone through the fitful rain—the ship was no more than two miles distant, Della guessed.

"Look, Addie! We'll reach them yet!" she said, pointing.

Addie had nearly fallen asleep, but at Della's words she sat up straighter. "Oh, we are coming closer. We are! But look how low in the water she sits."

Della bit her lip. She had already noticed that distressing fact and privately thought Captain Burt's claims that the steamer would float until morning were unwarranted. As they watched, a streak of flame shot into the lowering clouds—a distress flare.

"Isn't that a sail there, near the steamship?" Della asked, pointing. "Another ship has come!"

"Yes, but it's moving away," said Addie after a moment.

"Perhaps the men have already been transferred to it," Della suggested, though she knew there had not been time for that, not unless the other ship had dozens of boats of its own.

"Perhaps," Addie agreed, but Della knew they were merely trying to keep up each other's spirits. They stared at the steamer's lights, willing them to come closer. The other ship, visible only by its own lights, moved further and further away.

"Why don't they come this way?" Addie cried. "Surely they must see our lights as well."

Della shook her head. "They must also be crippled by the storm and unable to maneuver well. But they may well have taken passengers off our old ship while they were near."

Slowly, slowly they drew nearer the *Central America*. Both women anxiously watched their progress, hands clasped together for comfort. Then another rocket left the steamer, this time at an oblique angle, to disappear quickly into the sea.

"What do you suppose . . . ?" Addie asked, but Della merely pointed. They watched, horrified, as the lights of the steamer tilted, then disappeared, row by row, until all was darkness.

"No," Addie whispered. "Oh, no."

Della folded the other woman in her arms, though her own heart felt as though it had died as well. With vain, halting words, she tried to tell Addie—and herself—that some of the men must have escaped. Captain Burt approached them, his hat in his hand.

"Ladies, won't you go below now?" he asked quietly.

In unison, they shook their heads. "We have to know," Della explained brokenly. "Surely there will be some word—"

"When there is, be sure I will bring it to you immediately," the captain promised.

Numbly Della and Addie rose and allowed themselves to be led below. Women and children, some of them injured, were crowded into an inadequate cabin there, with seawater several inches deep sloshing with every movement of the ship. Old Aunt Lucy, the stewardess, was the most seriously hurt. Her breathing was labored, and Della feared she must be bleeding internally. For half an hour Della spoke softly to her, comforting her as best she could, until the stewardess slept.

Then she moved among the others, looking for some way to occupy herself by helping anyone who might be in need. Most, however, were either dozing or huddled in despair, far beyond any aid she could offer.

"I can't remain here," she finally said to Addie. "I'm going back on deck."

"I'll come with you." Together they climbed back up the narrow stairway and settled themselves on a hatchway near the prow. A moment later, without a word, Captain Burt brought them a large sheet of sailcloth and spread it for them to sit on.

"Thank you, Captain, for understanding." Della managed a weary smile of gratitude. The captain only grunted.

Though they were soaked through with rain and the occasional wave, neither woman moved as one hour stretched into two. The captain had just come up to plead with them again to go below when a hoarse shout was heard upon the waves.

Della sprang up with an energy she hadn't known she still possessed and ran to the rail. "It's Mr. Black, with the last boat," she cried.

The captain ordered a line dropped, and a few minutes later the *Central America*'s boatswain scrambled aboard. The activity had brought several other women up from below, and a fair crowd was gathered breathlessly by the time he stepped on deck.

"What news, man, what news?" asked Captain Burt impatiently.

John Black looked around at the anxious faces, and his expression killed all hope in Della's heart even before he spoke the dreadful words.

"The steamer has gone down," he said dully, "and every soul aboard her has been lost."

NINETEEN

How long in that same fit I lay,
I have not to declare;
But ere my living life returned,
I heard and in my soul discerned
Two voices in the air.

—SAMUEL TAYLOR COLERIDGE,
The Rime of the Ancient Mariner

DELLA CAUGHT ADDIE AS SHE COLLAPSED. "Are you sure?" she asked Mr. Black urgently. "What of the other ship we saw in the distance?"

"I can't speak to that," the man answered, "but the deck of the *Central America* was still thick with men when she went down. If any were taken off, it wasn't many. And there was no ship by her when she sank, that I do know."

The other ship must not have had boats, then, Della thought, though aloud she said,

"Then there may be hope still, Addie, however slim."

But Addie shook her head. This latest news seemed to have finally broken her spirit. Around them, other women wept, some silently and some audibly, pitifully railing against fate. Della helped the captain to quiet them and get them settled again below for what remained of the night. She urged Addie, Virginia, and even poor Mary Patterson to help, knowing that activity would distract them from their pain.

Addie joined in after only a moment's hesitation, but Virginia and Mary were too weak and weary from grief and seasickness to move. Della's own heart felt cold and lifeless within her breast. Soon, she knew, the agony must come, piercing the numbness. For now, though, she was willing to delay all emotion and concentrate on the tasks at hand.

The cabin was terribly crowded, so once tea and hard bread had been passed around, Della and Addie returned to the deck to sleep, agreeing that they would do better away from the palpable grief and sickness below. Captain Burt brought them another sheet of sailcloth to use as a blanket, and they made their bed on the same hatchway where they had held their fruitless vigil.

The next two days passed slowly, agonizingly, for all of them. Food and water being in short supply, they subsisted mainly on mush and molasses, sharing a handful of spoons and cups among a hundred people. The storm had finally blown itself out, and Della could not help but question the timing of the heavens.

Despite all the ship's doctor could do, Aunt Lucy died of her injuries. Della held the black stewardess' hand at the last, wishing she could have done the same for Kent in his final moments. Addie continued to pray at intervals for those sick and hurt aboard the *Marine* and for those who might have survived the sinking of the *Central America*.

Della envied her the comfort she drew from her faith, but could not bring herself to do likewise. She had finally found love, had been given a chance at a new life, only to have it snatched away. Providence had played them all a cruel joke, and she refused to ask anything more of it. The luck she had always been able to count on had finally run out.

On the third day they met a schooner, and its captain agreed to provide them with whatever food and water he could spare. He came aboard briefly to hear the tale of the shipwreck and survey the survivors, hungry, weary, and sunburned.

"You can have anything I have," he said gruffly, and Della was surprised to see tears standing in the hardened seaman's eyes. Were they really such a pitiful lot? She supposed they were.

The captain's sympathy had an odd effect on

her, both hardening her resolve to survive and causing unwilling gratitude to well up within her. She had always hated being dependent on anyone other than herself, but now she could not help but be thankful for the help offered her and her friends. The feeling bothered her.

Captain Burt did all he could to cheer the survivors, telling them of miraculous rescues at sea he had heard about. More than once Della heard him tell Addie that he believed she would see her husband again when they reached port. At one point she took him aside.

"Don't you think it wrong to raise her hopes like that? She's been through enough already, Captain."

He regarded her with a sad smile. "Hope is a valuable commodity, Mrs. Bradford. I'm sorry to see that you've lost yours."

A brief pain lanced through the numbness of her heart, but she quickly closed it off again. "I still have what I began with," she said, more to herself than to him. "It will have to be enough."

Three days later, they awoke to see a lighthouse in the distance. The captain informed them that they would reach Norfolk, Virginia, that day, if they could find enough breeze to spread a sail. After all of those endless days of wind and storm, the air was now breathless and the sea nearly flat.

Even as they spoke, one of the sailors spotted smoke astern, quickly moving nearer. It proved to be a steam tugboat. Captain Burt hailed her, requesting a tow into the Norfolk harbor. Word soon came back that the tug captain would comply—for the sum of five hundred dollars.

"That villain!" Captain Burt exclaimed. "We can't possibly pay that!"

But Della touched his sleeve. "Let me ask among the passengers. We may be able to collect that much between us."

The captain muttered angrily at the very idea, but Della knew the others were as sick of the sea as she was, and would be only too glad to pay whatever they had to shorten what remained of their ordeal. Nor was she wrong. Several of the passengers had managed to salvage either gold coins or notes, and in half an hour she returned to the captain.

"Tell him we have three hundred dollars."

Though he clearly resented doing so, Captain Burt relayed the message, and the steam tug sent a boat to rig a tow line. When they entered the harbor a short time later, a pilot boat came out to meet them, carrying astonishing news: Forty-nine men from the *Central America* had arrived that very morning in Norfolk.

Word spread like wildfire through the passengers, the news eliciting cheers and prayers. Della and Addie clasped hands painfully, afraid to hope. Half an hour later, the *Empire City,* the same steamship they had seen at Havana, came up and hailed them. Putting off a small boat, the steamer's captain himself came aboard. "Where is Mrs. Easton?" were his first words on reaching the deck.

Addie stepped forward, trembling. Della laid a hand on her arm for support as they breathlessly waited.

"Tell her her husband is awaiting her in Norfolk," the captain said then.

Turning toward Della for a moment, her face lighting with joy and disbelief, Addie let out a cry. "Oh! Oh! My prayers have been answered! Oh, Della!"

Della hugged her joyfully, though her own heart seemed frozen in suspense. Possibly, just possibly, might Kent be another of the survivors? The other women were already peppering Captain McGowan with questions about their own menfolk.

"The bark *Ellen* pulled several dozen men from the water a few hours after the sinking. Some are aboard my ship now, to continue on to New York. Look!" He pointed to where a ragged line of perhaps forty men stood along the rail of the *Empire City.*

The women crowded to the side of the brig, scanning the faces and calling out names. Della followed more slowly, examining each man's face in turn. Kent was not among them. Still, he might be with Ansel Easton in Norfolk, awaiting her. . . . But she would not allow herself to hope. Not much, anyway.

"I'm willing to take as many of you as would like to come aboard my ship," Captain McGowan said then. "You'll reach New York faster that way than if you continue on to Norfolk."

Addie refused, of course, now beside herself to see Ansel again, and Della decided to stay with her. Kent was not aboard the *Empire City*, so her only hope, if any remained at all, must be in Norfolk. Virginia Birch and Mary Patterson stood with downcast faces—their husbands were not among those lining the rail of the steamship, either.

"Perhaps they are in Norfolk," Addie said to them encouragingly. "You must come with Della and me to find out. Captain McGowan said there were a few other men who remained ashore."

But Mary shook her head. "Robert is dead. I feel it in my bones. I felt it the moment the *Central America* went down. I just want to get home to New Jersey now, to my mother."

Virginia looked undecided but finally opted to go with Mary. "If Billy was saved, he'll make his way to New York one way or another. If I stay back, I might miss him altogether. Perhaps he might already be on his way there."

Neither Della nor Addie was willing to shatter her fragile hope, so they did not attempt any further persuasion. Most of those on the *Marine* opted to board the steamer, where they would at least be assured of regular meals and a wash before reaching New York. The handful of survivors remaining on the brig bid the others farewell, some tearfully. Shared hardship had forged some strong—and unlikely—friendships.

Della even hugged Mrs. Benbow as she left the

ship, much as she had initially disliked the woman. Francis Cadbury, at Mrs. Benbow's side, only glared at her, however.

"Don't think you'll profit by what you stole from my sister," he said. "I'll see that you don't."

Della was more than happy to see him go. As for his threats, she was too heartsore and weary to care whether they carried any weight or not. If Kent had survived, nothing else would matter. And if he had not . . .

But she couldn't think that far ahead, not yet. Doing her best not to think at all, she joined Addie at the prow of the *Marine* to watch their progress into the harbor.

It was already dark by the time the ship reached quarantine, and a small boat carried the remainder of the survivors to the city. Seven miles they were rowed, to land at a lumberyard a few blocks from the National Hotel, where they were to stay. Della and Addie walked side by side near the head of the weary little procession as it wound through the streets.

By the time they reached the hotel, a crowd had gathered, trailing alongside to goggle at the curiosity and call out occasional questions or words of sympathy. Most of the women, however, were too tired and dejected to answer. Addie was the first to enter the hotel and immediately looked eagerly around for her husband.

"Ansel? Ansel, where are you?" she cried.

Della surveyed the waiting faces, but the one

she had hoped against hope to see was not among them. Around her, other women were also discovering that their husbands, or in some cases sons or brothers, were absent as well. One lady next to her dropped to the floor to sob out her grief, now that the hope that had buoyed her thus far had evaporated. Della swallowed hard but lifted her chin. She would not succumb to any such display—not before all of these witnesses.

"Mrs. Easton?" A man dressed as a sailor approached them. "Your husband isn't here. He persuaded Captain Johnson, of the *Ellen*, to row him out to the quarantine to meet you, more than an hour since."

"Why, we must have passed each other in the dark," she exclaimed, laughing through the tears that had formed in her eyes at her initial disappointment.

Della stepped forward. "Was anyone else with them?" she asked urgently. "Any other gentlemen from the *Central America*?"

The sailor frowned. "I don't think so, but I can't say for certain, madam. Only name I caught was Easton."

"Thank you," Della whispered. Her slender hope stretched thinner, despite Addie's encouraging words. She agreed to wait in the lobby with her friend until Ansel returned. Surely he would have some word about Kent, whether good or bad.

The two found a sofa in a corner and dozed as an hour passed, and then another. It must have been near midnight when a shout roused them.

"Addie! Where is my Addie?" Ansel Easton strode toward them, his arms outstretched, and Addie fairly flew to meet him. Della watched, smiling, as they kissed and embraced, murmuring words intended only for each other's ears. Not even to allay her own fears would she interrupt this reunion.

Finally, however, Addie recalled her presence. "Ansel, what of Mr. Bradford? Was he on the *Ellen* with you?"

His expression gave Della her answer even before he spoke. "I'm afraid not. There was so much confusion . . . I didn't see the bark until she was nearly on top of me, in fact. Bradford and I were together just as the ship went down, and he was well and strong then, but I haven't seen him since." His eyes expressed his sympathy more eloquently than his words could.

Della's heart seemed to shrivel within her, though she had expected no better news. Somehow she summoned up a stiff little smile as she thanked Mr. Easton, then told him how happy she was that he and his wife were now reunited.

Addie bit her lip. "Perhaps . . . perhaps another ship has rescued more of the men, but word has not yet come ashore. It's possible, isn't it, Ansel?"

He nodded, but there was no conviction in his

voice when he said, "Of course. Anything is possible."

"Perhaps." But Della felt utterly drained of life. "I believe I'll ask for my room now. Good night." Her hopes finally shattered beyond resurrection, she left them with dragging steps.

"Halloo! Is anyone else out there?"

Kent roused painfully at the shout and discovered himself lying on his back, bobbing like a cork on a darkened sea. Staring up, he saw a single star break free of the clouds for a moment, to infuse him with a measure of its hope before disappearing again.

Rolling onto his side, he discovered that his upper body was partially supported by a floating plank, and buoyed by his life preserver, while his legs dangled in the water, all but numb from the chill. One leg felt as though it might be broken.

"Here!" he tried to shout, but his throat was too dry to make a sound. Swallowing convulsively, he managed to work up enough spit for a second try. "Over here!" This time his voice carried far enough to be heard.

"Halloo?" came the voice that had awakened him. Looking hard in its direction, he saw no lights, nor any outline that betokened a ship.

"Who's there?"

He heard a splashing sound, rapidly drawing nearer, and then a raft of sorts came into view—really, a large section of what had been the steamer's deck. Five or six men lay across it, two of them using bits of planking to paddle. Abandoning his own bit of plank, Kent swam to it, made awkward by his injured leg. He caught hold of the highest edge so as not to overbalance the raft.

"Are we all that's left?" he asked incredulously as they helped him aboard.

"Hard to say until daylight. We've heard other shouts, further off than yours, but by the time we could reach them they were gone."

"Look! Is that a light?" asked one of the other men then, whom Kent recognized as one of the crew—a fireman, he thought.

They all looked and saw, far in the distance, the unmistakable outline of a ship, moving slowly away from them. At once they all began shouting as loudly as they could, and the ship turned. Instead of coming toward them, however, it seemed to stop, then proceed away at a different angle.

"They must be combing the area for survivors," Kent said. "Let's paddle in that direction."

The wind, however, was against them, and though they plied boards, arms, and legs, the lights of the ship receded further and further. Their shouts had not been without some effect, however. A few other survivors floating on the waves called out to them as they went, and soon the number of men on the raft had grown to ten.

Finally, exhausted, they agreed to save their strength for morning, when their chance of rescue would be greater.

Kent managed to doze, despite his leg and the painful lump on his head, which explained his earlier unconsciousness. When he woke again, gray dawn had arrived, but there was no sight of any ship, however they strained their eyes in all directions. A few of the men grumbled that they should have worked harder to paddle toward the lights in the night, and others that there were too many men on the raft for it to remain afloat for long.

"Don't be absurd," said Kent shortly, though he was as hungry and weary as any of them. "We're all quite safe for the moment, especially as the storm appears to be over at long last. All we have to do is hang on here until another ship appears."

Even as he spoke, another shout was heard from the sea. Turning, Kent saw a man, one of the few black passengers from the *Central America*, swimming toward them.

"We can't let him on," exclaimed one of the others. "We're already nearly swamped." And indeed, the raft was by now floating several inches beneath the surface.

"Of course we can," said Kent. "We certainly can't abandon him." He knew that some of the resistance stemmed from the man's color as well as simple fear, which reminded him vividly of Sharpe's prejudice against Della.

The others were adamant, however, and refused to allow the man, a Mr. Dawson, onto the raft. Kent glared around at them all. "After all we've been through, does your heroism end here?" They averted their eyes, but no one answered him.

With an exclamation of disgust, he turned to the man in the water. "Here is a rope, Mr. Dawson. Tie it around yourself, under your arms, so." He helped the man with the knots, as his own hands seemed too weary to manage them. "Now, with that plank you have, and the other end of the rope tied here to this raft, you should be well enough until another ship comes for us."

And indeed, less than an hour later, they did spot a ship low on the horizon. Perhaps it was the one from the night before, for it appeared to be moving back and forth, as though searching the water.

Again they paddled and shouted with every ounce of their strength. The ship was nearly five miles away, however, and though the wind had dropped enough to make paddling less fruitless than it had been last night, they had moved very little closer before the ship began, again, to move away. All too soon, it was entirely out of sight, leaving them alone on a vast expanse of ocean.

Several of the men became completely dejected now, despite everything Kent tried to do to cheer them. "I've lost the fortune I spent the past five years digging up," said one, a returning prospector. "I got a letter two months since that my wife went off with another man. Guess there's not much point in me hanging on."

With that, he rolled off the raft before anyone could stop him. He floated away, sinking deeper and deeper into the water until they lost sight of him. Ten minutes later, another man, who had been badly injured during the sinking, muttered something unintelligible and did the same. Kent made a lunge that wrenched his leg, managing to grip the man's sleeve for a moment before it tore in his grasp. As the other man wore no life preserver, he sank immediately, without a murmur.

Kent felt sick, both at the sight of such despair and at the foreboding that the same fate might well await them all. What would Della do at this juncture? he wondered. She'd make the best of things, of course. And so would he.

"Mr. Dawson," he said suddenly, "we have room for you now. Climb aboard." The others made no move to help him, but they did not protest as he pulled the colored man onto the raft. He thanked Kent heartily, and the two passed the next few hours exchanging life stories. Eventually one or two others joined in, and though the sun beat down on them and their hunger and thirst grew, they were able to keep despair at bay—for the moment.

As darkness closed in without any sight of another ship, however, hopelessness closed in along with it. Toward midnight, a man who had earlier introduced himself as James Birch, president of the San Antonio and San Diego Mail Line, sat up suddenly.

"I won't survive this," he said with conviction. "If any of you do, will you have the goodness to see my wife gets this? It's a gift for our little son." He pulled a small silver cup from his pocket and held it up. It glinted in the feeble moonlight.

"I'll take it, sir," said Mr. Dawson quietly. "But I'll give it back to you soon as we're rescued, so you can give it to your wife yourself."

By morning, however, Mr. Birch had disappeared from the raft, though no one had seen him go. They were now down to a company of eight, and no sign even of the wreckage of the *Central America* remained about them.

Kent's heart grew heavier and heavier. Never until now had he entirely lost hope of seeing Della again, but as the second day on the raft wore on, he couldn't help but think what her life would be like now, without him by her side. Whom would she turn to? Where would she go? Would Francis Cadbury carry out his threats?

The next few days passed in a blur of ever-increasing misery. Thirst became the very focal point of their existence, and one by one the men on the raft grew delirious, raving about food and water, imagining themselves ashore or back on the steamer. Two more died, either of thirst or of injuries sustained during the shipwreck. Another claimed he saw a ship and swam away, never to return.

On Wednesday, four days after the disaster, only three remained on the raft: Kent, Mr. Dawson, and Mr. Grant, one of the firemen. Kent spent much of his time staring into the water and attempting to net the occasional small fish that passed by with his shirt—so far without success. The other two faced in opposite directions and continually scanned the horizon for ships, but just as fruitlessly.

Turning away momentarily to rest his dazzled eyes, Kent was startled by a splash. A large fish had actually landed on the raft itself! For a moment he was too dazed to react, but then he reached out to seize it before it could slip back into the ocean. The others, belatedly realizing what had happened, turned to help him, and a moment later their prize was secured.

Mr. Grant was the only one with a knife, and with some difficulty he sawed through the tough skin of the fish, carving out a portion for each of them. Famished as they were, they still found it nearly inedible, but they forced themselves to swallow a few mouthfuls in hopes that they could somehow stay alive long enough for rescue.

The next day the fish was less tough, and though Kent gagged over it, he ate as much as he could, and cajoled his comrades into doing the same. By now, Mr. Dawson was becoming delirious, as so many of the others had before disappearing. Hourly, it seemed, he would implore the others to look again for a ship, as though one must surely be near.

"Very well, very well," said Grant after Dawson's latest supplication. "I'm scanning every inch of the— Well, I'll be damned! There's *something* out there."

Kent followed his gaze and saw, nearly a mile away, what appeared to be a small boat with an oar upraised. "Is that what it looks like?" The prospect of rescue had come to seem so remote that he doubted his own senses.

"I'm swimming to take a look," Grant declared. With his broken leg, Kent could not accompany him, but he and Dawson helped Grant to tie a life preserver about his middle, and then he struck off toward the boat. Dawson lay muttering, staring up at the sky, but Kent anxiously watched Grant's progress until he reached the boat.

Though the sun kept making his eyes tear, he thought he saw an arm reach out of the boat to help Grant into it. A moment later, it was unmistakable. There was another man in the boat, and he and Grant were rowing back toward the raft. As they drew close, Kent was able to read the name S.S. *Central America* on the prow of what could only be one of the steamer's lifeboats.

The man aboard her was Mr. Tice, who had been one of the assistant engineers. He was in no better condition than they, but as the boat was far sturdier than the raft, they all climbed into it, abandoning the piece of decking that had supported them for days. For a few hours, the men exchanged their stories of the shipwreck and its aftermath, but their parched tongues made talking difficult, and they eventually subsided.

Kent was never sure how they survived the next few days. Each of them had moments of delirium, but the others were always able to restrain whichever one threatened to leave the boat. No more food and no water whatsoever came their way. Over and over, Kent caught himself chanting the stanzas of the Coleridge poem *The Rime of the Ancient Mariner*:

> *Water, water, every where,*
> *And all the boards did shrink;*
> *Water, water, every where,*
> *Nor any drop to drink.*

It might have been Monday, though by then he couldn't be certain, when they were roused by a shower of rain. As quickly as their cramped muscles would allow, they set out the few pans and tins in the boat to catch all they could, then turned their faces to the sky, mouths wide. The shower was all too brief—when it ended, they had collected perhaps a pint of water to share between the four of them. All it had really done was rouse them to new awareness of their doomed condition.

Kent regretfully watched the rain move away. He was about to suggest they attempt rowing after the receding clouds when a flash of white on the waves caught his attention.

"A sail!" he croaked, his voice rusty from days of disuse. Without that mouthful of rainwater, he would not have been able to make any sound at all.

Rather than attempt speaking again, he pointed, then grabbed an oar. Mr. Grant took the other, and without a word they began feebly rowing toward the white triangle that was their very last hope of salvation.

TWENTY

Alone, alone, all, all alone,
Alone on a wide wide sea!
And never a saint took pity on
My soul in agony.

—Samuel Taylor Coleridge,
The Rime of the Ancient Mariner

Morning brought no renewal of hope to Della. Listlessly she peered out the window of her room at the National Hotel, which she shared with three other women from the *Central America*. What was she to do now? Where would she go? She couldn't bring herself to care, though she knew she needed to plan for her future. Life would go on, as it always did after a loss.

Wouldn't it?

Caring Norfolk townspeople had donated clothing and other essentials for the survivors of the shipwreck, and it was with genuine relief that Della put on a clean, if faded, gown after a thorough wash. Though still holding her emotions at bay, she now felt more equal to making decisions for her future.

Addie greeted her at breakfast with a hug, still glowing with happiness, though her eyes were sympathetic to Della's pain. "Ansel and I mean to go on to New York aboard a ship leaving this evening, and we wish you to accompany us. Ansel says that a few survivors transferred to another ship from the *Ellen* before she reached port."

"But Kent was not on the *Ellen*," Della reminded her.

"Ansel did not see him, but he says he cannot be absolutely sure. And it is always possible that another ship picked up more survivors, and that they may be even now on their way to New York. Do say you'll come with us, Della!"

Della hesitated. "Let me eat something, and I'll think about it. I promise to let you know well before you sail."

"Oh, of course! I'm sorry to be so pushy. Come, see the breakfast they have laid out for us!"

Docilely following her, Della surveyed the astonishing spread of food arranged on two enormous sideboards in the hotel dining room. Though she could not summon much enthusiasm, she ate enough and more to satisfy the lingering hunger from her long privation. While she ate, she considered her options.

The prudent thing, of course, would be to go back to California, perhaps to Sacramento, and to reestablish herself there. Or perhaps to travel northwest, to Ohio, where she still had cousins and, to the best of her knowledge, grandparents. Going to New York seemed pointless as well as risky.

The chance of finding Kent alive there was extremely remote, but if she went, she would be hoping all the while—and she was not sure her heart could take that. In addition, she would have Kent's family to face, not to mention his onetime fiancée and her vindictive brother. With no proof of her marriage to Kent, she might find herself in legal trouble on top of her other woes.

No, she would do better to avoid New York and to go anywhere else. That was the only way she could truly start her life over again. She'd done it before, after her mother died, and again after her father passed away and her sister married and left. She had no doubt that she could establish a successful business in Sacramento, Cincinnati, or wherever else she might choose to go.

Somehow, though, the thought of resuming her roving, solitary, mercenary existence seemed unutterably dreary after the hopes and dreams she had so recently allowed herself.

Where was the Della who delighted in living moment by moment, trusting to luck and her own wits? She seemed to have gone down with the *Central America*—with Kenton Bradford of the New York Bradfords, that East Coast stuffed shirt who had somehow become all the world to her.

She looked up from her breakfast and her thoughts at long last to find Addie and Ansel chatting quietly directly across from her. She opened her mouth to tell them that she could not accompany them to New York—that her destiny must lie along a different path. But then her glance fell on a young woman with a baby seated on the far side of the dining room.

Miracles, she realized, were all around her. Ansel Easton's rescue was one, as was that tiny life—and the other infants and children who had survived the shipwreck, who survived all of the hazards of childhood to grow up and live out their lives. Perhaps one more miracle, just for her, was not so unthinkable. She would trust in her Irish luck—and, yes, in God—one last time.

"I've decided to come with you," she said suddenly. "I'll go on to New York, just . . . just in case."

Though he rowed with all his dwindling might, Kent at first doubted they were making any progress toward the ship they had sighted. Soon, though, it became obvious that the sail was growing steadily larger—the ship must be heading right for them! Desperately fearful that it would veer away, they held their course.

Dawson and Tice waved their handkerchiefs while Kent and Grant rowed, Dawson praying aloud that the ship would see them. Then, before they could summon the energy to shout, it changed course slightly to meet them. They had been sighted.

As the British brig *Mary* loomed up, sailors shouting excitedly from her deck, Kent could focus on only one thought: He would see Della again after all.

Lines were lowered to the four men in the lifeboat while the crew of the brig shouted down for them to tie harnesses about themselves so that they could be hauled up. Kent's brief surge of exultation at their rescue faltered as he realized how feeble the days of starvation and exposure, followed by a frantic stint of rowing, had left him. Just tying the knots took every bit of his strength and concentration.

Tice could not manage his at all, so once Kent felt fairly certain his own ropes would remain tied, he helped the other man with his. Grant and Dawson signaled that they were ready, and the sailors began, slowly and carefully, to pull them aloft. Kent supported Tice until he was out of reach and then, finally, it was his turn.

Though the men above took care, still he had to fend himself off the hull of the ship as he swung on the rope. A few minutes later, they were pulling him over the rails to lie beside his comrades on the deck. "Where . . . where are we?" he managed to rasp out.

"Aboard the *Mary*, bound for Cork, Ireland," said a large man in a hearty Scottish brogue. "Captain Shearer, at your service. And where might you be sprung from?"

"California," mumbled Dawson.

"Havana," added Grant.

"The *Central America*," Kent explained. "Steamer."

The captain frowned. "California, Havana, *and* Central America?" He started to ask another question, but apparently changed his mind. "You're all near delirious with thirst, that's plain. Time enough for questions later. Cully, Williams," he called to two sailors, "bring them along to my cabin." Then, to the emaciated men, "We'll fix you up right enough, dinna ye worry."

Kent merely nodded, unable to speak further, and allowed himself to be half led, half carried to a spacious cabin. Dawson and Grant, beside him, asked for water, but the captain shook his head. "Not yet. We'll work up to that. First try a bit of this, to strengthen you."

Sipping at the cup someone held to his lips, Kent discovered it was warm, sweetened wine. He felt it course through his limbs, giving an illusion, at least, of vitality. Next came a mixture of thin gruel, but only a few spoonfuls. "Sleep now," said the captain. "We'll bring more later, with some water, and then we'll maybe have some talk."

Kent started to protest, but then felt his eyelids growing heavy. Yes, he could sleep. His mouth, less parched than it had been, relaxed, along with his limbs. He drifted off, to dream of his reunion with Della, of her sweet face and form, and of their future together in his familiar world of New York society.

New York was much as Della had imagined it—only more so. San Francisco had seemed a big city to her, teeming with life, but New York was on a far grander scale, and even more crowded. Arriving only a day behind the *Empire City,* she and the Eastons, along with a few others who had accompanied them, were quickly ferried to the New York Hotel to join the other survivors.

By now, a full ten days after the sinking of the *Central America,* the story of the shipwreck had reached all of the newspapers. Reporters and curious citizens crowded around the hansoms as they arrived at the hotel, shouting out questions.

"What was it like?" one man with a pad and pencil called out. "Were you terribly frightened?"

"Are there any other survivors on any other ships?" asked another. "How many were saved altogether?"

As the first two questions seemed fatuous and she didn't know the answers to the third and fourth, Della remained silent, though she heard Ansel Easton speaking to at least one reporter. Her energies right now were concentrated on reaching the hotel, finding the other survivors, and asking questions of her own.

Over the past two days, as they steamed toward New York, Della had wavered between hope and fear—fear that her hope would finally be blasted, fear of her reception in New York, fear of the future. Now she was here, and in only a few minutes she might have the answers that would determine her happiness, her prospects, forever.

She followed the others into the elegant hotel, through the wide lobby, and into a salon that had apparently been set aside for them. "Addie! Della!" Virginia Birch, looking far healthier than when they had seen her last, hurried forward to greet them.

"Virginia!" Addie hugged her. "And how is your little canary bird?"

Though her eyes were still shadowed with sorrow, Virginia smiled. "He seems no worse for his ordeal. I left him singing merrily in my room upstairs. Everyone has been so very kind. Why, yesterday when we arrived, even the drivers of the hansoms refused payment to bring us here."

"We've had the same," Addie assured her. "A lady in Norfolk wanted to give me a trunk, but I refused it, as I have nothing at all to put into one."

Della knew that Addie was merely trying to cheer up Virginia, much as she had tried to do for Della, but still her happiness seemed rather oppressive. She made no objection when the Eastons offered to see about rooms, leaving her to sit next to the other bereaved woman.

"I assume there's been no word of Kent?" she

asked Virginia, knowing the answer, but feeling obliged to make the effort.

Virginia shook her head. "Nor of Billy, either. Not that I expected it, really, but I had hoped. . . ."

"I know. So had I." Della sighed. "Addie kept talking of the possibility of other rescues by other ships, but—"

"Oh, there is something I must tell you at once," Virginia interrupted her. "Mr. Bradford's family—his mother, anyway—was here this morning, inquiring after him. I imagine she'll be pleased to see you, at least, and to hear what you can tell."

Della very much doubted that, but she smiled. "Thank you for letting me know. What does his mother look like? I don't believe Kent ever told me." She'd prefer to spot the woman before she was seen, if possible, and perhaps avoid what promised to be a most awkward interview.

Virginia thought for a moment. "Tall," she finally said. "Quite a handsome woman, really. She had on a large brown hat with white ostrich plumes, as I recall. And she— Oh! There she is now!"

Turning, Della saw an imposing woman in a brown-and-beige striped silk gown, cut in the height of fashion. As she watched, the woman questioned one of the other passengers, who pointed in her direction. Hastily Della averted her head, only to see Francis Cadbury bearing down on her from the opposite side.

"Trapped!" she muttered. Virginia regarded her questioningly, but she only shrugged. It was too late for explanations, anyway.

"Young woman!" came an imperious summons. Reluctantly she looked up to find the tall, haughty woman regarding her as though she were an insect, or perhaps a beggar on the street. And really, without Kent or a single possession of her own, was she much else?

Still, she lifted her chin defiantly. "Yes?"

"Am I correct in believing you to be one of the survivors from the sunken steamship *Central America*?"

Della nodded, determined to volunteer no information.

"I've been informed—erroneously, no doubt—" The woman sent a steely glance Cadbury's way. "—that you have claimed to be the wife of my son, Kenton Bradford, of the New York Bradfords."

So this was where Kent's self-consequence had come from, Della thought with an unexpected trace of amusement. Before she could reply, Mr. Cadbury spoke up.

"He claimed it, too." He sounded almost obsequious, Della thought. "They plotted it together."

Mrs. Bradford silenced him with a glance. "Well, young woman? Is this true?"

Before Della could answer, Virginia leaped to her feet. "Why, how very cruel! Of course Della was—is—married to Mr. Bradford. If his letter informing you was missent, it is no reason to browbeat her so. She has behaved most heroically, helping to save many of us from the wreck, myself included."

Della grasped Virginia's hand and pulled her back down to the sofa. "Thank you, Virginia, but I can speak for myself." She softened her words with a smile, which disappeared as she turned to face the others. "I was not aware that a marriage was generally considered a plot, but yes, I am Kent's wife."

"He is alive, then?" The hope that lit the older woman's face for a moment tugged at Della's heart. Overbearing as she might be, this was Kent's mother. She must be nearly as anxious about him as Della was herself.

Regretfully she shook her head. "I haven't seen him since the *Central America* went down, madam. It is possible that there may be survivors we have not yet heard news of, but I fear that is unlikely."

Mrs. Bradford closed her eyes, lines of pain etching her face. When she opened them again, they glittered with anger. "But you have the audacity to come here in his stead? No doubt you intended to make some claim upon his family and fortune as his supposed widow. You'll receive nothing, however, I promise you!"

An outraged exclamation from Virginia, followed by a murmur from the crowd that had gathered to witness the exchange, seemed to penetrate the woman's rage. She glanced around her, as though debating whether to continue.

"Mrs. Bradford," Della said softly, "I know that the loss of your son must come as a terrible shock, and I don't blame you for lashing out at me as a result. If it would bring Kent back to you, and if I thought it would make him happy, I would gladly disappear from the earth this instant. Unfortunately, I must learn to live with my loss, as you must learn to live with yours."

Mr. Cadbury sputtered something, but Mrs. Bradford seemed to realize that Della had offered her a way to save face before the crowd, which included several members of the press. "I—I'm sorry, dear," she managed to say after a moment. "You are right, of course. I am so overset that I don't know what I'm saying. I believe I will go up to my room to lie down—but we will talk later, so that you may tell me of my son's last moments."

Something in her eyes warned Della that there was much more she wished to discuss, away from the prying ears of the curious. Though she knew she would have to face Mrs. Bradford's questions soon enough, Della was happy to put off the inquisition.

"Of course. I was just about to dine with my friend Virginia, here, who has also lost her husband. If you are staying at the hotel, I'm sure we'll have a chance for conversation when you are rested."

Kent's mother raised one eyebrow skeptically, and the familiarity of the expression made Della suddenly swallow. Kent had looked at her exactly the same way on the day they first met. The resemblance softened her again toward this woman, though she saw no similar softening reflected in Mrs. Bradford's face.

"Indeed we will," she said at last. "I will be making a few other inquiries as well."

Though the others no doubt assumed those inquiries would be about the shipwreck and her son, Della knew that they would concern herself and her own shaky story. By now, it was even possible that word of her might have reached New York from San Francisco, where, as far as she knew, she was still wanted for murder. With a sense of foreboding, she watched Mrs. Bradford move away with Mr. Cadbury in tow.

"I hope you haven't already eaten," she said, turning to Virginia with forced cheerfulness. "And might there be an extra bed in your hotel room? I feel the need of friends about me, and Addie and her husband quite understandably wish to be alone."

Though her eyes bespoke her curiosity over what had just passed, Virginia agreed at once. "Dinner and then bed," she promised. "And you needn't tell me any more than you wish to."

Della smiled her gratitude. "Thank you. But it seems only fair that you know—most of it, anyway. Come, I'll tell you while we eat."

They found a quiet corner table in the dining room, and there Della told Virginia the story of her counterfeit marriage to Kent, finally culminating in a true wedding only two weeks ago. It was such a relief to finally unburden herself, she even found herself confiding her reason for fleeing San Francisco, and what she had done for a living. Finally the torrent of words ceased and she sat back with mingled relief and apprehension, waiting for shock or condemnation.

Instead, to her surprise, Virginia laughed. "That has to be the most unusual meeting I've ever heard of," she declared. "But I can see why you kept it quiet. Though some of our shipmates knew of it, I tried to play down my own past, too."

"Your past?"

Virginia nodded. "Did you never hear of the notorious Jenny French, showgirl and actress?"

"Yes, but I never saw . . . Wait, that was you?" asked Della in amazement.

"The very one," Virginia confessed. "As Billy was a showman as well, we didn't have to worry so much about his family's approval, but I remember one cousin of his, who— Well, that's of no moment now. But trust me, I do understand."

By the time they came down for breakfast the next morning, Della felt she'd known Virginia for years. They'd traded stories, each more outrageous than the last, until both were laughing helplessly, forgetting their grief for an hour or two. Finally they'd both fallen asleep, to dream of happier days.

The Eastons met them downstairs, and Della was just as happy to surround herself with friends against the possibility of Mrs. Bradford accosting her again. It still cost her a pang to see Addie and Ansel together, so radiantly happy, but she did her best to conceal it. Ansel was again doing his utmost to cheer them up, this time with more success.

"Billy was a true hero, Virginia. When we were all in the water during those endless hours of darkness after the ship sank, he kept our spirits up. Though he was sick and injured, he sang songs and recited limericks until we nearly forgot our plight."

Though a tear trickled from the corner of her eye, she smiled. "That sounds like my Billy."

"I should like a chance to thank him," Ansel continued. "Will he be joining us, do you think?"

All three women turned to stare at him. "Ansel, what are you saying?" Addie asked, aghast.

He looked confused. "Is he not upstairs? I assumed he would have reached New York by now, but perhaps he was delayed."

Della stared, and Virginia leaned forward to put a trembling hand on his sleeve. "Do . . . do you mean . . . ?"

It was Ansel's turn to stare. "Did no one tell you, Mrs. Birch? I just assumed . . . Your husband was among those rescued by the *Ellen*, along with myself. He and one or two others, to include my friend Robert Brown," he added to his wife, "went aboard another ship before we met the *Empire City*, thinking they might reach New York more quickly that way."

Virginia looked as though she might faint. Della hugged her, then kept one arm around her waist, supporting her until she was certain she would not collapse. "Is there any other news you've held back?"

Addie began to scold him as well, but he shook his head. "You must believe me when I say I never meant to occasion such a shock, Mrs. Birch."

But Virginia beamed through her tears. "It was the nicest shock I ever received, Mr. Easton, and I thank you."

Just then, a familiar, musical voice rose above the general murmur in the dining room. "Jenny? Is that my Jenny I see?" Turning, they saw Billy Birch himself crossing the room, though with a decided limp.

Virginia knocked her chair over as she scrambled to her feet, then hurled herself at her husband, nearly knocking him down as well in her enthusiasm. He joined them at the table, and for the next ten minutes, Della let the happy chatter wash over her. Finally, when she could wait no longer, she touched Billy's sleeve.

"Mr. Birch, have you any word of Kent? Did you see what became of him?"

His comical face grew serious. "Dear Mrs.

Bradford, I wish I had. I saw him on the wheelhouse, along with Easton here, just before the ship sank. But I never saw him after, nor heard his voice."

Della nodded. It was what she had expected. "Thank you," she managed to whisper before her throat closed entirely. Then, aware that her grief would dampen the others' justified joy, she excused herself from the table. Going upstairs, she packed her few donated toiletries, as Virginia and Billy would want this room to themselves.

She carried her small satchel back downstairs, uncertain what she should do next. Perhaps it would be easiest to simply leave this hotel and stay where there would not be constant reminders of her loss. She hadn't a cent to her name, however—the twenty-dollar gold pieces she had managed to tuck into her gown before leaving the *Central America* had gone to help pay for the tug into Norfolk. So where was she to go?

"There you are!" came a feminine voice. Turning, she saw Kent's mother bearing down on her like a ship in full sail. "I have been inquiring after you all morning. Come, I have had a room prepared next to mine. Let us go upstairs and talk."

"Of course," said Della tonelessly. What choice did she have?

All that day and the next, Della mechanically answered every question put to her by Mrs. Bradford, giving the story she and Kent had devised between them. Once or twice she considered telling the truth, but to do so would cast Kent in an unfavorable light, as well as put herself at potential risk.

So emotionally exhausted was she that she did not protest when Mrs. Bradford insisted on dressing her as befitted her station as Kent's widow, in expensive black silk. Mrs. Bradford made a great show of parading her "poor, widowed daughter-in-law" through the hotel to speak with reporters, always making certain her own name was mentioned in any interview.

After a few days, the press began to turn its attention elsewhere, every reporter having spoken with every survivor at least once. Most of those with friends in New York had already left the hotel, and the rest were making plans to do so. The Eastons and the Birches had gone, and Mary Patterson's mother had come to bring her home. No one Della could call friend was left.

"I've had enough of hotel living," Mrs. Bradford announced early on the fourth day. "I'm ready to go home. I suppose you may as well come with me, Della, for the time being, at least." She always called Della by her first name when they were alone. Distasteful as such familiarity must be to her, she was apparently unwilling to credit her with Kent's surname.

Though a few days' acquaintance had not served to endear her to Kent's mother, Della did feel a spark of interest in seeing the house where

Kent had grown up. And certainly it was preferable to being thrown penniless into the streets. "If that's what you wish, madam," she said, marveling in a detached sort of way at her own lack of spirit.

"Wish?" Mrs. Bradford looked down her patrician nose. "Not particularly. But it would look poorly if I left you to your own devices. I imagine we will find something suitable for you to do, however."

Della blinked. "Am I to be a servant, then?"

"Of course not. That would scarcely be appropriate. But I'm certain you would prefer to make yourself useful. You've not been used to a life of luxury, after all."

"Oh, no, madam. I'm just a poor Irish prospector's daughter." It appeared her spirit was not entirely dead after all.

Mrs. Bradford's eyes narrowed. "Sarcasm does not become you, Della. If this is all you have, let us go down. The carriage should be here by now."

Della followed, her heart a shade less heavy than it had been a few minutes earlier. Grief might have subdued her temporarily, but she knew now that though she had lost her hope of happiness, she had not lost herself. Her spirit, at least, had survived.

TWENTY-ONE

Like one, that on a lonesome road
Doth walk in fear and dread,
And having once turned round walks on,
And turns no more his head.

—SAMUEL TAYLOR COLERIDGE,
The Rime of the Ancient Mariner

After several days of sleep, interrupted only for increasing amounts of food and water, Kent felt recovered enough to take a hand in his own destiny. He sat up and discovered that his injured leg had been splinted and wrapped. A crude crutch leaned against the bottom of the bunk.

Rising, he put his weight on his left leg, the crutch under his right arm, and found he could walk without assistance. Dressing himself took more energy than he had expected, still weakened as he was by days of starvation. He persisted, however, and at last felt ready to venture out of the cabin, where his fellow survivors still slumbered, to search out the captain.

Blinding sunshine greeted him when he reached the deck, reminding him vividly of the early weeks of his voyage with Della. The thought strengthened his resolve. Blinking to clear his vision, he located Captain Shearer on the wheelhouse of the brig, talking with the pilot.

His progress was slow, and he feared the captain might move away before he could reach him. With an impatient exclamation, he tried to quicken his pace. "Sir! Captain! Excuse me," he called out as he neared the wheelhouse. "A word with you, if I might."

Captain Shearer turned in amazement. "Whatever are you doing up, Mr.— Is it Bradford?"

Kent nodded, saving his breath for more necessary words. "Did you say we were headed for Ireland?"

"Aye, with a shipment of sugar and molasses from Cuba. But you should still be abed, sir. It'll be days yet before you're strong enough to be walking about."

"I'll sit, then." He made good his words by lowering himself onto a pile of ropes by the foot of the stairs. Still shaking his head, the captain descended to stand next to him. "How long before we can return to New York?" Kent asked then.

The captain frowned, running a thoughtful hand over his graying whiskers. "I'll not be headed that way for a month and more myself, I fear. In a hurry to get there, are you?"

Assuming the *Marine* had made it safely to some port, Della might well have reached New York days ago. He thought of her in that great city—friendless, penniless, and grieving, thinking him dead. "Yes, I am."

"Hmmm. Well, then, I'll see what I can do. No promises, mind you, but I'll do my best. And now, return you to the cabin, or you'll be no good to anyone once you do get home."

With that, Kent had to be content. At least he'd done something.

Three days later, his action was well rewarded when Captain Shearer hailed a bark heading in the opposite direction. The other ship slowed, and after a brief exchange, its captain agreed to take the shipwrecked men aboard. By now, all four had regained enough strength to make the transfer without undue difficulty, and an hour later they found themselves aboard the *Laura,* out of Bremen, headed west to New York City.

Though the captain and crew pleaded with Kent to join his comrades below, he refused. For now, at least, he preferred to stand at the rail near the prow, watching the water flow beneath the blessed ship that was bearing him—he hoped—back to Della.

The Bradford residence was the most imposing house on a street of imposing houses, a street lined with stately elm trees and soaring brownstone mansions on the banks of the Hudson River. Della, after her first exploration, felt completely out of her element here. The house, the neighborhood, bespoke the Kent of the earliest days of their acquaintance—Kenton Bradford of the New York Bradfords, the proud stickler for social niceties and strict adherence to the customs of class.

The house was exquisite, with its broad balustered staircase, artworks by noted American and European artists in every room and hallway, and thick, richly colored carpets throughout. Never had Della seen such opulence, from the gilt-and-marble mantelpiece in the parlor to the intricately carved bedstead in the room she was assigned.

Somehow, though, she could not seem to envision here the Kent she had grown to love—the freer, more adventurous man with a lust for life. Still, this was his birthright, his history, so she tried her best to understand it. Memories were all she would have of him now, and she wanted to make his own memories hers, that she could have that much more of him to take away with her.

For she would not stay long. She had already determined that.

Mrs. Bradford did not want her here, a constant reminder of her son's loss and the questionable judgment he had shown in his final weeks of life. Della herself was a discord; she had more in common with the servants than with the mistress of the house. The only person who made her feel at all welcome was Judy, Kent's younger sister, but she was recently engaged and frequently away from the house.

"Thank you, Mrs. Glendover," said Della automatically to yet another neighbor who had called to express condolences to Mrs. Bradford and herself. "You're very kind."

"Poor, poor dear," the woman murmured, though Della noticed the appraising glance that raked her. "And you too, of course, Willa," she added to her hostess. "Have you contacted Charles yet with the news?"

Della had no doubt that Mrs. Glendover knew perfectly well that Kent's younger brother hadn't been heard from in years. How easily these society matrons hid malice under the guise of polite concern! Mrs. Bradford's reply surprised her, however.

"Not yet, but you'll be pleased to know that I had a letter from him only last month. He intends to be home before winter. That will be a great comfort to me, as you can imagine."

"Oh. Oh, of course. What a relief for you, I'm sure." Blocked in her attempt to gloat over the black sheep of the family, Mrs. Glendover settled for gleaning gossip. "I suppose he'll be taking over the business now?"

Mrs. Bradford hesitated—not surprisingly, from what Della knew about Charles—before saying, "Yes, I imagine he will. All of this is still so much to adjust to, you know." She artfully applied a handkerchief to her eye.

At once Mrs. Glendover was all apologies, and a few moments later she took her leave. Before Della could ask about Charles, however, more callers were announced. She forgot all about Kent's brother at the sound of the very names she'd dreaded hearing.

"Mrs. Cadbury, Mr. Francis Cadbury, and Miss Caroline Cadbury," the starched-up butler, Joseph, intoned.

Della sat very still as the three entered the room. Francis looked just as she remembered him, only better dressed. Mrs. Cadbury was a shorter and plumper matron than Mrs. Bradford, but she had the same fashionable air and the same proud tilt of her head. Della's attention, however, was focused on the last member of the party—Kent's erstwhile fiancée.

Caroline Cadbury was exquisite: blond, statuesque, cultured, and dressed in the absolute pinnacle of fashion and taste. Her chin echoed her mother's in haughty aspect, but she was still the most beautiful woman Della had ever seen. No wonder Kent had been attracted to her. When she spoke, her voice was low and well modulated, as lovely as her face.

"Mrs. Bradford, is it true?" she asked, stepping forward to clasp both of her hostess' hands in hers. "Is there really no hope?"

Freeing a hand, Kent's mother again plied her

handkerchief. "I fear not, dear Caroline. It has been so long since the ship went down. . . . I trust Francis has acquainted you with the details."

Caroline and her mother both nodded. "Such a miracle that my dear boy was saved," Mrs. Cadbury exclaimed. "And such a pity that, for all his heroism in rescuing others, he could not save poor Kenton." She sat on the sofa next to her longtime friend, and in a moment they were weeping in each other's arms.

Della couldn't resist arching an eyebrow at Francis. Heroism? He intercepted her glance and looked vaguely uncomfortable for a moment, but then his sister followed the direction of his gaze.

"And this would be the, er, widow you told me of, Francis? I must say, madam, I am most eager to hear *your* story." Her voice, warm and sympathetic when she spoke to Mrs. Bradford, now dripped ice. Della would find no sympathy here—not that she had expected any.

For a moment she wished she had never come here—that she had slipped away into the crowds of New York before ever meeting Kent's mother. But then she drew herself up. She would not allow these people to browbeat her. Just because they had been born to wealth did not make them better people than she was. Quite the opposite, in fact.

"I suspect my story may differ in some particulars from your brother's," she said. "But if you'd care to hear it, please have a seat."

Looking both startled and a bit wary, Caroline joined her on the other side of the spacious room, just out of earshot of the others.

"I'm sorry not to have happier news to share," Della began. "Believe me, I wish as much as anyone that Kent had escaped the sinking of the *Central America*. He was—very dear to me."

The woman across from her stiffened. "How dare you? Kenton Bradford was my fiancé."

"And my husband," said Della calmly. "Did your brother not tell you that?"

"He did, but I could not believe it. Kenton would never have ignored our engagement, not the Kenton I knew. You must have . . . bewitched him somehow." Her glance clearly indicated that she couldn't imagine how. "In which case, I must hold you responsible for his death as well as his betrayal."

Another murder charge? Next they might claim she had used her potions to bend Kent to her will! "That is absurd, of course. Kent would have been on that ship whether I was with him or not. In fact, he had arranged his passage before we even met." Belatedly, she realized she probably should not have offered that bit of information.

Caroline pounced on it at once. "Ah. So this *was* a hurried, patched-up business, as I thought, and not something Kenton had a chance to think through logically."

Della could scarcely deny that, but the smug satisfaction on Caroline Cadbury's face nettled her. "When was love ever logical?" she asked. "His engagement to you may have been impeccably logical, as I hear it would have been a financially advantageous match for you both. But love, I assure you, trumps all such reasoning."

Miss Cadbury's face flamed scarlet. "I have heard enough!" Rising, she said loudly, "Mother, Francis, I wish to go." She then turned back to Della, her eyes glittering dangerously. "You won't be accepted anywhere, you know," she whispered. "I'll expose you as the gold-digging little harlot you are."

"Thank you so much for your sympathy, Miss Cadbury," Della said aloud, showing no trace of emotion in her face or voice. "It is just what I expected of you, from everything Kent told me."

Mrs. Bradford looked confused but rose to bid her guests farewell. "I had thought you would be staying with us," she said, "but if you would rather not, I won't insist."

Mrs. Cadbury looked uncertainly at her daughter. "I'll, er, let you know where we are, Willa, and will certainly see you again before we return to Philadelphia. I fear right now dear Caroline is rather overwrought, poor thing."

Caroline's face was dark with fury. "Come *on*, Mother!" she exclaimed, then remembered her manners long enough to take a more cordial leave of her hostess.

Once they were gone, Mrs. Bradford turned to Della, her lips tight. "What did you say to upset poor Caroline so? She is like a daughter to me, and is understandably grief-stricken by this news."

"Why, nothing," said Della innocently. "Nothing at all." Grief, she realized, had not been among the emotions displayed by the exquisite Miss Cadbury.

It soon became clear that Caroline had lost no time in carrying out her threat. When Della accompanied Mrs. Bradford to Kent's memorial service the next day, appropriately attired in black dress and veil, she was greeted by cold stares. Whispered comments followed her down the aisle of the church as she moved to her place at the front.

Across the aisle, also attired in black, sat Caroline Cadbury, graciously accepting the sympathetic murmurs directed her way. Della tried to tell herself she cared nothing for the opinions of these people. Still, because of them, she forced herself to hold back her tears during Kent's eulogy, even though she knew that would only reinforce their impression of her.

A reception at the Bradford house followed the service, and again Della was ostracized, while Caroline was petted and coddled for her loss. Even Kent's sister Judy, normally kindhearted, spent most of her time with her older sister, Barbara, who appeared to be one of Caroline's intimates. As soon as she could reasonably do so, Della slipped upstairs to her room.

Finally alone, she let the tears she had suppressed all day flow at last. But while a good cry offered her momentary release, it did nothing to solve her larger problem. All too soon, she dried her eyes. Rising, she went to stare out the window onto the civilized street below while she considered her options.

New York society was not for her. She'd known it from the start, had told Kent she would never fit in. Now the verdict was clear. She could not stay here—it was not her world. Nor did she want it to be.

In California, she'd seen drunkenness, debauchery, cheating, and stealing, but never this cold heartlessness, which masqueraded under a veneer of etiquette. Even the most lawless prospectors in the far-flung mining camps had more humanity than these people, and more honesty. Della knew instinctively that she could never grow to mimic or even tolerate the hypocrisy she'd seen displayed today. No, she would have to leave. The only question was how.

She looked about her, considering. As Kent's wife, a measure of his wealth was presumably hers by right. But she had no way of knowing how much, and she would not risk taking anything that might belong to his mother or sisters. No, she'd done enough damage by coming here at all, oversetting everyone's memories of Kent by her very presence.

At least she could partially undo what she had

done. She could tell them what they wanted to hear—that Kent had never really married her, that she had forced him to pretend aboard the ship. She would tell the truth, all except for their wedding aboard the *Central America*. There was no proof now of their marriage, anyway.

She would even embellish the story, painting herself blacker and Kent more shining. What did it matter? These people were determined to hate her anyway. This would give her an excuse to separate herself from them at once. And while she was at it, she might as well give his mother and sisters an untarnished memory of him to keep.

Quickly she packed the few things she felt she could rightfully keep: the two dresses given her by charitable folk at the hotel, a few toiletries, and a few pennies she had found in the bottom of a drawer. Setting the worn leather satchel, also a gift of charity, just inside the door of her room, she headed back downstairs.

The hum of voices had muted by now, and when she opened the door to the large parlor, she saw that only Caroline and her mother remained, along with Mrs. Bradford, Kent's sisters, the husband of the elder and the fiancé of the younger, and one other young man she did not recognize. They all turned toward her as she entered, their faces displaying various expressions of coldness, disinterest, or curiosity.

"Madam, I need to speak with you," she said

to Mrs. Bradford before she could lose her nerve. "It's a matter of some importance."

The matron raised one patrician eyebrow. "Indeed? Out with it, then."

For a moment she hesitated, then decided she might as well make her confession to all of them, as they'd know it soon enough anyway. "I fear I have perpetrated a falsehood upon you. Kent and I were never married."

Every eye in the room was now fastened upon her, a stunned silence greeting her words. Without prompting, she continued, twisting a handkerchief between her hands as her only support.

"I . . . I played a trick upon him, pretending we were husband and wife, to escape some trouble with the law in California. Only his innate chivalry kept him from denouncing me. We had never met before boarding the ship from San Francisco."

"I knew it!" crowed Caroline triumphantly. "You little—"

But Della ignored her, focusing only on Kent's mother, who regarded her with mingled horror and dawning relief. "I came to care a great deal for Kent, but I knew his sense of honor would prevent him from breaking his existing engagement. He never behaved toward me as anything other than a gentleman. Your son was a remarkable man, Mrs. Bradford."

The older woman's face began to crumple in upon itself, as though the truth of Kent's death had only now been brought fully home to her. But only for a moment. Recollecting herself, she straightened. "Why—why do you wait until now to tell me this?"

Della sighed. "At first I was still too stunned to know what I should do, and then I was afraid. But I can't allow Kent's memory to be tarnished by my actions. He meant too much to me." She put a hand on the doorknob. "I won't trouble you again."

"Wait!" Caroline's voice arrested her as she began to turn the handle. "You're not going to just let her walk out of here like this, are you? She has deceived all of us, and is no doubt a common criminal, wanted, by her own admission, by the law in California. She should pay for what she has done!"

Mrs. Bradford, now recovering from her shock, nodded. "Indeed she should. Why, I have introduced her to everyone as my daughter-in-law, much as it mortified me to do so. The social embarrassment, once this comes out, will be devastating. Charles"—she turned toward the young man Della hadn't met—"pray go fetch an officer of the law, so that we can determine what should be done with her."

"Do you think that's really necessary, Mother?" he asked. "It doesn't sound as though she's harmed anyone." He regarded Della with interest and a tinge of admiration.

She studied him with equal interest, nearly forgetting her own precarious situation. So this was the black-sheep brother Kent had told her about. He didn't look like a wastrel. In fact, now that she looked closely, he showed a startling resemblance to Kent, though he was shorter and lighter in coloring.

"You have no idea what she's done, Charles," his mother retorted. "You haven't even met her. She's played us all skillfully, like the brazen actress she no doubt is." She faced Della again. "Yes, I discovered who your 'friend' at the hotel really was. A common San Francisco showgirl!"

Della opened her mouth to defend Virginia, then closed it. Nothing she could say to these people would make any difference. She had made her confession, and she was glad of it, but now she would have to take whatever consequences came. "I'll wait in my room until you decide whether to allow me to leave or not," she finally said.

"Indeed you will," agreed Mrs. Bradford. "Joseph, escort her upstairs and see that she remains there," she added to the butler.

Her heart strangely lightened despite her uncertain future, Della preceded the servant up the stairs. Whatever happened, she'd be away from these hateful people soon, no longer pretending to be a part of their superficial, petty world. Even the sound of a key turning in the lock once she was in her room did not dampen her relief at that thought.

She went back to the window, and a few moments later saw Charles ride away, presumably to fetch the police. A slow hour passed, which she spent devising and rejecting plan after plan on how to make her living once she was on her own again. Nothing she might do seemed to hold any appeal. Even the thought of world travel had somehow lost its charm.

Staring vacantly at the street below, her attention was caught by a horseman at full canter. It was Charles, returning, but she could see no law officer with him. Reaching the house, he leaped from the saddle and ran up the front steps, disappearing from her line of vision. She heard the door below her open and close.

Curious, she crossed to her door, but remembered when the knob would not turn that the butler had locked it from the outside. She rattled the knob impatiently, then called out, but there was no response. She sighed in resignation. Whatever it was, it most likely did not concern her. If it did, she would find it out eventually. Wishing she had something to read, she went to sit on the bed—but only for a moment.

A piercing shriek from downstairs made her fly to the door again, this time to press her ear to the panels, but she could hear nothing further.

Again the front door slammed and, hurrying to the window, she saw Charles remount his horse and ride off. A moment later, a carriage came clattering around the corner. It stopped, and Mrs. Bradford and her daughters scrambled into it. Then another carriage came up behind to consume Caroline and her mother, and both followed Charles at a brisk pace.

"Something is definitely going on," Della exclaimed aloud to the empty room. Perhaps it was merely a forgotten social event or a particularly juicy bit of gossip, but their urgency suggested something more important—if anything *was* more important to these people.

Immediately Della berated herself for such a thought. Most likely a relative had suddenly fallen ill. But whatever it was, she had no intention of remaining locked in this room indefinitely. A sycamore tree stood some twenty feet away, and one of its broad branches stretched nearly to her window. Retrieving her small satchel, Della hitched up her skirts and opened the window.

The climb was harder than it looked. Tossing down her satchel first, she steeled herself for the jump to the branch, four feet away. Telling herself this was nothing compared to what she'd gone through to be rescued from the *Central America*, she leaped and caught the branch across her middle. Scraping her hands and legs, she scooted to the trunk, then had to half climb, half slide to the ground, for the tree had no lower branches. Once down, she picked up her satchel and began walking at a brisk pace, her one goal to put as much distance as possible between the Bradfords and herself before they returned.

TWENTY-TWO

Oh! dream of joy! is this indeed
The light-house top I see?
Is this the hill? is this the kirk?
Is this mine own countree?

—Samuel Taylor Coleridge,
The Rime of the Ancient Mariner

Newspaper reporters crowded around Kent, Grant, Dawson, and Tice, seated in Castle Garden, where they'd been brought as soon as the *Laura* left customs. Already it seemed as though the whole city knew of their rescue, perhaps due to that enterprising young reporter who had rowed out to the ship early this morning to ask questions of the captain.

"What was it like, adrift upon the sea, facing certain death?" someone asked Kent for what must have been the twentieth time.

"I don't recommend it," he replied, to a general chuckle.

Mr. Dawson took advantage of the crowd's brief distraction to slip between two newspapermen. In a moment, he had limped away, leaving only three to answer the questions. Five minutes later, a squeal announced the arrival of Mr. Tice's wife. Kent watched the tearful reunion with a lump in his throat. Where, *where* was Della?

Since setting foot on land, he had scanned every face, hoping to see her. Where might she be by now? Would she have heard the news yet, or had she given up hope and left New York, perhaps with one of her friends from the ship? Or had she ever come here at all? He'd seen a list of other survivors. Maybe Della had gone with the Eastons or the Birches. Or—

"Kenton! Oh, oh, Kenton, my dearest boy!" The crowd parted again, to allow his mother through. Before he could say a word, she launched herself at him, hugging and kissing him as she repeated his name over and over.

Kent returned her embrace, but he couldn't help glancing over her shoulder. Judy was there, and Barbara, and . . . Caroline. And was that, could it be, *Charles?* Of Della he saw no sign.

"I know, Mother. I thought I was dead, too, for a while there. But I'm fine now." He tried to keep the burning impatience out of his voice.

"But you're so thin, Kenton! Come, I must get you home and start fattening you up at once. You poor, poor dear! Oh, I still can't believe it!" She released him, but at once his sisters rushed forward to twine themselves about him.

"Careful, careful, I still have a few bruises, not to mention a broken leg," he said teasingly. They exclaimed in concern, loosening their grip slightly. Kent looked over Judy's shoulder at Charles. "This is a surprise," he said warily.

His brother grinned at him, and suddenly it was as though the seven years since they'd last met evaporated. "I only got here this morning," he explained. "Just in time for your memorial service, in fact. You should have been there. Such raptures over what a fine young man you were."

When his sisters finally disengaged themselves, Caroline stepped forward. "I'm so relieved to see you alive, Kenton," she said with a smile that somehow failed to warm her fine blue eyes. "You can't imagine what agonies I suffered while we thought you were lost forever."

"Indeed," said her mother from behind her. "Especially with that insufferable young woman pretending to be your widow—"

Kent's head snapped up. "Della? Where is she?" Again he scanned the crowd.

"Not here, I can assure you," his mother replied. "I'm sure your gallantry is to be commended, my love, but really, you should have had the girl arrested, rather than shielding her. Who knows what she has done?"

"She's done nothing," he snapped, then again demanded, "Where is she?"

His mother hesitated, but Charles spoke up. "Back at the house." Then, with a speaking glance at Caroline, whom Kent knew he had never liked, he added, "Under lock and key."

"What?" Kent roared. But the sudden exertion made him cough, marring the effect of his righteous indignation. Charles slapped him on the back to help him recover, while his mother and Caroline both chattered at once.

"You have no idea how she duped us. I introduced her everywhere as your widow!"

"The way people treated me—with pity! The poor, jilted fiancée. I was mortified."

Kent glared, silencing them both. "Della is the woman I love, and my wife. Take me to her at once."

Two sets of eyes widened in disbelief.

"But she admitted—"

"She said—"

Both women began to sputter protests, but Kent grabbed his crutch and hobbled toward the waiting carriage, ignoring the pain in his leg. "At once," he repeated.

Suddenly becoming aware of the interested onlookers, most of them reporters, his mother abruptly ceased her protests and motioned for the coachman to help him inside. Charles mounted his horse with a grin. "See you back at the house! This should prove extremely entertaining."

Judy seated herself next to Kent. "No harm has come to her, I promise you," she said softly, with a nervous glance across at their mother and at Barbara, who looked nearly as forbidding. "I liked her from the start, and am very glad to know she is not a criminal after all."

Kent gave her shoulders a quick squeeze. "Thank you, Judy. I'm glad of your support, for I suspect that over the next few days, Della will need every friend she can find."

His mother merely sniffed, clearly hoarding her words for later. Kent tapped on the roof and shouted for the coachman to hurry. Whether Caroline and her mother followed in their carriage, he neither knew nor cared.

The afternoon was beginning to fade when they reached the house half an hour later. Despite his urgency, Kent gazed fondly at the imposing facade of the place he'd spent most of his life and had despaired of ever seeing again. He and Della would be happy here, he was determined—no matter what.

It was Charles who helped him from the coach, supporting him until he could orient his crutch properly. "You're pretty good with that thing," his brother commented approvingly.

There were hundreds of questions Kent wanted to ask him, but they would all have to wait. Right now, nothing mattered except Della.

Mounting the stairs with difficulty, he wondered what had prompted her to say that their marriage was a sham. If she intended to repudiate their marriage, why had she gone with his mother at all? Gaining the front door, he stepped into the broad marble foyer.

"Della!" he shouted. "Della, I'm home!" He turned to his mother, who had entered just ahead of him. "Which room?" he asked.

She frowned and her chin trembled, either with anger or with disappointment. "Joseph, bring our guest down to the parlor. Kent, I must insist that you rest that leg."

He took a step toward the stairs, but the old butler was already halfway up them. Damn his leg, anyway! "Very well," he said sourly, impatient at the delay. He followed her into the parlor and allowed Judy to place a pillow under his foot, propping it up on the divan. His mother and Barbara also fussed about him, but he waved them away, his eyes fixed on the doorway where Della would appear at any moment.

"What's taking her so long?" he muttered after two minutes passed, then three. "Charles, would you . . . ?"

"Of course."

His brother rose, but before he reached the door, Joseph entered. "Madam, the young woman is gone. I took the liberty of searching the room, and it appears she may have climbed out of the window."

"How long?" Kent rapped out over his mother's outraged exclamation. At the butler's questioning look, he clarified. "How long ago could she have left?"

He looked confused. "I can't really say, sir. I haven't checked on her since showing her to her room, some two hours ago."

"Since locking her in her room, you mean." Kent shot an accusing glance at his mother. "Come, we must—ugh!" The exclamation was forced from him when he tried to rise too quickly, inadvertently putting weight on his right leg. "Charles?" It rankled him to ask for assistance from his scapegrace younger brother, but he saw no choice.

"Of course." Charles leaped to his feet. "I'll help you to the gig, since I assume you can't ride with that leg. Then I'll go ahead on horseback and begin making inquiries around the neighborhood. Surely someone will have seen her."

Kent nodded his agreement—and gratitude. With Charles' help, he was soon seated atop the family's small gig, the reins in his hands. Where would Della have gone? He turned to his mother, who had followed them out of the house.

"Why would Della have left?" he asked her. "With what had you threatened her?"

She twisted her handkerchief between her hands. "I—I sent Charles for the police. I thought—that is, Caroline insisted—"

"That she suffer for embarrassing you both," he finished. "Did you not tell her about me before you left?"

His mother shook her head.

Kent closed his eyes, biting back the words he wanted to say. Poor Della, with no one to turn to, nowhere to go, thinking she was about to be arrested. But it gave him a clue as to where she might have gone. She'd be trying to get as far away from here as possible.

He shook the reins, but just then a carriage pulled up and Caroline jumped out. "Kenton! Please, you must listen to me," she began.

"I think not," he said shortly, and touched the whip to the horse's back, driving past her without another word.

The nearest transportation Della could find would be nearly a mile away, at the hansom station. Or she might have headed for the new railroad depot, a mile and a half in the other direction. At the crossroad, he stopped, considering. Which way had Charles gone?

Just then he spotted his brother riding toward him from the left. As he drew close, he called out, "Mrs. Milliken believes she saw her, nearly an hour ago, on foot. She was headed west."

Kent frowned. "The railroad, then, I suspect. I'll go that way, but I'd appreciate it if you would go east and check the hansom station, just in case Mrs. Milliken is mistaken."

With a salute, Charles rode off again. Turning to the left, Kent urged the horse to a quick trot. He had no idea what schedule the railroad followed, but he prayed he would reach the station before Della could depart. What despair must she be feeling? With all he had gone through, at least he had been secure in the belief that Della was safe. She had no such lifeline to cling to.

Ten minutes later, he pulled the gig to a halt in front of the railroad depot. No train waited on the tracks, and a quick survey of the handful of people sitting on the platform showed that Della was not among them. Kent looked down. The ground seemed far away, and he was not at all certain he could reach it without assistance—nor could he get back into the gig alone once he left it.

"Hello!" he called to a uniformed man near the tracks. "You there! May I speak with you a moment?"

The man ambled over to the gig. "Can I help you?"

"I fervently hope so," Kent replied. "Have you seen a young woman within the past hour or so? Red hair, probably dressed in black." He hadn't thought to ask what Della wore, but as his supposed widow, black seemed a good guess.

The man tilted back his head to peer up at Kent from under the brim of his hat. "Yep, she was here. Tried to talk me into lettin' her board the next train, saying she'd pay at the other end of the line. Felt sorry for her, young widow and all, but rules are rules. Can't afford to lose my job."

Kent let out a breath he hadn't even realized

he'd been holding, feeling suddenly weak with relief. "Can you tell me where she went?"

Scratching his chin, the man considered. "I wasn't paying real close attention. There were other folks in line to buy tickets, you see. Perhaps one of them will remember." He motioned to the group on the platform.

"Would you mind asking them?" Kent asked. "I'm—" He gestured to his wrapped leg.

"No problem at all." Walking over to the others, the man asked a few questions, then came back. "Gent there says he seen her walking off down the tracks, westward." He pointed. "If she's hoping to reach the next station that way, she's a ways to go. It's near twenty miles away."

Kent peered down the track but saw no sign of anyone. A path beside the tracks was wide enough for his gig, however. "Thank you, sir. Thank you very much." He reached into his pocket, only belatedly realizing that he had no money with him. So instead he tipped his hat, then snapped the reins to head after Della. In a few minutes, a very few minutes, they would be together!

•

Della pulled out her handkerchief to mop her brow again. What was the matter with her? Back in California, she had often walked ten or fifteen miles in a day, simply because it was the cheapest way to get anywhere. Had she lost all her stamina?

No, she had just lost heart, she realized. She

had no real goal in mind now, but was simply trudging west along the railroad track with the vague plan of establishing herself somewhere else under a new name. What else was left for her to do?

Briefly her disobedient mind lingered over the bright plans she and Kent had woven together—plans she had vowed she would never think of again. She should have known such a life was not for her. Love, stability, knowing what tomorrow might bring . . . "I'd have been bored inside of a month," she told herself fiercely.

But even as she spoke the words aloud, her nose began to tingle, that too-familiar prickle started behind her eyes, and a tear slipped down her cheek, followed by another. She quickened her pace, as though she could outrun her grief, sobbing as she went.

Why? Why did life have to be so *hard?* Some people—like Caroline Cadbury—never seemed to face hardship. Why did she? Again she mopped her brow, then blew her nose defiantly, rejecting her self-pity.

She had no desire whatsoever to be like Caroline, she reminded herself. Vain, shallow, hypocritical, petty, and cruel. At least Kent hadn't died without knowing real love—something he never would have received from his fiancée. Della had given him that much.

The tears threatened again, but just then she heard the crunch of wheels on the graveled path behind her. Without a backward glance, she slipped into the trees to her left, hoping whoever it was hadn't seen her. She'd been foolish to argue with the railroad station attendant. He would remember her now, if anyone asked, and might even have seen which way she went.

The trees weren't thick here, but a large oak a dozen yards from the path offered a reasonable hiding place. Ducking behind it, she squashed down her hoops with her hands and turned to watch the vehicle that approached. It was a one-horse gig, with a single driver. He had been moving quickly, but now he was slowing. He must have seen her.

She pulled back behind the tree and held very still, though she knew the spread of her black skirt must be visible. Though she hadn't gotten a good look at the driver, she thought it might be Charles Bradford, in which case he would be looking specifically for her, under his mother's direction. If he followed her on foot, she'd never escape him. She thought quickly, trying to formulate an argument that might convince him to let her go. He'd seemed more sympathetic than the others. . . .

"Della?"

Yes, it must be Charles, for the voice sounded heart-wrenchingly like Kent's. She pressed her lips firmly together and remained where she was. Maybe he would drive on.

"Della, please come out," came the voice again, so familiar it made her vitals contract in sudden pain. Maybe she should dare a quick peek, just in case. . . . No! That was foolishness—mere wishful thinking.

"I don't think I can get out of this thing by myself," her pursuer continued, "and I'd hate for our reunion to occur with me flat on my face."

She began to shake, wanting to believe, afraid to believe, but completely unable to resist looking, even knowing it was probably a trick. "Kent?" she whispered, peering back toward the gig.

He saw her at once, but instead of leaping down, he waved, then motioned her to approach. She did, one disbelieving step at a time, poised for flight the moment the illusion dissipated. But it did not. With every step, the man in the gig looked less like Charles and more like . . .

"Kent?" she repeated, her voice rising with hope and emotion that threatened to overflow into rapture.

"Yes, Della, it's really me. I'm alive. And you're safe now." He smiled, and it was really, truly Kent's smile.

"Oh! Oh!" She began to run toward him, faster and faster, heedless of her hoops. Then, just a step or two from the gig, she tripped over her skirts and fell face first into the dust and gravel. Even that could not dampen her spirits, however, and she pushed herself up at once. "Oh, Kent!" she sputtered happily.

"I guess I should have tried to climb down after all," said the familiar, beloved voice. "Now you've ended up flat on your face instead." She looked up to find his arms outstretched.

Ignoring the dirt and scrapes on her hands, she gladly put them into his and lightly sprang up into the gig. He folded her against him in a tight embrace, and then she was kissing him, hugging him, things she'd despaired of ever doing again. "Kent! Oh, Kent!" was all she could manage to say between kisses.

Not until he released her did she notice his leg. "What—" she began, but he silenced her with another kiss. For a long moment, she could only revel in being transported so abruptly from purgatory to paradise, but finally reality intruded again.

"How?" she asked wonderingly. "How can you be here? It's been weeks. . . ."

Kent held her face between his hands, gazing deeply, lovingly, into her eyes with his own dear golden brown ones. "And I spent every minute of that time dreaming of you—of this moment. It's the only thing that kept me alive, Della. You kept me alive."

She gazed back rapturously, still barely able to believe any of this could be true. Looking at him more closely now, she realized how gaunt he was, his cheeks sunken and his arms thinner than she remembered. And his maimed leg . . . "It's a miracle," she breathed. "But what happened?"

He pulled her to him again, draping one arm around her shoulders so that she could nestle against his side. "It's a long story, and even I don't remember all of it. After the wreck, I drifted for days—nine days, they tell me—along with three others. There were more of us at first, but . . ."

His voice trailed off, and he swallowed hard before he continued. "Finally we were rescued, and after changing to another ship, we eventually reached New York just before dawn this morning. The details you can read in the papers, for I'm sure every reporter in the city has heard them twenty times by now." He grinned, repudiating the undoubted horrors of his experience.

Della gazed up at him, her heart too full for words. Addie's prayers had been answered, and then Virginia's, and now hers. Ten minutes ago she had cursed her ill fortune, but now she knew she must be the luckiest woman alive. Luck of the Irish.

Kent's next words sobered her a bit, however. "Now let's get you home so we can pick up where we left off, shall we?" He released her so that he could have both hands on the reins, carefully turning the gig around on the narrow path.

"Home? You mean . . . your mother's house?" Though she tried, she could not keep the apprehension from her voice.

The turn accomplished, he flicked the horse into a trot, then pulled her against him protectively. "I won't let them mistreat you," he promised. "With me there, they won't dare."

Dusk was falling, and Della realized that though she'd been gone two hours, Kent could not have been home for long. He must have set out after her almost the moment he arrived. She would not mar his homecoming with her fears. So instead of speaking, she snuggled against him for the brief drive back to the house she had sworn she would never enter again.

Several people erupted from the house as they pulled to a stop. Della saw Mrs. Bradford, Kent's two sisters, and Caroline Cadbury and her mother. Della stiffened, but Kent only tightened his clasp about her shoulders.

Charles rode up just then and jumped down from his horse so that he could help Kent disembark from the gig. Then he swung Della down with an encouraging wink. She smiled back uncertainly, grateful that at least one person other than Kent might not condemn her. Then she turned to face the others, forcing herself to meet their eyes.

Of the group assembled on the wide front step, only Judy's face held any trace of sympathy. The expressions of the others ranged from distaste to outrage. Della's heart, so recently soaring, began a faltering descent. Still, she would not let them see that they intimidated her. Holding first Caroline's gaze, then Mrs. Bradford's, she lifted her chin.

Kent took her hand firmly in his. "I believe you all know Della Gilliland Bradford—my wife."

Mrs. Bradford's lips tightened into a thin,

implacable line as her eyes met Della's. "We'll discuss her true name and status later," she snapped. "Right now, Kent, you must come inside and rest. Dinner will be served in an hour."

Della realized that Kent's mother was on the verge of collapse, for all the uncompromising front she put on. And no wonder. In one day, she had seen her long-lost younger son return, mourned her elder son, heard Della's confession, then had her dead son abruptly raised back to life. Now Della, by her very presence, was adding to the woman's strain.

"I'll go upstairs and change," she suggested as the others headed for the parlor. "Black no longer seems appropriate."

Kent gripped her hand for a moment, unwilling to let her go. His eyes held a question.

"I'll be fine," she whispered. "Go join your family."

Though he still frowned, she slipped away from him and hurried up the wide, curving staircase, her satchel in her hand. Though hope had reentered her life with Kent's reappearance, she had no more idea now of what her future might hold than she had an hour before. One thing she was still sure of—she would never survive in Kent's world.

TWENTY-THREE

And now 'twas like all instruments,
Now like a lonely flute;
And now it is an angel's song,
That makes the heavens be mute.

—Samuel Taylor Coleridge,
The Rime of the Ancient Mariner

Reluctantly, with one last glance at the stairway up which Della had disappeared, Kent allowed his sisters to lead him into the parlor. He couldn't blame her for wanting to change out of her black dress, especially as it had been dirtied when she fell, but he hated to let her out of his sight for even a few minutes.

"It seems the girl has *some* sense," his mother remarked sourly as Judy again arranged Kent's injured leg on the divan. "Now we have a chance to talk without the awkwardness that would attend her presence. Kenton, I beg you not to do anything rash."

He glared at her. "When have you ever known me to do anything rash, Mother? I'm not—" He broke off with a glance at Charles, who appeared not at all offended.

"You're not me," his brother finished for him with a grin. "But it looks as though you may finally be coming to your senses, if Miss, er, Della is any indication."

Kent wasn't sure whether he wanted Charles' support or not. "Just why did you decide to return home after all these years?"

Charles shrugged. "I've had enough of the roving life. I'm almost thirty years old, after all, and have seen half the cities in the world by now—and made myself unwelcome in most of them," he added with another grin. "It's time I thought about settling down. This seemed the obvious place."

"And I suppose you'll want your interest in the business back?" Remembering what he'd gone through when Charles first left, Kent couldn't quite subdue his resentment.

"I'd like to lend a hand, at least. I've learned a few things. But there'll be time enough to discuss business later, when there are no more interesting topics afoot. How did you really meet Della?"

Warily Kent glanced around at the others. "What did she tell you?"

Caroline, who had been listening impatiently to the exchange, seemed to take this as her cue. "That she tricked you into pretending she was your wife, so that she could escape the consequences of her crimes in California. She also said that your sense of *honor*"—sarcasm dripped from the word—"prevented you breaking your engagement to me."

Despite the tension in the room, Kent smiled. Dear Della. Thinking him dead, she had obviously tried to furbish up his memory for the sake of his family, with no thought for herself.

"We were married aboard the *Central America*, by the captain," he told them. Both his mother and Caroline gaped. "And Della committed no crimes," he continued. "She *was* falsely accused, and San Francisco justice is uncertain. She felt it safest to leave until the facts were known."

"Kenton, dear, how can you be sure?" his mother asked gently, her earlier haughtiness replaced by what seemed to be genuine concern. "You've known her such a brief time, and have only her word for what her past has been. It's perfectly clear, at any rate, that she is not of our social class. Do you really believe she can make you happy?"

"Yes." Kent did not waver for a moment. Out of the corner of his eye, he saw Charles nodding approvingly.

"But what of her happiness?" asked Caroline shrewdly, leaning forward to place a hand on

Kent's arm. "She has seemed most uncomfortable among your old friends and even your family. Suppose she cannot adjust to the position in the world she must assume as your wife? She hasn't had the upbringing for it."

"As you have?"

She inclined her head with a modest smile. "Well, yes."

Kent had never fully realized before just how artificial Caroline was. And to think he had once accused Della of being a consummate actress! Caroline would even pretend sympathy for Della if she thought it would bring her what she wanted—his money and position.

But now his mother joined in. "She's right, Kenton. Your little Irish girl would be a fish out of water in our social circle. She would be embarrassed at every turn, shunned by many and ridiculed by the rest. Her disgrace would reflect upon you as well. First social contacts would be broken off, and then business ones."

"Her disgrace?" he echoed. "She may not have been born to a wealthy, prominent family, but that is no sin. With my support, I have no doubt she will get on well enough here in New York. She is charming and witty, and will make friends quickly."

"No sin?" Caroline repeated waspishly. "Francis tells us the two of you shared a cabin for weeks while at sea—*before* this alleged wedding. I assume no proof of such a ceremony now exists?"

Kent looked at her through narrowed eyes. "No, the papers were lost, of course. I take it you are willing to overlook my lapse if I will repudiate her and marry you? How commendable."

Apparently realizing her mistake, Caroline tried another tack. "I only want what's best for you, Kenton, just as your mother does. Surely you can understand that."

"I understand all too well. I think you had better go now, Miss Cadbury, before I feel compelled to explain. And you may want to tell your *heroic* brother to stay out of my way as well."

Both his mother and Caroline's began to sputter, but Caroline herself rose and headed for the door. "Very well, Kenton, but you will live to regret this. You and your little Irish harlot will never be accepted under any other genteel roof in New York or Philadelphia, mark my words. Come, Mother." With a toss of her golden curls, she swept out of the room, her wide black skirts brushing both sides of the doorway.

Mrs. Cadbury hesitated for a moment, dithering, but then followed her daughter out, with one apologetic glance over her shoulder at Mrs. Bradford. The moment the front door closed behind them, Kent struggled to his feet.

"I'm going to go see what's keeping Della," he said, hobbling out of the parlor before even Charles could rise to assist him. Reaching the stairs, he looked up—to see Della on the landing, in an outmoded sky blue dress. Catching sight of her expression, he quickly asked, "How long have you been standing there?"

"Long enough," she said quietly. "Or perhaps too long. Kent, this should be a joyous time for you, and I'm ruining it."

"Ruining it! You are my one true source of joy, Della. Don't you know that yet?" Gripping the rail, he started up the steps toward her. She made a motion to come down to help him, but he shook his head fiercely. He would not be treated like an invalid in his own home!

Della watched silently, her eyes wide with concern, as he made his way up the last few steps to the landing. Then she motioned to the small settee placed there. "Sit with me here, and we'll talk."

Though he shot a suspicious glance her way, he was just as glad of an opportunity to rest his leg. "What about? The plans we made before still hold. You will take your place here as my wife. If you prefer not to live in this house, we will buy another, or have one built—"

"No, Kent." Her face was as uncompromising as her words. "I heard what your mother said, and she was right. I'm completely out of place in New York society, and to be honest, I'm not at all sure I *want* to fit in, even for your sake. These past two weeks . . ." Her voice trailed off, but he could see in her eyes a reflection of what she had endured. Anger welled up in him.

"What did they do to you? What did they say? I'll make every one of them—"

"No, Kent," she repeated, with a firm shake of her head. "Before, when we were still on the ship, I let myself believe it could work. That somehow our love could overcome all obstacles. I believed it because I wanted to, not because my reason convinced me. But now I know otherwise. Even united, we cannot change the ways of the world—the ways of *your* world."

Alarmed, he grasped her shoulders. "What are you saying, Della? You're my wife. You promised to live with me until death us do part. Are you now reneging on that promise?" He could not lose her now—he would not!

Her green eyes filled, and one lone tear slipped from lash to cheek. "I want to be your wife—to live with you—more than anything on earth. But to alienate you from your family, your friends, your whole sphere . . . How could I live with myself?" she whispered.

He gripped her shoulders more tightly. "I don't care about any of that! I love you, Della."

"And I love you. But answer me this, Kent, honestly: If our positions were reversed, if your marriage to me would threaten my comfortable future, tear me from all I'd ever held dear, all the rights and privileges I'd been raised to, would you allow that?"

He opened his mouth, then closed it. Of course he would not. He could never intentionally be the instrument of Della's ruin.

"Now you understand," she said softly.

But he shook his head stubbornly. "No. It's not the same. I admit that I may not be able to shield you from every insult, but having you by my side will enrich my life immeasurably, not destroy it. Together we *can* effect a change—not at once, perhaps, but eventually. You'll see."

Della sighed, her face still troubled. He tried to think of more he might say to reassure her, but just then Joseph appeared at the foot of the stairs to announce dinner.

"Thank you," said Kent. "We'll be right down." Taking Della's hand firmly in his, he led her slowly down to the dining room, determined to prove his intentions.

Della had to admit that the meal was less tedious than most she had endured at this table. Kent, Charles, and Judy chatted among themselves, occasionally including her in their conversation. Mrs. Bradford and Barbara, however, were at best icily polite. And this was a mere family dinner. What might society at large have in store for her?

"Railroads," Charles was saying, gesticulating with his fork and ignoring his mother's disapproving glare. "Railroads will be the wave of the future, you'll see. In ten years they'll be as important as ships, or more. In twenty they'll make traditional shipping obsolete."

"You say they're in extensive use in the South, to ship sugar and cotton?" Kent asked, his interest clearly piqued. "I'm familiar with the passenger lines here in the Northeast, and a line from Sacramento to the gold fields seemed to be prospering, but I hadn't seriously considered them for real cargo shipping."

Charles went on to describe what he had seen in the South and in England, where he had spent a year during his wanderings. Kent looked thoughtful.

"I'll make some inquiries tomorrow. Mother, didn't you say there would be a reception at the Burroughses' next Tuesday? That will be an excellent chance to sound out our shareholders . . . oh, and to introduce Della, of course." He turned to smile at her.

She returned it mechanically. Already Kent was mentally reentering the world he had left behind. This was his milieu, where he belonged, amid the press of business and politics. She tried to envision herself at his side, meeting wealthy, prestigious personages—and failed utterly.

It had been one thing to pretend to that position aboard a ship where no one knew her past. It would be something else entirely to continually justify—and apologize for—her antecedents. For here they would be known. Caroline Cadbury would see to that.

". . . and tomorrow we'll go shopping," Judy was saying to her. With an effort, Della recalled herself to the conversation. "With your unusual coloring, I daresay you can make quite a splash in the right gowns."

"A splash? Er, perhaps." Judy meant well, Della knew, but her best course would surely be to appear as inconspicuous as she could, a mere shadow behind Kent.

Mrs. Bradford sniffed, then echoed her own thoughts. "Nonsense, Judy. Her only hope is to dress as conservatively as possible. Though even that is unlikely to counteract the gossip, which is even now making the rounds."

Kent frowned, distracted from his discussion with Charles. "Gossip? We'll nip it in the bud, if it indeed exists. Judy is right. We'll dress Della to the nines and let her burst upon the scene. She'll bowl them all over with her beauty and charm." He smiled warmly at her.

She tried to return it, but her thoughts were rebellious. She would not be dressed like some doll, to be paraded on Kent's arm while the society matrons snickered behind her back. And Kent would be as much an object of their ridicule as she. No, she could not allow that to happen. Pretending to listen to the conversation that flowed over her, Della began to plan.

By the time the ladies retired to the parlor, leaving Kent and Charles to their talk of railroads, she knew what she had to do. If she was careful, by the time Kent realized she was gone she would be well on her way to Ohio, where she could attempt to start her life over. There was a train leaving the station at midnight, and she meant to be on it.

* * *

"So, how long do you think that leg will keep you on the sidelines?" asked Charles once the ladies had left the dining room.

"Not long, I hope. Mother has summoned Dr. Portman, and he should be here shortly. We'll see what he has to say about it."

Charles nodded, then obligingly filled a glass for Kent from the sideboard before reseating himself across from his brother. "Now that you've heard the details, what do you think of my proposals?"

"I think you're probably right. Bradford Shipping needs to expand into railroads. I have a new appreciation for the risks of relying solely on ships." Kent took a sip of his brandy.

"I can imagine you do! And that being the case, I have another proposal for you. One I think you should consider, for your Della's sake."

Kent regarded his brother warily. "What do you mean?"

"I heard a bit of your conversation before dinner, and I was watching you both during the meal. It's clear you love her to distraction, but you're not always as observant as you could be."

Charles had always been shrewd, Kent recalled, able to read people so well that he could manipulate them without their even noticing it. Rather like Della, he realized with a start. "I'm listening," he said.

Kent's eyes widened as Charles outlined his idea.

As she had expected, Kent's mother and sisters made no objection when Della excused herself for the evening only moments after they all reached the parlor. Judy murmured something about how tired she must be, but the others looked frankly relieved to see her go—doubtless so that they could talk about her.

Not that she cared—not now. Soon enough, she would never have to worry about such things again. Ignoring the hollow ache in her heart, Della tiptoed past the dining room, then up the stairs to her room. Kent would likely retire as soon as the doctor had gone, so she didn't have much time.

Just inside her doorway, she stopped. Where was her satchel? Quickly she searched the room, only to discover it was neither under the bed nor in the wardrobe. Kent must have had it taken to his room, she finally realized. That would complicate things further . . . but no. She'd have had to go there anyway, to get the money she needed for train fare.

Cautiously she stepped back into the hallway and looked in both directions. Which room was his? Slowly, quietly, though every nerve screamed for her to hurry, she peered into first one room, then another. She feared that if she was stopped, she'd never again summon the courage to leave.

The third door she opened, the second one

down from hers, revealed her satchel on the edge of a four-poster bed in the center of the room. Glancing around, she saw that it was indeed a masculine chamber, richly appointed in mahogany and deep green fabrics. She breathed deeply. Yes, it even smelled faintly of sandalwood—of Kent—though he couldn't have inhabited this room for half a year.

Soon, all too soon, she would never smell that scent again. The thought brought unbidden tears to her eyes. Was she really doing the right thing, wounding them both for the sake of Kent's worldly advantage? Such things mattered little to her . . . but she knew they were important to him. He'd been bred to wealth and influence. They were his birthright, and she had no right to deprive him of them.

With shaking hands, she quickly opened first one drawer, then another. In the desk by the window, she found what she sought—fifty dollars in bills. Tucking them into the pocket of her skirt, she went to the window and peered out into the darkness. No convenient tree limb stretched within reach. She'd have to return to the other room to make her escape.

Again she tiptoed down the hallway, trying vainly to ignore the searing pain in her heart. She was doing the right thing. She *must* be doing the right thing. As she put her hand on the knob of her former room, she heard voices at the foot of the stairs. With a gasp, she turned the handle and whisked inside, closing the door as quietly as she could.

She listened for a moment but heard no sound of footsteps on the stair or landing. The voices were muffled now, but she thought she could barely distinguish Kent's among them. Perhaps the doctor was even now taking his leave, which might mean Kent would come upstairs at any moment. If she was going to leave, it had to be now.

"Farewell, my darling," she whispered to the closed door. "I'll love you forever. Try to forget me, so you can go on with your life—the life you were meant to have."

Her voice broke on a sob, and she hurried to the window. As before, she first threw down her satchel, then clambered over the sill herself. In the dark, it was harder to gauge the jump to the tree branch than it had been before—and her vision was further obscured by tears, now flowing freely. Impatiently she dragged her sleeve across her eyes, then leaped. And missed.

She caught the branch with her right hand, but her left flailed wildly. Frantically she clawed at the branch, but came away with only a handful of leaves—and then she was falling. In the split second before she hit the ground, she had time only to wonder what Kent and his family would think when they found her in a heap on the ground. She tensed for the impact.

"Got you!" Instead of the hard ground, strong

arms broke her fall. "It's a good thing only my leg was broken, isn't it?"

But even as Kent spoke, her weight overbalanced him, and he fell in an ungainly heap, with her atop him—just as in their cabin aboard the *Central America*.

The moment she caught her breath, Della scrambled up. "Are you hurt? Your leg—"

"It's fine. The doctor says I can even dispense with the crutch in a week or two. Della—" He tried to rise.

She helped him up without thinking. Then, "Kent, what are you doing out here? How did you know?"

"Charles suspected, and it seems he is still more perceptive than I. Did I ever tell you that you remind me of him sometimes?" The moon and the light from the windows showed his smile, but also the shadowed confusion in his eyes. "Della, why? I thought we had agreed to face down the society snobs together."

Suddenly her flight seemed more cowardly than noble. Still, she tried to explain. "The more I thought about it, the more unlikely it seemed. I knew I would be miserable, and it seemed inevitable that I would make you miserable as well, at the same time alienating you from the world where you belong."

"So you were leaving, to go—where?" To her surprise, his expression was sympathetic rather than condemning.

"Ohio," she confessed. "If I still have family there, it seemed a place to start. From there . . . I don't know. I—I was going to take the midnight train."

Now, though, she would not be on it. A different future awaited her—one by Kent's side, but rejected by his peers. She sighed, both relieved and depressed.

"Will the noon train tomorrow do instead?"

She blinked up at him in confusion. "What?" Would he let her leave after all? Was he sending her away? Though she'd thought it was what she wanted, her throat tightened in sudden pain.

"I'd really rather have a couple of days to put everything in order," he said in a perfectly calm, conversational tone. "But if you're as anxious as all this, I'll do my best to be ready to leave tomorrow morning."

She stared incredulously, comprehension beginning to dawn. "You can't mean—?"

"I finally realized that you were right. You'll never be truly happy in New York—and neither will I. I've changed, Della, thanks to you. The money, the position, the privilege—everything I grew up with seems hollow to me now. I want to see more of the world, to explore new ways of doing things. Together we can do just that."

"Then—" She still scarcely dared to believe. "Then you'll come with me?"

He nodded, his eyes holding hers so that she could read the love there. "Charles will handle the

New York office while I develop a new branch of Bradford Shipping—a railroad branch. Will you help me, Della?" Now his eyes held a plea that went far deeper than his words.

Suddenly Della understood. He wasn't asking her to stay in New York with him. Instead he wanted to go adventuring—with her by his side. In answer, she pulled him to her for a lingering kiss that he returned with mounting enthusiasm.

"May I carry your luggage upstairs, madam?" he asked with mock formality several moments later.

"I'll carry it myself," she replied, her heart lighter than it had been in weeks—perhaps years. "You still have that crutch to manage, remember?"

They reentered the house by a side door, and Kent wordlessly led Della back to his room. For a long moment they stood just inside the closed door, gazing hungrily at each other. Then Kent gestured toward the bed. "What will we do with all that space?" he asked with a grin.

"Let's experiment."

Between kisses, they quickly stripped off each other's clothing, their urgency mounting. How long had it been? But Della's mind was too focused on Kent and on the pleasure to come to count days. The bed, that beautiful, enormous bed, beckoned. She sat down on the edge of it to pull off her stockings—the only garment she still wore—then grabbed Kent's hand to pull him down next to her, careful of his wrapped leg.

With a chuckle, he stretched his length beside her, taking her into his arms again. "Like this?" he murmured, then rolled atop her. "Or this?"

"Mmm." His body felt heavenly against hers. But before he could enter her already moist cleft, she pushed against his shoulder, rolling him onto his other side, in the center of the bed. "Perhaps like this."

"Or even this." With a heave, he rolled further, until she was on top of him. Each motion tantalized her senses, her breasts brushing his chest, his shaft caressing her eager nubbin. He felt wonderful.

"This will do—for now," she said, then shifted slightly, parting her legs until the very tip of his shaft entered her waiting depths. She paused, moving slightly, so slightly, teasing him until his eyes began to glaze. Then, with one swift thrust of her hips, she impaled herself on him.

Together they gasped, then their mouths met and fastened, and they became one. Rocking, writhing, in moments they both spiraled up to the peak, to explode in an ecstasy both had thought they would never experience again.

Even before her body stopped shuddering with pleasure, Kent again rolled Della over, still deep within her. "Now let's try it this way," he suggested, supporting himself with his arms and his good leg. Again he began to move within her, his shaft still engorged with passion despite his release.

Now they took the time to pleasure each other more thoroughly, hands and mouths caressing, exploring curves and hollows, until finally they mounted to another crest and together sailed over its top.

Sated for the moment, but still joined, they pulled back briefly to gaze lovingly at each other.

"Kent, I wish I could tell you how happy you've made me," Della breathed.

"You've just shown me," he said with the smile she loved.

She smiled back, her heart in her eyes. But then practicality intruded. "Oh! How is your leg?"

"I forgot all about it." He grinned fondly at her, then sobered. "I think you've cured me, Della—in more ways than one. You've shown me that money isn't everything, and that what seems most valuable on the surface is often only fool's gold. Love is what really matters."

With a sigh of pure contentment, she snuggled against him as they began to plan their future together.

AUTHOR'S NOTE

While Della, Kent, and their personal story are fictional, the events and people surrounding them were real. All of the ships mentioned were actual ships, and most of the characters were actual passengers aboard them, including the Eastons, the Birches—even the canary. My goal, of course, was to spin an engaging romance rather than to give an exhaustive account of the *Central America* and its fate. Therefore, although I have remained faithful to the historical sequence of events, I focused on those aspects that best fit my story and limited myself to what my characters would have experienced during the voyage, sinking, and rescue. (For example, I added Kent as a fourth man on the real raft carrying Dawson, Grant, and Tice.) I wish to acknowledge my gratitude to the San Mateo County Historical Museum and the accomplishments of the S.S. *Central America* Project, which were of great assistance when I first began my research on the S.S. *Central America* several years ago. I'd like to dedicate this story to Captain Herndon (for whom Herndon, Virginia, was named) and the other valiant men and women aboard that ship, who were the true heroes and heroines upon whom I based Kent and Della. May you never be forgotten!